Early to Rise

Early To Rise

a romantic mystery

LINDA RICHTER

Early To Rise
Copyright © 2022 Linda Richter

Visit our website at
www.StillwaterPress.com
for more information.

First Stillwater River Publications Edition

ISBN: 978-1-955123-83-9

12345678910
Written by Linda Richter
Cover Art by Lindsay Whelan
Published by Stillwater River Publications,
Pawtucket, RI, USA.

Dedicated to my dear friend Richard Pacheco,
who believed in me and supported my creative process
every step of the way.

Thank you to all of my friends and family.
You support my writing habit by loving, listening,
reading, editing, and motivating. Special thanks to my
daughters Eva and Zoe, who make me want to get up
and write every day.

Early To Rise

One.

Monday

~~~~~~

L AINE PULLED A rain poncho over her short, brown
curls, grabbed a trash bag and headed for the beach.
At first she tossed empty cans into the bag with
diligence. But soon the lazy drizzle and foggy outlines of
rocks lulled her to inward meanderings. Her green bag
trailed behind her like a child's forgotten toy.

As she walked on the damp sand, images of her life a year
ago popped into her head. Twelve months ago, engaged to
the chef of Boston's prestigious Clubs restaurant, wedding
bells chimed in her future. The savory smell of Toby's lasagna
smothered in tomato vodka sauce had been to die for.

I'm actually drooling. She wiped her chin. *Better not think
about the lasagna, or the tortellini either.*

Now she lived alone in a tiny cottage perched at the edge
of the sea. Canned soup and grilled cheese sandwiches made
up her gourmet diet. Life held more surprises than she'd
bargained for.

*I still have my first day as children's director at the Bay Nature
Center to contend with. Enough of my trip down memory lane
and back to the present.*

Laine glanced down at her almost empty trash bag. *Some
beach cleaner I am.*

Scooping up a bottle and a soda can, she dropped them
in the bag and hurried back to the cottage.

LAINE SMILED when she opened the door to her bedroom. *My purple heaven. Not a bad job with the paintbrush, and my watercolor paintings look great against the lavender walls. Alas, no one else will see them, since I don't plan on having raucous sex any time soon. And if I do, the hunk better gaze at my body, not my artwork.*

In the living room, the plum velvet couch looked incongruous against the knotty pine walls. No, not incongruous. Eclectic. Perfect for curling up on a cold winter's night, especially with her heated fleece throw.

Laine sighed with contentment as she combed her hair. A lot less fussing now that her hair ended mid-ear instead of mid-back. A dab of gel, a couple of finger scrunches, that's all she needed. She'd gotten her hair cut the day before her move from Boston to Seaglass Bay. New life, new do.

LAINE CLIMBED into her Honda and started down the winding country road. The first day at a new job gave her jitters. At least her brown suede suit and green hat gave her confidence in her appearance. A perfect outfit for a nature center.

In fact, I look alarmingly like a tree. I hope I don't meet up with a territory-marking dog. Can't get peed on my first day. The silly thought eased her tension.

Laine drove at a sedate pace, taking in the scenery through the veil of light drizzle. The trees, fields, and marshes soothed her soul.

ANXIETY CLENCHED her gut as she pulled into the crushed shell driveway and gazed up at the white Victorian building. The nineteenth century structure looked more imposing than it had online. The picture on the website, taken in summer sunshine, made the building look like a bright and sunny place.

Today in the October drizzle, the white paint looked dingy. Laine wouldn't be surprised to find bats in the belfry behind the filmy windowpanes on the third floor.

Laine crunched along the oyster shell path, reminding herself to straighten up. Ever since fifth grade when she was tallest in the class, she'd slouched. The posture teacher's mantra stuck in her mind: "Stop the slump or get a hump."

As she opened the oak door of the Bay Nature Center, a sudden, strong gust of wind propelled her into the room. Papers lifted off a nearby desk and swirled across the floor. Laine grabbed for the door, and pushed it closed against the wind. Then, turning to apologize, she tripped over her own feet and careened back into a rolling chair.

"Damn it all to hell." Laine yelped as she and the chair hit the wall.

"Now that's what I call an entrance." A woman with a striking jet-black mane and a fringe of bangs sauntered towards her.

Laine sputtered an apology and stood, trying to straighten her clothes.

"Not to worry. You just provided my morning entertainment." The woman's snicker held a touch of bitch. "Hell, maybe my entertainment for the week. I'm Fiona Glaze, administrative assistant, which is really a glorified term for secretary. And you must be Laine. You've got wet leaves in your hair. You look a lot like a tree. A fancy tree."

Shoot, maybe not all of the bats are in the belfry. Laine caught her breath.

"Hello."

Fiona gave Laine the once-over. "Are you going to a convention after work? We're informal here at the BNC."

Oh crud, I'm wearing the wrong clothes. And I felt so confident about my outfit.

Fiona wore a roomy, gem-studded, black sweat suit. When she turned her head, her long, straight hair swung back and forth like a pendulum. Fiona's glossy locks mesmerized. Back and forth, back and forth.

I am now turning into an organic chicken. I am now turning into an organic chicken.

"Let me show you around." Fiona's voice brought her back. Fiona pointed out the three office spaces hogging most of the right side of the room.

"Your desk is the one in the back, closest to Brooke's office."

"Okay, cool."

A round oak table and eight chairs managed to fit on a Navajo wool rug in the center of the room. Against the left wall, nature books were crammed into free-standing shelves. Framed maps of the waterways covered the rest of available wall space.

Partitions separated the three desks. But the areas seemed roomy, and the computers fairly new.

Laine couldn't ask for more. She wouldn't have privacy to pick her nose, adjust her pantyhose, or have a quickie, but she'd manage.

"Brooke's expecting you." Fiona rapped three times on the wood paneled door. The copper plaque on the door read "Brooke C. Treadwell, Executive Director."

Laine gave herself another mental shake to straighten her shoulders.

Fiona opened the door and waved Laine in. "Here's our new children's coordinator."

Laine straightened her back even more at the mention of her title. She thought she heard trumpets blare in the distance as she entered the sanctum sanctorum.

Brooke Treadwell, a tall woman in her forties, rose from behind her desk and extended her slender hand. She gave Laine a cool handshake, just short of brusque.

"Please sit down." Her voice sounded cultured, well-modulated. "Fiona, could you bring us a pot of my special green tea?"

Laine sat, feeling damp and wrinkled and cursing the inclement weather. Brooke probably made everyone feel that way. The woman must have been born with a laundry and dry-cleaning attachment. Even her jeans sported well-pressed creases. And her short gray hair looked fresh,; like it came straight from the salad crisper.

"Welcome to the Bay Nature Center. Sorry your first day is so rainy and gloomy." Then Brooke explained the center's mission, a recap of what Laine had learned from the internet.

Laine cast surreptitious glances at the exposed wood beams, chrome lighting, and gray leather chairs. Black and white nature photos hung on the walls. One of a dancer in the snow caught her eye.

That can't be an original Stevins photo. They cost a mint.

Several bouquets of vibrant red roses preened in sleek black vases on the well-polished table.

Hothouse roses are expensive this time of year. Brooke's got a few bucks to throw around. Of course, maybe someone bought them for her.

Fiona reappeared with a green ceramic teapot and poured dark liquid into two matching cups.

"The Bay Nature Center is open Monday through Saturday," Brooke continued. "Your work schedule is flexible, as long as you put in your thirty hours."

Oh goody, I can come to work on weekends if I get lonely. Who am I kidding? When I get lonely. Laine lifted her cup, wondering if she should crook her pinky. She sipped the steaming tea. And the inside of her mouth puckered like a prune as tears sprang to her eyes.

What the hell? The cup didn't contain tea; it held a witch's poison brew.

Laine started to gag, but forced herself to swallow the bitter hot liquid.

Brooke sat sipping her tea, a complacent smile on her face. "Are you alright? My special blend has a lot of medicinal properties and can take some getting used to."

Laine forced herself to breathe. "It's…interesting. I've never had green tea quite like this."

I've never had anything quite like this. What is this, some sort of test? If I don't die on the spot I can keep the job?

"I have it specially made. It has more caffeine than coffee. I like a strong flavor."

Yuck, it's disgusting. Laine set down her cup, wondering if she could accidentally spill it on the floor. But it might take off the polyurethane finish.

"Are you familiar with the bike path proposal for Seagulls Bay?" Brooke took another sip of the tea. Her eyes didn't even water.

"Yes. I read Seaglass Bay was awarded several million dollars in state grants."

Brooke nodded. "Last week we received our final approval for a bike path along the old railway bed."

"Congratulations. That's wonderful. When do they start building?"

"We have a few loose ends to tie up first."

"I could have a bike safety poster contest."

Brooke gave a slight smile. "I admire your enthusiasm, but let's not get ahead of ourselves, okay?"

"Of course." Huh? At the last nature center she worked in, a grant from the state for a bike path was big news, cause for celebration and activity.

"Let me show you where we hold our indoor children's groups."

Laine followed Brooke downstairs, into a spacious activity area. Books, fish skeletons, and fish tanks jammed the shelves lining the wall.

Several long tables stood in the center of the room, set up with art supplies for the kids' projects.

Brooke glanced at her expensive looking watch. When she nodded, she moved her head forward once towards her chest, then back into place. The awkward movement commanded attention.

Laine's returning nod jerked her head like a series of small brain convulsions.

"I'm running late for a meeting," Brooke announced. "If you need anything, Fiona will assist you."

Laine thanked Brooke and followed her up the stairs. She walked into her cubby and eased into her very own desk chair. Seated, she clasped her hands together on top of the desk and murmured a few words.

"What are you doing?" Fiona poked her head around the corner. "You look like you're praying. You're not one of those holy rollers, are you?"

Laine smiled. "I'm having a special moment. I'm into firsts, and this is my first time at my desk at the Bay Nature Center."

"Knock yourself out, kiddo." Fiona disappeared back around the corner, her hair sweeping in an arc to the other direction.

Fiona's hair acts obsessed. No way normal hair undulates like that.

Laine cleared her head of snake dancing thoughts and booted up the computer, eager to get started. She spent the next two and a half hours reading about the history and workings of the Bay Nature Center.

At lunch break, Laine sat with Fiona at a table in the basement. Beset by first-day jitters, she'd gone without breakfast. Now, feeling ravenous, she devoured her bag lunch—a tuna, lettuce, and tomato pocket.

Fiona's lunch consisted of a frosted donut and a large cup of coffee. Looking like a cat, she delicately licked icing from her finger.

"Have one, kiddo." She pushed the donut box in Laine's direction. "They're homemade at Barry's Bakery. If my perfume smelled like those donuts, I'd have every man in Seaglass Bay after me."

"At least the cops." Laine bit into a honey-glazed donut and watched it deflate like a flat tire. She and Fiona shared a laugh. Perhaps they could be friends, even though no one had called her kiddo in a long time—maybe ever.

A framed news photo on the wall caught her eye. Laine rose to examine it in greater detail.

A woman with hair sticking up in alarm stood next to a beefy, red-faced man. The young woman held a sign opposing nuclear power.

"Who are those characters in the photo?"

"The young and the idealistic. It's Brooke Treadwell and David Emson in the seventies. They hated each other then, and they hate each other now. They're on opposite sides of every environmental battle. The difference is Brooke always wins."

Wow, the Brooke I met is sleek and styled. She's certainly tamed her tresses into submission since the seventies.

As if reading her mind Fiona said, "Brooke goes to my stylist now. He's a miracle worker."

Must be if he's the one making Fiona's hair into snake charming tresses.

"I'm glad I'm on the winning team. Who is David Emson?"

"Where do I start? He's a developer who owns the land behind our nature center, and plans to build some fancy McMansions on three acre lots. He is no friend of the Bay Nature Center. He's so full of himself; if his head swells any more, it'll pop right off his neck."

Laine grimaced. Head popping wasn't her thing.

"Now for the important information. The nearest takeout is the Corner Kitchen."

"Good to know."

"Don't bug Brooke until she's had her morning cup of green tea. And we call the Bay Nature Center 'BNC' for short."

"Thanks. I've never had green tea like that. I think I sprouted chest hair."

Fiona laughed. "It's called Dragon Fire Brew. Brooke gets it from some fancy tea shop in Providence. I think she likes to watch people's reactions when they drink it."

Laine smiled, thinking about how she must have looked after one bitter sip.

"So what do you think of our fair city so far?"

"It's not a city at all. I love it. After living in Boston, it's great to see trees and water."

"Boston, huh? How long did you live there?"

"After college until now. I worked at a nature center a few miles outside the city."

"This village must be culture shock for you. Have you met any of our illustrious citizens yet?"

Laine shook her head. "Not really. I'm still taking time to settle in."

"It takes forever and a day for Seaglass Bayers to accept newcomers. Believe me, it's not like the Bayers are anything to write home about. There's Sofie Pacheco, having an affair with a married guy. And Stanton Coles's wife ran off with their baby daughter years ago. Now all he cares about is money and seducing younger women. Last but not least, we can't forget Sam Holliston." Fiona almost spat his name. "He thinks he walks on water, but he's nothing but a low-life gardener. This town is full of people with skeletons in their closets."

Fiona opened her mouth to expose a set of pointy whites. "I can tell you loads more, if you want."

Attempting lightness, Laine said, "I appreciate it. I'll let you know if I need help fleshing out any characters." Character *assassination* more likely. She knew Fiona Glaze's poison words had the power to taint her first impressions.

"Believe me kiddo, you will. If you need advice, or to chat, come see me. I'm always at my desk."

"Thanks."

Fat chance. Scratch "we could be friends." This cat has claws.

Laine spent the early afternoon designing a youth page for the BNC newsletter. She wrote an article about recycling. When she read her finished article she almost put herself to sleep. What ten-year-old would want to read this dry stuff?

Laine didn't have pencils to chew so she played this little piggy on her fingers.

Finally the clouds parted and light dawned. She would design a clown named Recycle who rode on a recycled cycle and told the same jokes over again because he liked to recycle them. She'd have to work more on that idea.

They could also have a youth page written by kids for kids. She sent an email to area schools asking for nature stories, jokes, and poems. A fun junior news page.

WORK ENDED for the day, and Laine said a polite goodbye to Fiona and drove through the still pounding rain to her cozy cottage.

As soon as she took off her coat, she started a fire in the stone fireplace and then buried her nose in her latest female detective story. The fast-paced novel kept her enthralled. An hour later, she tore herself away long enough to grab several slices of leftover cold pizza to eat while she read. When she finished the book, she dropped it to the floor with a sigh of satisfaction.

Nice how the detective always gets her man. Even better how she calls the shots.

LAINE SNUGGLED into bed, scrunching the pillow against her cheek. She fell into a deep, unbroken sleep in the cottage by the sea.

Two.

Tuesday

L AINE HUMMED an old Beatles' tune while she slipped into faded jeans, a jersey and sweatshirt. The sky spat drizzle, so she grabbed her yellow rain slicker from the hook beside the door; then glanced at her reflection in the hallway mirror. Her short hair looked toss and tumble, and the rain slicker sported rips in several places. In Boston she used to dress up to go to the bodega for a candy bar. Laine sighed with contentment as she headed for her beach walk.

As Laine walked, she pondered her luck.

The good luck is true luck, but the bad luck is my own damned fault.

Remembering her past sent her spirits sinking and she bit her lower lip in frustration.

Cut it out. You're NOT a victim. You create your own luck.

Her good luck included the beach cottage at Beaker's Point. The cottage belonged to the BNC, and the rent made up part of her salary. Like a clergyman who resided next to the church, she lived in a cottage two hundred and fifty yards from the beach.

Laine smiled as she peered down at her shiny new BNC badge. The job included ten hours a week for patrolling and cleaning the beach, plus thirty hours coordinating children's activities. That left time to read, jog, and think.

And get lonely.

No! Cut it out, Laine. Alone doesn't mean lonely—unless it's midnight and I have a craving not even dark chocolate can satisfy.

When she'd read the announcement for the position at the BNC, Laine had sent in her résumé, thinking she had slim odds of landing the job. At least twenty other qualified applicants had applied. But the BNC board loved her work at the large environmental agency in Boston and hired her after just one interview. Now here she stood, smack dab on the loveliest stretch of beach in Massachusetts.

Laine turned back to gaze at her new home. Any doubts about moving from Boston to the sticks melted at the sight of the cottage. A love affair had begun with the weathered hobbit-house poised near the edge of the sea.

Memories of Toby and the bad luck he'd brought to her life still left a hovering dark cloud. When they first met, almost two years ago, their first months together consisted of a mad rush and glow of cards, flowers, and candlelight dinners. The food tasted superb since Toby, ever the proud professional chef, didn't mind bringing his work home with him.

Even now, Laine considered food her aphrodisiac of choice. A man covered in béchamel sauce, or a guy with a 401(k)? No contest.

For six months, Toby's indefatigable romantic energy amazed and delighted her. Most of the other guys she knew remained clueless in the romance department. She remembered the movie date where the guy bought two popcorns and ate them both, never offering her one kernel. Toby always brought her a bag of her favorite chocolate caramel popcorn—that he made himself.

Laine loved the way Toby opened doors and brought her thoughtful little gifts. Warm memories flooded her of the night he turned his kitchen into an Italian bistro and dropped down on one knee to propose. On the happiest night of her life, she agreed to marry the most sensitive guy she'd ever met.

The very next day Toby received a dream job offer from Los Angeles. Toby's chance to be a chef at one of California's top ten restaurants. But it was okay if Laine didn't want to resettle.

Indignant, she'd told him of course she'd move across the country with him. Laine loved adventure and she loved Toby. She gave two weeks' notice at work, sure she'd find another environmental job on the West Coast.

Laine remembered the giant yard sale where she'd sold most of her worldly possessions. She still missed her brass bed and plush green loveseat. When she had nothing left but two trunks, she took off for sunny California.

A week later, coming home early from job hunting, she surprised Toby in bed with another woman. She cried; he comforted. She raged; he apologized. He confessed he'd been cheating on her all along. But the other women meant nothing; he adored Laine above all others. She was the only one, the one he cooked for. Some men had extra needs for sexual release, didn't she understand that?

Laine threw a copper pot full of veal marsala at him. Her parting image was Toby rescuing baby veal pieces from the floor, his shirt spattered with red sauce. In that snapshot of a moment she saw the real Toby, a man driven to excess in every part of his life. Laine took the next plane home, never wanting to look back, but doing so much too often. Love affairs end, and this chef left a bad taste in her mouth.

Laine's self-proclaimed skills of intuition and observation had failed her. She had mistaken style for character.

Oh puh-leeze. Give me a break. I knew all along what was happening. Clue number one happened the day she arrived at Toby's apartment to pick him up for a date. No answer to her ring or knock, so she opened the door. Pillows covered the floor, the couch cover askew. The wastebasket was tipped on its side. Had the house been burgled? Judging by the two empty wine glasses on the table, Toby and the thief had gotten quite chummy.

Laine found Toby on the back terrace, sitting tête-à-tête with a young woman in a skin-tight dress. Her extra-long eyelashes reminded Laine of curled black pipe cleaners.

"Hey babe," Toby said. "This is Collette. She's the new sous chef at the restaurant. We're creating some signature recipes."

Laine reminded him of their date for the gallery opening.

"Oh, shit, babe. I'm sorry, I completely forgot. Would you mind going alone? I've really got to go over these recipes with Collette. I promise I'll make it up to you later."

Of course she didn't mind. She knew his cooking career was important. But she never did see Collette at the restaurant. There were other instances of the wrong panties in the wrong places and whispered phone calls. Her mind had recorded these details, but her heart refused to accept the inevitable. Toby had done everything but plaster the message on a billboard. Caution: boyfriend sleeping around.

Laine was pissed at herself because intuition called and called, but she never answered. Of course, the whole thing made sense. How could someone as gorgeous and charming as Toby have fallen in love with her in the first place?

No! Those feelings belonged to the bad days. The bad days were behind her.

She'd left Toby last November, about a year ago. Seaglass Bay presented her with an opportunity for a fresh start. After sighing herself back to the present, she stooped to untangle a deflated balloon from a stick of driftwood. Continuing to walk, she contemplated the balloon and its possible deadly effects on hungry sea turtles. Her attention caught by sand and shells, she crashed right into a solid mass.

"Whoa." Laine jerked back, suddenly finding herself looking up into a pair of deep-set brown eyes, framed with curly brown lashes.

The man stared; then his mouth formed an ugly snarl. "Where the hell do you think you're going? Can't you read signs? This is private property." His deep voice spewed hostility.

"Hold on, I can explain."

"I don't want to hear any lame-brained excuses. Go back to Boston or wherever you came from."

Huh? How did he know she came from Boston? She'd never seen this a-hole before. While he ranted, Laine's eyes swept the shoreline. With a start, she realized she'd walked well past the BNC boundaries to end up on private property.

Ahead on the beach, an inlet held a dock jutting out to a wooden houseboat. A denim blue window box filled with mini gourds gave it a cozy, well-kept touch.

The houseboat must belong to this territorial idiot. Fine. Okay, so she trespassed. But the rain came down harder, and she didn't have time to chat about her misdemeanor.

"Sorry for stepping on your precious property. I walked too far, that's all. I can assure you it won't happen again." As she tossed her head, her slicker opened at the neck to reveal the BNC badge on her sweatshirt.

"Oh, hell." He frowned and ran his hand through his dark brown curls. "Jeez, I'm really sorry. I thought you were one of those nosy tourists. I didn't know you were the new BNC hire. You should have said something."

His tanned face softened, but now anger surged within Laine.

"I should have said something? You didn't give me a chance to speak. You took one look at me and started yelling your head off."

"I didn't yell. I'm—"

"The rudest man I ever met," she finished for him; then turned to leave.

"At least be careful. The rocks around here get slippery in the rain."

She wheeled back to face him. "I can take care of myself, thank you very much." Before he could say another word, she turned on her heel and walked away with long, energetic strides.

"Hey, come back, please. I said I was…" His voice got lost in the mist.

Laine kept walking. She needed to prolong her visit with the Miss Manners reject like she needed a hole in the head. More pressing matters held her attention, like getting home to dryness and warmth. But, a mile of wet beach separated her from her cozy cottage and the sky loomed overhead, an ominous blue-black slab of cloud.

Three.

Later Tuesday

LAINE QUICKENED her pace. A sudden burst of rain prevented her from seeing the slick, black rocks in her path. She hit one with her foot, righted herself and then bumped into another. She stumbled and fell on her side, her left leg twisting beneath her. A spasm of pain rocketed up her leg. Pulling herself up, she tried to take a step and cried out as pain burst from her ankle. She eased herself back down on the sand, not wanting to cause more pain.

Laine considered yelling for help, but who would hear her in the pelting rain? In inclement weather, the beach could stay deserted for hours, even days. She tried to remember what she knew about hypothermia.

Don't panic. Breathe deeply. In for the count of four, hold for four, then out for four.

In a few minutes she would try to stand. Her breath calmed her and soon the rain abated. Laine uncurled and shivered, unable to stop. Her bones felt like they were made of sand and water. Wriggling into a more comfortable position, she wrapped her arms around herself and concentrated on efficient huddling.

An orb of sun began to poke through, a miscreant yoke in a gray egg. Faith surged—someone would come!—but a crack of thunder and another burst of cold rain quelled, then quashed, all hope.

Laine sat, cursing the whole eastern seaboard through chattering teeth when strong arms lifted her up.

"Thank God," she moaned. She squeezed her eyes shut. Even Count Dracula would be better than staying here and freezing to death. Maybe she should take a peek. Opening her eyes, she focused on her rescuer.

Brown eyes as dark as molten lava stared back.

Oh great. The eyes belonged to the territorial dude from the houseboat. The last person she wanted to see.

"You again." It was all she could manage.

"Yeah, it's me. Let's get you to the houseboat." His low voice now held gentleness. "Hold on tight, we'll get you where it's warm."

Laine looked up at his face, at the strong chin, full lips. A good face, tanned for late October. She'd let him save her, and not wait for Prince Charming.

Progress went slow, since her soaked clothes weighed about a hundred pounds. Pain shot up her leg with each step. Then, in spite of her protests, the man picked her up and carried her along the beach and down the dock to the houseboat like a sack of potatoes.

INSIDE, he eased her onto the couch in the warm, dry room. Laine sank against the cushions.

The man took off his rain slicker and busied himself getting tea and a thick terry towel. He was tall, six feet at least, with a lean body. He wore form-fitting jeans and a blue chambray shirt with the sleeves rolled up. His muscular arms resembled those she'd admired resting on car windows in traffic. Good arms for holding, working and playing. Okay, time to change the subject. She didn't need a man right now, and definitely not this one.

"How did you know to come looking for me?"

"I got worried about you. Those rocks really are treacherous, and you didn't seem in the mood for my advice."

You think? "Thanks, I appreciate you coming to find me." Damn, she didn't even know his name.

"I'm Laine Camara."

"I'm Sam Holliston, longtime Seaglass Bay resident and pain in the ass."

You got that right. "By the way, I'm getting your couch soaking wet."

"Don't worry. The maid will take care of it." He laughed at her look of surprise. "I'm joking. More important, you're shivering. We should get you out of those wet clothes right away." He eyed her with speculation. "I have clothes that might fit you."

Yeah, probably something left over from the string of ladies you invited to your houseboat. He disappeared down a narrow hallway before she could comment on his intriguing statement. Laine took a moment to study her surroundings.

The compact living room and kitchen—what did one call it on a boat? Ah yes, galley—were well organized by the looks of it. Baskets of shells and smooth stones gave a sense of ambience. The place exuded cozy charm. Almost romantic; not that she intended on getting romantic with this Neanderthal any time soon.

Sam returned holding a gray sweat suit. "Why don't you change, and then we'll have a look at that ankle. If you need help taking off your pants, let me know."

"I'm perfectly capable of taking off my clothes, thank you," she retorted, with as much dignity as she could muster.

"Hey, I'm trying to help. Give a shout if you need me." He disappeared into another room.

Laine muttered thanks for giving her some privacy.

Not that I'm a vision of loveliness at the moment. I probably look like a drowned rat.

After undoing the button on her jeans she tried to pull them off. They stayed plastered to her thighs like wet sealskin. Her swollen ankle protruded from the left cuff.

Shrugging into the sweatshirt, she called, "Yoo-hoo. I think I'll wait until I get to the doctor's office to change my pants."

Sam reappeared, his face a mask of concern. "This is no time for modesty; we've got to get those jeans off. I'm an emergency medical technician. I do this kind of thing all the time."

"I'll bet you do."

"Look. Your lips are blue and your teeth are chattering. I don't want to risk you getting pneumonia or hypothermia. Do you want to see my EMT certificate? Plus I was a boy scout."

"Oh, all right." Laine agreed with reluctance. "But only because I don't want to spend all day arguing about it."

Swell, rescued by a pervert.

Sam rummaged through a kitchen drawer. "This should do the trick." Holding what looked like a utility knife, he knelt on the floor beside her. "Don't move."

"Believe me, I wasn't planning on it," she grumbled. Why was she feeling tingly while he sliced through the left leg of her jeans? Because it sent tingles of sexiness, having a handsome stranger cut her pants off, that's why. Kinky, but still sexy.

When he finished, she looked up and their eyes met. Then she watched his gaze rove over her in an unprofessional way.

"You sure you're an EMT?"

"I am. Want to see my badge?"

"No, forget it. I believe you."

"These should be easier to get off now."

Thank goodness I wore my nice panties and not the unraveled pair. Aunt Rose always said to wear clean underwear in case of an accident.

This is the most embarrassing thing that's ever happened to me.

I'm going to use all my old pairs of underwear as dust rags. I'm grateful these are my old jeans, because I don't have room in my budget this week for a new pair. Oh, and by the way, this is the most embarrassing thing that's ever happened to me.

Sam peeled off the jeans and stared at her panties. He started to laugh.

"What's so funny?" True, she hadn't had good luck in the man department, but no one had laughed at her panties.

He pointed.

Laine realized with growing horror, that she wore her joke panties. A strategically placed ice-cream cone adorned the front. Underneath, words stated, "lick me."

Laine groaned. *Why did I ever wear these this morning? Of all the pairs of panties I own, I had to pick these.*

"Don't worry, my lips are sealed." Sam smiled, producing a dimple on his right cheek. "I won't tell anybody that you wear kinky panties."

His impish amusement made him even more attractive.

"They are not kinky," she said, calling up reserves of dignity. "They show my sense of humor, that's all."

"Whatever you say."

Sam Holliston, the name rang a bell. Ah yes, Fiona.

"It's been a pleasure taking off your pants, for medical purposes of course." He took her hand, and their eyes met again. His grip was warm, the gentle pressure almost seductive. One more second and he'd have her hand to his lips, for Pete's sake. She jerked her hand away.

How could I feel attracted to him? I guess I shouldn't be too hard on myself. It's been a year since I've had anything remotely resembling a date, let alone sex. The exact dates are marked on my calendar in red.

Sam's manner became brisk. "I'll call the doctor while you get into my pants. Put on my sweatpants, I mean."

A wicked warmth suffused Laine as he blushed. *Got caught in your own trap.*

He wandered off in the direction of the bedroom while she pulled up a pair of his sweatpants.

"We'll have Doc Cremble take a look at that ankle. To make sure nothing's fractured," he said, returning to the room. "He says to come over now."

"That's amazing. In Boston it takes a month to get an appointment with my doctor. And that's for an emergency." Laine knew she babbled. It must be her ankle. It couldn't be cranky houseboat man.

Sam shrugged. "He's a family friend. Plus we're not in the city, in case you haven't noticed."

No shit Sherlock. She looked down at the baggy sweats. "These are at least fifty sizes too big. I'll have to tell the good doctor I did not escape from the circus."

"I'm glad you can joke about this."

"It's better than complaining. 'Laughter is the best medicine,' as Aunt Rose always said."

"Aunt Rose?"

"My aunt Rose took care of me after my parents died. She has sayings for everything. I call her the 'Maxim Queen.'"

The sayings drove Laine crazy when she was younger, but now she drew comfort from them. She even kept a box full of Aunt Rose's sayings to refer to when she needed inspiration.

"How old were you when . . . ?"

"They died? Thirteen." Other people always found it harder to talk about her parents' deaths. "But I had Aunt Rose's maxims to guide me through."

"I'm sorry. That's rough."

"They died in a car accident soon after my thirteenth birthday. They were on their way to a concert."

A concert where Dad performed.

Sam lifted her with care and carried her to his truck. He tucked an afghan around her waist.

"We've got to keep you warm." Sam slid into the driver's seat, cranked up the heater, and backed out the driveway.

"Are you comfortable, Laine? You warm enough?"

She liked the way he said her name, lingering on the L. La, la, la.

Laine nodded. *Oh, boy, I'd love to play doctor with him. Except, what about his hissy fit on the beach? He may be cute with those damp curls framing his face, but he's got a temper.*

Sam gave her such a look, she wondered for a sickening moment if she had said the words aloud. She changed the subject to be on the safe side. "I grew up with Aunt Rose in a trailer park in New Hampshire. Our trailer wasn't much bigger than your houseboat."

Laine never felt ashamed of having lived in the trailer park. Aunt Rose had made it a magical cozy place and that was all that mattered.

Sam smiled. "I bet it had much better decorations than my houseboat."

"Oh yeah." Laine thought about the beaded curtains and murals on the walls and lava lamps Aunt Rose favored. "Definitely."

SAM PULLED into the driveway of a white house with black shutters and pots of mums on the porch.

"Aren't we going to the doctor's office?"

"This is his office." Sam got out and opened her door. He lifted her from the passenger seat and gently swung her to the ground.

This is the life. I could get used to this.

She hobbled inside with Sam's help.

"I called ahead. Doc should call you in soon. In fact, here he is."

Doc Cremble looked to be in his late fifties with a shock of thick white hair. Casually dressed in jeans and a striped, button-down shirt, only the stethoscope around his neck gave him away.

He introduced himself and led her to a treatment room. After a minute of probing and prodding he pronounced the injury a simple sprain. "Looks and feels worse than it is; but stay off your feet for a couple of days."

If her ankle still hurt, she could wear a support bandage.

Doc Cremble smiled. "You couldn't find a better man to nurse you back to health," he said. "He's one of the best."

"Who? What? Oh, you mean Sam. I only met him a couple of hours ago. I don't know him very well."

Doc cocked his head and smiled. "My mistake."

Why did his smile make him look like the cat who ate the canary?

BACK IN the truck, Sam asked what she was smiling about.

"Every cloud has a silver lining."

"Aunt Rose again?"

"Exactly. I have so much reading to catch up on. I can't wait to pack my ankle in ice, climb into bed, and open up a good book."

Unless I had something better to do.

Her thoughts strayed again to Sam's physique, and this time she did sigh aloud. "You said you work at the houseboat. What kind of work do you do?"

"I'm a landscaper. I like to draw up my plans for gardens and parks at the houseboat because the ocean inspires me." His voice warmed to the subject. "The open space is like a clean sheet of paper."

Laine imagined the view from the houseboat; a river out one window, ocean out the other. "It must be an amazing view when it's not raining."

"You got that right. In New England, you can garden for only a few months of the year. Gardeners get pretty wound up during planting season." His eyes lit up, indicating he was one of those people.

"Do you have a garden of your own?" Maybe he had a water garden near the houseboat.

"You can't grow much in sand and marshes. I've got a house closer to town where I experiment with different plants. I'll show you sometime."

Laine nodded, but remained silent. Fiona had called Sam a low-life gardener. What would a high-life gardener be like? Fiona sure needed an attitude adjustment.

Sam pulled into her driveway and helped Laine to her door. On the porch, they stopped to admire the scenery.

"God's country." Sam gazed out towards Beaker's Point.

Laine nodded agreement. Between Seaglass Bay and Cuttyhunk Island stretched several miles of sea and horizon.

"The sky looks like it's smudged with a charcoal pencil." Laine held onto Sam's arm.

"Are you an artist?"

"I dabble in watercolors." Since the paintings were in her bedroom, he wouldn't get anywhere near them.

"Look." Laine pointed towards the water. "That sailboat's in trouble."

Sam followed her gaze. "Trouble is right. It looks like it's about to capsize. Crazy fools should know better than to trust late October weather. I'll call the Seaglass Bay harbormaster for help."

He pulled his cell from his pocket and within a few seconds he reported the boat in a calm take-charge voice. Maybe he really was an EMT.

"I'll drive to the Point to see if I can lend a hand." Sam pocketed his phone. "Why don't you rest? Elevate your foot. I'll come back and check on you later . . . if that's okay. Good eye, by the way."

"I want to come with you. I'm dry and warm and I can rest my foot on the dash."

Sam nodded. "Fine by me, but you'll have to wait in the truck."

Laine agreed. She sure didn't feel up to walking. But she wanted to see how this drama played out. After all, she'd spotted the boat.

My first real adventure in Seaglass Bay. Besides getting my pants sliced off by a moody hunk, that is.

They drove to the Point and arrived just behind the ambulance. Sam introduced her to Mike, the ambulance driver.

She remembered the other EMT, the lanky guy in the passenger seat, from one of her beach walks.

"Hi, Hank. How are you?"

"I'll be better when we know everybody's safe and sound."

The harbormaster's Boston Whaler motored past at a fast clip. Mike climbed out of the ambulance and made a great show of wiping the mirror, managing to flex about a hundred muscles in the process. He asked Laine how she liked living at the cottage.

Before she could answer, he wondered aloud if she got lonely at night. "If a pretty little girl like you needs company, I'm available."

"Watch out for Seaglass Bay's ladies' man, or horndog, as we guys call him," Sam said. "Mike, she's not a girl, she's a woman. You'd know that if you got your head out of your ass and into the twenty-first century."

"C'mon. Girls love old-fashioned guys, right Laine?"

Laine rolled her eyes but couldn't help smiling at the incorrigible man. Hank saved her from answering by asking her about the BNC.

She was in the middle of a reply when the Coast Guard call came in. The twenty-six-year-old male they'd picked up exhibited signs of hypothermia.

Mike and Hank shifted gears into efficient work mode as they readied the stretcher and wool blankets. In under a minute, the harbormaster boat pulled in at the landing.

Mike and Hank placed the young man on a stretcher.

Sam helped the other EMTs wrap the man in wool blankets; then returned to the truck and Laine. "His name's Tim Hadley. He's conscious. That's a good sign."

"But his face is blue."

"It's the beginning of cyanosis. Hopefully he wasn't in the water too long. What an idiot."

"Hey, just because I didn't know about cyanosis doesn't mean I'm an idiot."

"Sorry. I'm talking about sailor boy, not you. You've got to be an arrogant fool to go boating on an afternoon like this."

Maybe he's young and adventurous.

WHEN THEY reached her cottage, the view overwhelmed her yet again.

The ribbon of Coast Road led to the rocky beach. A sturdy maple stood about twenty-five yards from the cottage, a few leaves still waving from its branches. Scrub pines dotted the landscape wearing varying shades of green. A ginkgo tree stood at the side of the house closest to the street.

The ginkgo leaves fluttered in the gentlest of breezes. Every time the wind kicked up, the tree swayed back and forth like a drunken prom queen. When Laine moved into the cottage the tree had a full crown of burnished gold leaves. Then one morning she woke up and the leaves had fallen to the ground. Every last one of them.

"Maidenfern cottage is something else."

"What did you call it?"

"Maidenfern. Maidenhair ferns look like ginkgo leaves."

Laine smiled. "My first house with a name." *As a matter of fact, my first house since I was thirteen.* Since then there'd been Aunt Rose's trailer and the Boston condo.

"Many of the nineteenth century homes around here were built for and named after New Bedford whaling captains," Sam told her.

"Is that why they have those widow's walks on top of the houses? So the wives could go up to the platforms and watch for their husbands at sea?"

"That's the romantic version. I think those cupolas were a popular feature of Italianate architecture. Whaling captains could well afford them during the whale oil heyday. Don't get me started. I'm a history buff and I could bore you to tears."

"I don't think so. I love history, especially of the local area. Makes me feel connected to my home."

Sam's dimples came out full force. "I'll never run out of things to talk to you about. That is, if I . . ."

"My cottage is named after a fern. I like it," Laine interjected, to save herself any further awkwardness. Sam didn't look like the type to feel awkward.

He helped her hobble inside and get settled on the couch. "I'll make you a cup of tea, if you've got any." He placed a pillow under her leg.

Laine hesitated, wrestling with her mixed feelings for this man. Annoyance, doubt, the beginnings of respect mingled with attraction.

"I promise I won't call you an idiot."

"I've been called worse things," she said with a smile. "My ankle's throbbing." She told him where to find the tea bags; then listened to Sam bustling in the kitchen.

A few minutes later, he handed her a steaming mug of tea. "I'll get you a cold pack if you've got one."

"I don't think so. I don't have any ice cubes either." She pressed her finger against her bottom lip for a second. "I have four pints of Ben & Jerry's. My emergency stash."

"Which flavor can you part with?"

"Hmmm." Life often held difficult decisions. "Chunky Monkey, I guess."

Sam pulled the ice cream from the freezer. As requested, he gave them each a large spoonful before wrapping the container in a towel and handing it to Laine. She held the ice cream to her ankle and waited for the cold to stop the pain.

Sam poured himself a cup of tea, pulled the rocker next to the couch, and sat down.

"Thanks for everything," Laine murmured as she warmed her hands around the hot mug.

"Don't mention it. How's your ankle?"

"Much better on ice cream." She raised her teacup. "I'm into firsts, so here's to my first house that has a name."

Sam raised his mug. "Here's to you. I think you had some other firsts today."

Laine colored as she remembered her jeans getting sliced off. "Yes I did."

They sat quiet for a few moments, sipping tea.

"So, am I still the rudest man you've ever met?" Sam's cheeks dimpled with his smile.

"Maybe. But you've certainly exonerated yourself quite a bit today."

"That's all a man can ask for. When you're back on your feet, come to Serena's on the peninsula." He carried the cups to the sink.

"Who's Serena?" she asked, sneaking peeks at his snug-fitting jeans.

"You mean what's Serena. It used to be a coffee shop."

"Is Seaglass Bay the coffee capital of the world? There's a coffee shop for every ten people."

"Yeah, I know. People around here like their coffee. Really what they enjoy is getting together for some gossip. Coffee is as good a reason as any. Unfortunately, Serena's coffee tasted like low tide. So she got the idea to open a bar. How hard could it be to pour beer and wine? She mixes up her mixed drinks though, sometimes."

"I can imagine what she does with a screwdriver."

Sam chuckled. "Every Wednesday night a few of us play folk and blues. It keeps us out of trouble." He hesitated a moment. "Stop in on Wednesday night if you feel up to it."

It seemed like ages since she'd been out at night. It had been ages.

"So is it a date?"

"It's a date." Laine blushed. "I didn't mean a real date, I meant as friends."

"You're making it worse." Their eyes met, and in that instant Laine moved closer to Sam. She lifted her face to his.

A passing truck sent vibrations through the house, breaking the spell. Laine opened her eyes.

What am I thinking? I almost kissed a man I met several hours ago. This is crazy. So what if he's hot.

They pulled back at the same time and stared at each other, as starstruck as two teenagers.

Laine turned away first. "I'm feeling a little woozy. Must be hormones. Or low blood sugar."

"I'm feeling woozy too, but I don't think it's hormonal." Sam scratched his head. "I think it's something else entirely."

Laine broke the silence. "The sky cleared up out there." When in doubt, talk about the weather.

Sam looked out the picture window. The view seemed to rouse him. "That's New England for you. I spent a winter in Arizona designing a park a few years back. The first morning, I walked into the coffee shop and mentioned the sunny weather. They told me the weather was always nice, and looked at me like I had two heads. I'll take New England any day."

Freak snowstorms and surprise almost-summer days in November made up New England's weather. "Me too. I'm going to climb into bed."

And ponder the error of my ways.

"I have landscaping plans to finish. Of course, maybe you need help getting into bed."

Her heartbeat quickened, but she forced her words to sound light. "No thanks. Although I'm sure your EMT training would come in handy."

He grinned. "That's for sure. I'll call you tomorrow and see if you need anything. Is that okay?"

Laine nodded. "Thanks again."

As Sam's truck pulled out of the driveway, she breathed in his lingering pine needle smell. She breathed so hard, she almost hyperventilated.

That man is dangerous. I can't let myself get too close.

Conflicting thoughts pranced around inside her head.

Too soon. Only been a year since my last fiasco. He's too handsome. Plus he looks like a real rascal. I want an unattractive boring man who won't ever leave me. Did that thought just cross my mind? How lame.

HOBBLING INTO her bedroom, she eased down onto her double bed, thinking of her long, love-dry year. And the pricking of attraction to a man she'd met only a few short hours ago sent shivers up her spine. Maybe they could have a one-night stand. They wouldn't be standing for long, though. Laine gave herself a mental slap for her shallow thoughts, but it didn't stop her fantasies.

How about his angry tirade when I walked on his property? Maybe he's a territorial male, or was he hiding something?

Laine snuggled under the covers. *He's a bad-tempered country boy. No, he made a simple mistake. Everyone makes mistakes. He woke up on the wrong side of the bed.* She'd done that herself. He was sick of tourists traipsing around and who could blame him? She'd ask him more about it when she got a chance.

Aunt Rose always told her curiosity killed the cat and put humans into a mess of trouble. Laine didn't believe it. Curiosity kept her healthy and alive, didn't it?

My cottage even has a name. Maidenfern. It sounds like an old fairy tale filled with wisewomen making potions.

She imagined a painting of ferns with female faces blowing gently in the breeze. She wanted to explore that image by painting a watercolor. If she didn't get up and do a quick sketch she would forget it by morning. That was her last thought before she fell fast asleep.

Four.

Wednesday

LAINE WOKE up the next morning on a bed full of potato chip crumbs. She inhaled the damp sea salt smell permeating the cottage. She chuckled, remembering how Toby made her promise to stop eating in bed after he woke up with a chip up his ass. Now that she saw him in the rearview mirror she realized how full of himself he had been. She didn't miss him. As raindrops streaked the windowpane, she raised herself with an effort and swung her legs off the bed.

Wincing, she touched her foot to the floor. Standing in spite of the pain, she stretched her arms, peered into the mirror, and admired her violet-flecked brown eyes. Her dusky skin glowed again, and the copper highlights in her newly cropped brown curls sparkled. At least she could have a good hair day.

Turning from the mirror, she surveyed the books on her bookshelf. On impulse, she picked up the self-help book; her Bible for the past year: *Women Who Love the Wrong Men Who Don't Love Them Back*. Smiling ruefully, she tossed the paperback towards the trashcan. The book slapped the wall and hit the floor.

I'm sick of reading about relationships. I've probably read enough to qualify for a PhD in dance-away lovers, feeling-stuffers, and codependents. If I never see the words 'heart connection' and 'emotional distancing' again, no problem. I'd rather read about osprey habitats any day of the week.

A picture of Sam floated into her mind and she willed it to go away. If she had the choice she'd kick November right off the monthly lineup. November, the month her parents died, thirteen years before. November, the month she broke up with Toby, exactly one year ago. November, the month of Thanksgiving, that drove home that she only had Aunt Rose for family.

Stop right there, girl. Cut the "poor me" mantra. Close the door on your past.

Laine sighed, thinking of her Aunt Rose. Aunt Rose stood at just under five feet, but her fiery red hair and dynamic personality made her appear much taller.

Laine sucked in a deep breath and returned to more immediate concerns. First she called the Bay Nature Center. When Fiona answered, Laine started to explain about her ankle.

Fiona immediately interrupted. "I heard Sam Holliston took you to see Doc Cremble."

"Really?" Fiona should be a private eye, the way she ferreted out information. The nature center wasted her natural talents.

"Are you home in bed with a sprained ankle or with Sam Holliston?" Fiona gave a mirthless laugh. "Figures Sam Holliston is sniffing around the new girl in town. He's gone through every other woman in town. Watch out for him; he's a loser, a boozer and a user." Fiona giggled as if impressed with her attempts at poetry.

Laine ended the conversation as fast as she could.

After spending a couple of peaceful hours lying in bed watching nature films, she hobbled over to the couch for a change of scene. She considered opening a can of soup when someone rapped at the door.

"Who is it?"

"It's Sam." His voice sounded muffled through the closed door.

"C'mon in," she said, annoyed at her quickening heartbeat. "The door's unlocked." *Maybe my heart's racing because I'm hungry. Maybe it's a vitamin deficiency. I must make a mental note to schedule an appointment with Doc Cremble.*

As soon as Sam stepped inside, a tangy aroma wafted towards her.

"I brought lunch. Curry chicken salad in French sourdough bread from the Corner Kitchen." Framed in the doorway, Sam's presence brightened the room. Hell, it brightened the neighborhood. His tanned face and muscular body radiated health and virility.

Laine stood up. "It smells delicious." She shuffled toward the door and took the bottle from Sam's outstretched hand. "Wine?"

"Seaglass Spirits. There's a winery right here in the village."

"How does it go with painkillers?" She hobbled to the couch. "I'm kidding. I haven't taken any meds today."

"I probably should have called first. I'm used to dropping in on people. My city friends tell me it's a small town thing."

"Don't worry about it. Hand over the sandwich, STAT." Laine's mouth watered in anticipation. "This is great, and I'm starving. Eating is my favorite pastime in the whole world. I mean, it's one of my top favorite things," she amended in answer to Sam's amused expression.

I'm acting like a maniac. I'll blame it on the ankle. Not enough blood getting to my head.

"Sit down." She patted the couch beside her. "There's plenty of room."

They sat in companionable silence and munched the crunchy baguettes.

"It looks like they stuffed an entire chicken into my

sandwich." Laine wiped her mouth and abandoned all pretense of etiquette as clumps of chicken salad plopped onto the white paper wrapping.

"I like how you decorated the place," Sam said in between bites.

"Thanks. Look around if you want."

Sam stood, stretched, and gave himself the ten-second tour. He peered through the open door into the bedroom.

"Did you paint the watercolors?"

"Guilty as charged. I hung them in my bedroom so nobody would see them."

Sam raised his eyebrows.

Laine blushed. "I don't mean nobody. I mean not too many people. God, foot-in-mouth disease must go with the sprained ankle."

Sam laughed. "I like your sense of color and attention to detail."

Laine's face glowed with pleasure.

"Why did you choose to use watercolors?"

No one had ever asked her that before and she liked the question.

"You mean instead of oils and acrylics? I guess it's because watercolors can be soft and suggestive or stronger and more colorful. I've always liked the idea of white space. Lots of room for the imagination."

"Nice. I see you also painted the bedroom walls."

"How do you know? Did the last gal who lived here sprain her ankle too?"

"You cut me to the quick." Sam placed his hand on his heart and tried to look affronted. "I knew the guy who used to live here. The latrine green walls looked pretty gruesome."

Laine smiled. "They did. Luckily I had time to paint before I started my new job. It was like living inside a poopie diaper." They both laughed.

"I like the purple."

"Thanks. My room was lavender when I was a kid. Now, wherever I live, I paint my bedroom lavender for good luck. I guess it sounds silly," she added, noting Sam's amusement.

"It's not silly. I do something like that."

"What?"

"I stick at least one myrtle plant in every garden I design. When I was six, I dug a bunch of myrtle from a neighbor's yard without asking. I thought plants were free for the world. I planted it under our maple tree. It spread all over the front yard. After three years, we didn't even have to mow the lawn anymore. Everyone stopped to admire it in the spring. Maybe that's why I went into landscaping. It was something I could do, something I enjoyed, and it made people happy."

Laine smiled.

He believes in good luck like I do. But what about that little anger management problem he displayed yesterday?

"Why did you get so pissed off when I trespassed on your property?"

"You mean, why did I rant and rave like a total asshole?"

"Something like that."

"I'll tell you. This past spring, a Boston magazine featured an article of fantastic secret getaways. The reporter listed the beach near my houseboat as a prime spot. The asinine photographer took a picture right in front of my property and put it in the paper. Secret getaway, my ass." He shook his head in disgust.

"There's already a town landing near my house, a place where townsfolk can picnic, launch their boats, or walk through to the river. I think public access is great. But the tourists who trespassed on private property drove me nuts."

Laine nodded in understanding. "You thought I was a tourist, huh? Did my binoculars and Hawaiian shirt give me away? Or my camera and fanny pack?"

"Very funny. Like I said, townsfolk are fine. But sometimes in the summer, the tourists are thicker than seagulls. I prefer the seagulls."

"I guess you're of the shoot-first-ask-questions-later school."

"I know. I'm a bad boy." Sam hung his head in mock shame.

Laine laughed. "That's okay. This feast almost makes up for your sins. I do have a favor to ask, however."

"Whatever your little heart desires." Sam raised his eyebrows ever so slightly.

Is that lust in his eyes? Stick to the program, girl.

Laine cleared her throat. "Tell me everything you know about the BNC."

Sam plopped down next to her on the couch. His arm brushed against hers, sending goose bumps up her spine.

"Sure thing. What do you want to know?"

"The history of the center, public opinion, anything that will help me understand the BNC and the Seaglass Bay community better. *Plus, there's something odd about the place that I can't quite put my finger on.*"

"Okay." Sam leaned back and made himself comfortable. "A wealthy couple, Joe and Ethel Mackinaw, left a sizable chunk of wetlands to the Bay Nature Center when they died. The rest went to their daughter, Katherine."

"When was this?"

"About seven years ago. Before that the BNC sat on fifty acres. Now it's two hundred and fifty. The BNC's mission is to study and protect the beach and wetland areas. The

BNC land includes the building and the two hundred and fifty surrounding acres. Katherine immediately put her hundred and fifty acres up for sale. The state wanted to buy and preserve her part of the property, but they couldn't come up with enough dough. David Emson, Seaglass Bay's largest developer, bought the land. He's got about twenty-five or so large house lots for sale on what's now called Emson Estates."

"Katherine wasn't an environmentalist like her parents?"

"Hell no. She moved to Manhattan as soon as she turned eighteen. She couldn't wait to get out of the sticks. That's why the Makinaws left a chunk of land to the nature preserve. Katherine always had more interest in profits than plovers."

Laine nodded. Being curious about everything, she had plenty more questions. Did Katherine get along with her parents? Did she still live in Manhattan? But she put aside those thoughts for now. "Tell me more about the bike path."

"It's supposed to run through a section of the BNC, then along the old railway bed before ending up on a path to the beach. It's going to be awesome. I'll have to get my bicycle out of the basement and make sure I still know how to ride."

"They say it's one of those things you never forget how to do."

They stared at each other without speaking for what seemed like a full minute. An assessment, and maybe an acknowledgment of a kindred spirit. Laine wondered if she still remembered how to have sex.

"So how do people in town feel about the BNC?"

Sam pushed his thick dark curls back from his forehead. "They trust Brooke to make good environmental decisions for the town. They basically go along with whatever she decides."

"I wonder why it's so quiet all the time. The last nature center I worked at was bustling with activity."

"Yeah, well the Bay Nature Center has never really been a friendly kind of place. People are intimidated by Brooke and Fiona can be . . . abrupt."

That's not the word I was going to use.

"They aren't exactly user friendly."

Laine laughed. "That's for sure."

"Everyone's busy with work and families, so they leave Brooke and Fiona to supervise all conservation matters. This bike path is the first time the public has been this involved."

Hmmm. All this quiet autonomy gives them time to do their work and create mischief if they choose.

"Anything else?"

Laine shook her head. "Thanks for bringing the delicious feast." *A red-blooded male sitting next to me—and the only thing swollen around here is my ankle.*

Sam picked up the empty food wrappers, all but licked clean. He leaned over and kissed her lightly on the forehead.

What a tender thing to do. But I don't know if I'm ready for tender.

"You better go." Her voice sounded husky. "I need to rest."

"Right." He stood up. "I better get back to work."

He's a gentleman. Oh, shucks.

He hesitated before he said, "Call me if you need anything."

Anything?

"Anything," Sam said. It creeped her out the way he seemed to know her thoughts.

AFTER SAM left she crawled back into bed and surveyed her lavender walls and dark blue silk throw pillows with pride.

I had a live one standing in the doorway of my room. It's really true: if you build it they will come.

Laine tried to distract her thoughts by watching cooking shows, flipping from one to the next. They made it look so easy. When she was up and at 'em, she'd try some recipes. Or maybe she'd just keep on watching other people cook on TV. Less calories and cleanup that way.

Laine reached for the leather box on her bedside table, pulled out one of the sayings from Aunt Rose and read aloud. "Early to bed, early to rise, makes a man healthy and wealthy and wise." It seemed a particularly apropriate saying since she was lying in bed at the moment.

Laine recited her own version of the saying. "Early to bed, early to rise, your girl goes out with other guys."

The saying made her miss Aunt Rose, so she picked up the phone and dialed. Aunt Rose didn't disappoint. She worried and fussed about Laine's ankle, and gave decorating tips for the cottage.

"Make hay while the sun shines," Aunt Rose suggested. "Sew hems and buttons. Paint another watercolor. Don't forget to text me some photos of Seaglass Bay. I want to put names to the places and faces you talk about."

"I'll have to sprain both my ankles to have time to do all that. I miss you."

"Absence makes the heart grow fonder."

"Abstinence makes the heart go yonder," Laine said automatically. When she lived with Aunt Rose, she developed the habit of redesigning Aunt Rose's maxims.

After warm goodbyes, Laine guiltily turned off the TV and picked up a research guide to native birds. A few minutes later, she laughed and reminded herself she was a big girl. Aunt Rose lived many miles away, definitely not in peeking range. *Make hay while the sun shines, indeed. I'll make play while the sun shines.*

LAINE SPENT the rest of the day reading mysteries and romances and eating like a pig. An early orange sunset turned out to be a ruse, for evening brought wind and rain.

A TV mystery failed to hold her interest and she kept nodding off. She climbed into bed and let the sounds of rain and wind rock her to sleep.

LAINE DREAMED she sailed a small catboat. A man swam towards her. She could make out his head, sleek as an otter. Fins flapped behind him. He swam closer until suddenly he grabbed the gunnels, tipping the boat toward him. She realized it was Sam the moment she pushed him back into the water. She screamed, thinking she had drowned him.

Sam disappeared under the waves. Then she remembered his tail. He was a water creature. He would survive.

Five.

Thursday

～～～～～～～～～～～～～～～～～～～～～～～

THE NEXT MORNING, Laine woke up with the flannel sheets wrapped around her legs. She untangled herself, and eased out of bed. After wrapping her ankle with care, she wriggled into a pair of wide-legged jeans, a sweatshirt, and slipper clogs. She climbed into the car, careful of her ankle, and drove to the BNC offices.

When Laine entered the office, Fiona gave her the once-over. "You sure dressed down today. Your hair has that tousled, just-out-of-bed look."

Laine straightened her shoulders. *If you can't beat them, handle them with humor.* "I finally had to kick Armando out of bed," she said in her most serious voice. "He was good, too."

"I hope Armando is your cat."

"I don't have a cat. Armando does purr, though." Fiona's jaw dropped, much to Laine's amusement.

Brooke appeared in the doorway of her office. "Hello Laine; how's your ankle?"

"Much better, thanks. I have to cut out jogging for a week."

"Obviously not your other activities, though," Fiona muttered under her breath.

"I'm glad you're back. I want to introduce you to Tim." Brooke reached for an intercom on the wall. "He's our resident intern."

"Resident hottie," Fiona muttered.

"Tim, could you come up here for a minute please?" Brooke spoke into the intercom.

A mumbled male assent came through.

"He spends most of his time in the basement tending to the touch tanks."

"Dungeon," Fiona whispered.

Fiona would be wicked funny if she weren't so wicked. Brooke seemed to completely ignore Fiona's snide side comments.

Footsteps sounded on the stairs. A few seconds later a young man stood before them, pushing hair out of his eyes.

"Tim, meet Laine, our new children's director."

Laine did a double take as she stammered a hello. She had seen this man before. That time his eyes had been closed. Hell, he'd been an unbecoming shade of blue. Here in the BNC office stood none other than Tim Hadley, the man from the capsized sailboat.

Tim Hadley smiled and shook her hand. He explained he studied environmental management as a graduate student at the local state university.

Fiona's phone rang and she made a beeline for her desk. Brooke went back to her office. Tim visibly relaxed after her office door clicked shut. His shoulders sunk down an inch or two.

Interesting. Brooke made him nervous, too. Interesting, but not surprising.

"What kind of research are you doing?" Laine asked.

"I spent the last few months making sure the bike path won't damage any endangered species' habitats. My next project is studying the harbor seals on Shout Rock."

"I think Shout Rock is a stone's throw from my cottage."

"This winter you can take binoculars out to your front porch and catch a harbor seal or two sunning on the rocks.

They're really something to see."

"I'll be sure to do that."

As he talked, Laine noticed how cute he was. Not rugged like Sam, but fresh-faced and boyish.

He reminds me of someone, with the straight streaky-brown and blonde hair lopping over his eyes. Oh yes, the guy in the X-rated flick I saw at a college party. The movie, directed by a woman, had featured cute guys, especially one with dark eyes and sun-kissed hair. Was it natural or did he have it done? There was only one way to tell if he was a natural blonde.

Laine let slip out a giggle.

"What's so funny?" Tim scratched his head.

"Nothing, I'm in a good mood today," she explained, stammering.

I could have sex on the brain. Must be some kind of vitamin deficiency. Better hurry and make that appointment with Doc Cremble.

Tim smiled and led her downstairs. He pointed out several tanks filled with lobsters, blue crabs, starfish and other sea creatures.

"These are the touch tanks. Visitors can reach in and pick up the creatures." He watched as she stuck her fingers in the tank to feel a slippery scup.

"Kids of all ages love this part."

Laine noticed an expensive looking red racing bike leaned against the wall. "Is that yours? I don't know much about bikes, but this looks like a beauty."

Tim beamed. "Thanks, I got it for Christmas last year."

"You must be psyched about the bike path."

"I am. In fact, I've created a virtual tour of the proposed route. It's up, if you want to take a peek."

Oh good. At least someone is showing an interest in the bike path.

As LAINE returned to her desk and checked out the website, Brooke shot out of her office and flung a folder at Fiona. Then without a word, she strode out the door.

That woman had the warmth of a glacier. Laine knew the type. All their passion went to preserving nature with nothing left over for human beings. As Aunt Rose would say, different strokes for different folks.

Laine went back to the virtual tour and marveled at the plans. The path would go through beautiful country, including trout ponds and wetlands. It promised to be a real boon for Seaglass Bay.

AT ONE O'CLOCK, Laine's office hours ended. Suddenly wanting company, she asked Tim to go to lunch.

"Thanks but I can't today. I have to study for a research exam. I'm a poor boy trying to get his master's degree."

A poor boy with an expensive sailboat and a serious racing bike. Laine filed the information away.

AFTER LAINE ran a few errands, she stopped in the village to get a mug of soup at the Corner Kitchen. She parked the Honda and as she walked towards the café, she saw Brooke and Fiona inside, sitting at a window seat. Brooke saw her and waved. *Shit, I can't very well make a run for it.* Laine entered the restaurant.

"Hello Laine. Why don't you join us?" When Brooke waved her regal hand, it seemed impossible to refuse. "In fact, lunch will be my treat."

Laine sat down, put off-guard by this show of friendliness.

When the waitress appeared, Laine ordered the lunch special of fish and chips. The spaghetti dish looked yummy but she couldn't take the chance of sauce dripping down her chin in front of her boss.

After sharing a few pleasantries, Laine explained her plans for open house day. Children would hike and then return to the BNC for cocoa and crafts.

"I'll buy fifteen pairs of binoculars," Brooke said. "The children will get a much better view of the birds using them."

"That's great. I really appreciate your support."

"Make sure you use the binoculars for the birds," Fiona added in a catty tone. "They're not for spying on your neighbors."

Laine managed a smile. "My nearest neighbor is a quarter of a mile away. They'd have to be mighty powerful binoculars." Shit, the woman was incorrigible, even while dining in a restaurant. *Give it a rest, girl.*

Laine munched on her fish and chips. Delicious. She congratulated herself for not wolfing them down or moaning obscenely while she ate. The fries were to die for. She noted Brooke's meal did not include fries.

Laine held a theory that two types of people divided the world: those who ate fries, and those who didn't. A restaurant's quality could be determined by the French fries. These were hand-cut with the skins on. She'd have to come back alone when she could eat with wild abandon.

While Laine continued her love affair with the fries, Brooke scribbled a number on a slip of paper and slid it across the table.

"Give Stanton Coles a call," she instructed. "He travels to South America every few months to photograph and sketch birds. I'm sure he'll want to be involved with the children's programs."

Laine reached for the paper, but Brooke snatched it back and added another number.

"Sofie Pacheco designs soft-sculpture mammals for museums. She'll be another great resource for you."

Over coffee, Brooke regaled Laine and Fiona with stories of BNC victories. As far as Laine could tell, the BNC won almost every environmental battle in town. Clearly, Brooke held the power to sway many townspeople. Most of them were busy working, raising kids. They trusted Brooke and the board to make the right choices for the town's natural resources.

What's it like to have so much influence over people? I can't imagine having that kind of clout.

As LAINE drove home she thought about Fiona and Brooke. Fiona talked behind people's back, a gossip, and Brooke acted a bit stiff. Okay, she acted so stiff she probably needed fabric softener just to bend over. But everyone had faults. Laine had been known to have a few herself, though she couldn't think of any at the moment.

LAINE PLANNED to go for a beach walk when she got home. Instead, she found herself taking a detour and driving slowly along the shore road. The overgrowth of scrub pine and cedar made Windham Landing difficult to find, but she finally spotted the entrance. According to Tim's virtual tour, the bike path route began here.

Laine parked the car in a clearing and grabbed her old windbreaker from the back seat. After fumbling with the zipper, she searched around for the path.

To the left of the landing a narrow path vanished into a tangle of *Rosa rugosa*. Shivering, Laine stuffed her hands in her pockets and ventured down the path, careful not to trip on underbrush.

I wouldn't want to chance this deserted path at night. Not if I'm by myself.

As she walked, her internal antennae kicked in. Small details jumped out. The crunch of leaves under her boots, the rustle of a squirrel in the branches, the wind picking up.

According to Brooke, the path led to the old railroad bed. In the thirties, the Seaglass Express brought hordes of summer visitors to the elegant Bay Manor Hotel. Ladies in their summer dresses and floppy hats disembarked from the hot train and breathed in the cool, salty sea air. Now the hotel had become secrets in the sand, washed away by the '38 hurricane.

A clearing glimmered beyond the trees. Laine glimpsed part of the site of Emson Estates. The land gently sloped to the Seaglass River around the bend from the ocean.

Emson will make a killing on these house lots. They're bordered by the river and the nature preserve. A short jaunt to the ocean for boating excursions and picnics.

The sound of voices caught her attention. She tiptoed forward, hoping for a view of the speakers.

Hidden by pines, two men talked and gestured. She didn't recognize the round-faced man with curly grey hair. The other gentleman, his stately bearing evident even at a distance, looked familiar. She'd seen him somewhere, but she couldn't remember.

She leaned forward to eavesdrop. So intent on deciphering a word or two, she tripped and stumbled into the underbrush. Catching herself before she fell to the ground, her involuntary yelp of surprise attracted attention.

The men turned toward the sound, eyes scanning the brush for intruders.

Oh swell. I can't hear them, but they can hear me.

"Who's there?" One of the men started in her direction.

Damn. Laine didn't think they could see her behind the tangle of brush. Still, she turned and glided in silence, back the way she came. Her ankle didn't feel up to the task of running yet. Even so, bad ankle or not, she had no intention of sticking around. The men didn't look like they welcomed any intruders on their clandestine meeting. Bad things happened to girls like Little Red Riding Hood when they lingered in the woods to chat with the wolf.

BACK IN the car with windows rolled up and doors locked, Laine breathed a deep sigh of relief. She wiped her sweaty palms on her jeans.

That was an exciting adventure. I can tell because my heart's actually thrumming like a hummingbird. Either I was a spy in my last lifetime, or I've been reading too many mysteries. So I have a thrill-seeking side. So what? No crime in that. At least I'm not hang gliding during a hurricane or breaking into department stores wearing a ski mask. I'm just spying on people. Good wholesome fun.

Something about the two men in the woods seemed menacing, but now that she sat in the safe car she thought maybe she imagined it.

When she arrived home, she checked her voicemail and listened to Aunt Rose demanding that she choose between fried or roasted turkey for Thanksgiving.

The fried turkey would be difficult to make, the message said, since Aunt Rose didn't have a turkey fryer. She would be glad to buy one though, if that's what Laine wanted. If Laine preferred, she could even have a turducken. Aunt Rose explained a turducken was a turkey breast stuffed with duck and then chicken. That would also be hard to make, but Aunt Rose would do it if that's what Laine wanted.

Laine appreciated Aunt Rose's thoughtfulness. Aunt Rose knew Laine's most difficult moments struck on holidays. Many residents of the mobile home facility where Laine grew up gathered in the recreation hall for holidays. Everyone tried to make things festive for her, but those were the times she missed her parents the most. It sounded like a sob story, but in groups and healing centers she'd met countless others with similar situations, many even worse.

The holiday table laden with succulent turkey, gleaming candlesticks, and togetherness, didn't grace as many tables as the media made people think. She knew she was lucky. After her parents died, Aunt Rose had taken her in and treated her like the daughter she never had. Aunt Rose had become a version of Miss Piggle Wiggle, the storybook character who fixed everything with part good sense and part magic.

Laine immediately called Aunt Rose to cast her turkey vote.

"I vote for plain old roast turkey. Not that anything is plain the way you cook it. Fried turkey sounds interesting, but this year I feel a hankering for all the old traditions. Turducken if you are bored with nothing to do."

"That will be the day. Have you met anybody in Seaglass Bay yet?"

"Yes, I met my coworkers at the Bay Nature Center."

"I mean Men. You know, those people with hairy faces and big—"

"Aunt Rose," Laine interrupted.

"I was about to say egos, dear."

"Oh, them. There are a couple of guys, but they are friends, nothing more. You know how I feel after Toby. One of the men is down to earth, and the other man has a big sailboat."

"A big what?"

"Behave yourself, Aunt Rose. I said a big sailboat."

"I hope you'll have lots of tidbits for me when you visit. Now I'm old and boring, I live vicariously through you."

"You aren't boring." Laine laughed.

"Well use it or lose it, I say."

After they said their warm goodbyes, Laine made a cup of licorice tea. It should lessen her cramps, for she could feel them starting. Then she lit a fire in the fireplace. True, she cheated with fire-starter logs, but when that fire blazed, pride suffused her, as if she'd chopped down the tree herself. How good to be nurturing herself, instead of struggling to keep her head above water.

LAINE CALLED Stanton Coles, the birder, and they set a time to meet and share ideas. After they said goodbye, she breathed a sigh of relief. Phoning people she didn't know made her uncomfortable. When the conversations went well, she thanked her lucky stars. Buoyed by her success with Mr. Coles, one more call seemed in order.

Sofie Pacheco designed soft-sculpture mammals for museums and nature centers. While waiting for the ring, Laine remembered why the name sounded familiar.

Ah yes, Fiona's poison gossip, something about dating a married man.

Sofie answered on the second ring and invited Laine for a visit.

Pleased with herself for completing difficult tasks, she curled up and read while she ate her supper—a virtuous salad, augmented by a generous heap of potato chips. Hard to believe chips were actually junk food, especially these baked ones. Maybe licorice sticks for dessert counted as junk food too. But no, she'd bought organic licorice. Several of her food vices might be healthful. She had read somewhere that no one ever died from lack of junk food. She'd have to see it to believe it.

Laine returned with anticipation to her newest strong-woman detective mystery.

On page eighty-seven, the woman hopped out of bed at five in the morning, rushed to dress, and then kissed her sleeping lover. She tucked her gun into her jacket pocket.

"Don't go," he begged, trying to pull her back into bed. "I want to make love to you again and again."

"Never bother me when I'm on a case," the female detective said. "I'll call when I have time. Maybe I'll even let you make me dinner again, if I'm not too busy."

This novel sure beat the relationship self-help books.

Laine snuggled up in front of the dying embers. Finally, she secured a stray licorice stick between two pages to mark her place, and ambled to bed.

Warmth and comfort suffused her, more than it had in years. The sea air acted like a natural sedative.

I could stay here forever in my own private cave. Forever is a really long time. Maybe I should return Sam's call.

Laine jerked herself back from the edge of sleep and dialed his number.

"Hey, returning your call," she said to his voice message. "Oh yeah, this is Laine. Okay, bye."

"Don't look at me like that," she scolded the bedside clock. "I can't help it if my message sounded lame."

Laine had gotten into the habit of talking to inanimate objects since she couldn't afford pet food and vet visits. Someday she'd have a pet, but for now the clock and toaster met her communication needs.

"What am I supposed to do? Tell him to come over and ravage me? Don't answer that." *If I keep thinking along those lines, it's going to be a long night.*

Six.

Friday

~~~~~~

IN THE MORNING, Laine pulled on her navy blue jogging outfit and headed for the beach. Of the resolutions she made after moving to Seaglass Bay, she intended to keep the one to walk at least once a day. She still needed to go easy on her ankle, but she could walk a half a mile if she took it slow.

On most days, Laine jogged to the concrete foundation—all that remained of a cottage after the '38 hurricane tore up the shoreline. Today she walked at a leisurely pace, her eyes on the lonely and austere stretch of beach.

The beach displayed a different mood every hour of every day.

"I am the only person here. Me, and the rocks, and the sea," she sang while she walked. "Me, the rocks, and the sea." Much nicer than hiding in a sea of faces in Boston.

Laine's thoughts wandered to yesterday's wood trail spying adventure. Who were those fellows anyway? A good chance existed the round-faced guy was David Emson, since he owned the land. The other guy looked like a prospective buyer.

According to Sam, the lots would sell for at least a million dollars each. No low-income housing for Emson Estates. Laine wondered if any of the lots had sold yet.

After her short but enjoyable walk, she spent the rest of the morning doing chores. In the olden days in Seaglass

Bay, that would have included sewing clothes and salting codfish. These days it meant a trip to the grocery store, drugstore, and laundromat.

After lunch she patrolled Beaker Point. The unseasonably warm day shimmered in hazy sunlight.

Laine stopped to chat with hikers and answer questions about winter gulls. She told a group of children, many different types of seagulls called the beach home.

"People throw trash right in the seagulls' living room, so we have to help keep it clean," she explained. Much as she loved the children and their eager curiosity, she finally said goodbye. She had an appointment with Sofie Pacheco. If she didn't hurry, she'd skip fashionably late and go straight to unfashionably tardy.

Driving down the dirt road to Sofie Pacheco's house, she imagined Sofie as a country girl wearing something along the lines of a comfortable denim smock and clogs. Her voice had sounded friendly enough on the phone.

As Laine's car approached the house, the woman sweeping leaves from the porch straightened up and waved. Laine laughed out loud as she took in Sofie's outfit. Country bumpkin indeed.

Yes, Sofie did wear clogs, but there the similarity between real and imagined ended. The clogs had three-inch heels, not that Sofie needed the height. Her form-fitting red sweater didn't quite meet the top of the hip-hugging black slacks. To top it all off, her glorious hair formed a halo of thick dark curls.

As Laine stepped onto the porch, she noticed white powder covered Sofie's clogs.

Following Laine's gaze, Sofie looked down at her shoes and smiled. "It's flour. I made bear claws. Come in and try one with a cup of tea."

"Bear claws aren't actually made from bears, are they?"

"No." Sofie laughed. "They're made with apples and honey. They're called bear claws because I press my fingers in the dough before baking, and the cookies come out looking like little paws."

A few minutes later, Laine munched on a bear claw, fragrant with lemon and cinnamon, and sipped spearmint tea. "I'll try not to take much of your time." Although she wanted to stay all day eating goodies and breathing in the mouth-watering cooking smells.

"Don't worry. I've started sewing a dolphin and I'm at the avoid-getting-to-work stage. It's tiresome, but I must wait for the muse to strike." Sofie pantomimed hitting herself over the head and they both laughed.

Laine looked around the room and sighed with pleasure. "I love your cast-iron pots hanging from ceiling hooks."

"They aren't merely cookware; they're weapons. Cast-iron pans are a major murder weapon in Sweden during the dark season. You know, the husband complains about too much salt in his food and *wham!* The wife clobbers him over the head with a fry pan. Anybody tries to break in here, and I'm ready."

"Thanks for the warning."

Bouquets of dried herbs and strings of garlic and red onion hung from the ceiling beams. A window shelf held wine glasses catching the sunlight, reflecting bright stained glass shapes and colors across the room.

"I want a kitchen like this someday," she told Sofie. "It's so homey and inviting."

"Thank you."

"This is a dream kitchen." Laine described her apartment in Boston. "White walls, white floors, white ceilings, and white appliances. I could hardly tell them apart."

"That does sound like a lot of white. I guess it takes a stranger's eye to make you appreciate what you have. Although I don't think you'll be a stranger for long."

Oh yay. Maybe I'll make a friend. That's another one of my resolutions.

AFTER THEY finished their honey-dipped pastries, Sofie showed Laine the small upstairs space where she created her mammal masterpieces. Fabrics and sketches of sea creatures filled the room. Sofie's desk stood in front of a large picture window, overlooking stone pathways that curved between stone and wood sculptures.

"That's my herb garden. Sam Holliston helped me design it."

Laine's heart started up, skyrocketed to her throat, made a quick U-turn, and traveled back to her chest.

"It's beautiful. I've met Sam." Laine mustered a casualness she didn't feel.

"No kidding. Did you?" Sofie gave her a sidelong glance.

Laine, eager to change the subject, asked Sofie to tell her more about the marine soft-sculpture business.

"I graduated from the Rhode Island School of Design," Sofie explained. "I wanted a job where I could be my own boss. I'm not meant to work for other people. In high school, I worked at a donut shop. One day I went to spray whipped cream on a customer's hot chocolate. The can malfunctioned and I accidentally sprayed all the customers. I gave the mayor of Bedford Falls a whipped cream beard, and she was none too pleased."

Laine laughed at the image of customers decorated in whipped cream.

"That was only the first of a string of unusual work experiences. Anyway, I decided self-employment was the way to go. One day at the Boston Aquarium, I got the idea to create anatomically correct soft-sculpture sea creatures. It was rough going at first, but now I get commissions from museums and nature centers all over the country."

Sofie lifted the teapot and refilled both their cups. "Pretty soon I'm going to have to hire some help, hopefully a young eighteen-year-old stud. But that's enough about me." She drizzled a spoonful of honey into her tea. "How do you like the BNC?"

"I like my work so far. Tim, the intern, is cute in a surfboard beach boy way. Brooke has a stick up her ass, and Fiona is a bitch. Other than that they are fine."

Sofie threw back her head and roared. "Tell me what you really think. Here's my advice: don't say anything personal to Fiona. She's like a one-woman welcome wagon speeding in the wrong direction down a one-way street."

"My sentiments exactly." Laine chuckled. "I think she absorbs secrets through osmosis. She and Brooke are tough to warm up to. I don't share anything personal with Fiona unless I want to read about it in the morning paper and watch it on the evening news."

Sofie nodded. "No kidding. You got that right. She's always trying to get dirt on me. I find it a challenge to hide from her."

"The BNC is a strange place."

"How so?"

"It feels more like a funeral home than a nature center except for its planned activities."

Sofie guffawed. "Funeral home. I like that. I know what you mean. It's not a warm and fuzzy place. Brooke has been the director for so long, and although qualified and competent, she's rather a cold fish."

"I wonder if that's all it is. Something doesn't feel right. They got a grant from the state to build a bike path and they are dragging their heels."

"No kidding? That doesn't sound like Brooke. She's usually raring to go."

"Not this time. What about Sam?" Laine tried to sound only mildly interested. "Do you know him well?"

"I sure do. Sam is my sister's husband Rick's stepbrother's cousin. I see him at family functions."

"Oh, I think I got that. What's with this town? Everybody is either related or has known each other since grade school. It's incestuous."

Sofie smiled. "It's like that song about being my own grandpa. But let's get back to Sam. He's a terrific guy, and sexy as they come. He's got his demons though."

Laine wondered what his demons were but Sofie stayed mum on that score.

"Some women love that rugged type," Laine said, giving in. "He's probably got half the women in town after him."

"Actually more like two-thirds."

"At least I know Fiona Glaze isn't one of them."

"No kidding. Is she talking trash about him again? She has no right after what happened between them."

"What happened between Fiona and Sam?" Laine asked, now trying the direct approach.

Sofie pantomimed zipping her lip shut. "That happened years ago, back in the college days. Anyway, no matter what Fiona says, you'll never find a better man."

"Who says I'm looking?" Laine ignored the butterflies in her stomach. "I don't even like the rugged type." *Uh-huh.* "What about you? Are you attracted to him?"

Sofie dropped her jaw in exaggerated shock. "We're almost related, remember? Besides, I'm into older, cultured men. If we meet any men, I'll take the father and you can have the son."

Laine smiled as she gathered her notes. "That sounds fair."

"Why don't you come for supper day after tomorrow?" Sofie suggested. "Next week I'll be completely immersed in my project. But this week I'm in my 'avoiding work' phase. Besides, there's no time like the present."

Aunt Rose really would love Sofie's maxims.

"I'd like that. What can I bring?"

Seven.

~~~~~~

S AM CALLED the next morning to invite Laine for a
drink at Serena's, and she tried not to act as if she
had won the lottery. After ending the call, she did a
tiny dance of glee around the cottage.

"I'm not gloating. I'm doing my exercises," she reassured
the asparagus fern. "I know I need to go slow. I don't have
a great track record with men, or man I guess I could say."

But Sam was handsome and rugged. Sam smelled nice.
Sam looked at her with dark brown eyes that made her
heart go gushy all over.

Work at the nature center went by very slowly as she
counted down the hours until she'd see Sam.

Evening eventually arrived, with a rose-stained horizon
for fanfare. Laine threw on jeans and a sweater, but then
took extra care with hair and make up. A search online
dug up several inconsequential tidbits about her favorite
actors and musicians to make sure she arrived fashionably
late. She arrived at Serena's to find Sam waving to her
from a booth near the door. He stood as she approached
and gave her a hug, proving he'd been top of his class in
hug school.

Catching her breath, Laine plunked down across from
him. To her chagrin, she found herself tongue-tied.

*Where are my scintillating conversation skills? I need a
refresher course.*

"It's crowded for a weekday," she tried. *Oy. And how about those Red Sox?*

"That's because it's buy-one-drink-get-the-second-free day."

"No wonder you brought me here. Cheap date." Their laughter broke the tension.

"So Laine, tell me how you spend your time. When you're not working, I mean."

His way of asking the question made her feel important. With eloquence, she expounded on her various interests: hiking, painting, and reading. He listened intently, almost as if she doled out state secrets. She could have purred with pleasure.

Weren't guys supposed to listen to women? So what if it was just a ploy to get women into bed? If her damp panties were any indication, Sam's ruse made a good start.

Laine brought her thoughts away from panties and back to her hobbies. "I want to learn how to cook," she finished. "My specialty right now is grilled cheese."

She realized she knew very little about Sam, besides his being good with quips and cutting through jeans with a knife. She asked about his interests and was surprised to find they shared many pastimes and favorite mystery authors.

"You read the books with the strong women detectives? Seriously? Like Sarah Paretsky, Sue Grafton, and Laura Lippman?"

"Cross my heart. I even read Janet Evanovich. But lest you think that makes me less manly, I also read hunting and fishing magazines."

"Thank God, you had me worried there for a minute." She loved thinking of Sam reading books by her favorite authors.

"Do you read romance novels, too?"

"Definitely not. I must draw the line somewhere. Of course, if a book has a tiny bit of romance in it, I don't mind." He went on to list the rest of his interests.

"Wow," she said when he finished. "I've never been hang gliding, white water rafting, or hot air ballooning."

"We can remedy that." The fine crinkles around his eyes deepened when he smiled.

Crow's feet and laugh lines look so much better on guys. Not fair.

"I've never climbed Mount Washington or done a Vermont bed and breakfast biking tour."

"That also can be arranged."

We'd wake up in each other's arms in the bed and breakfast. He'd suggest skipping the biking and instead want to have wild monkey sex on the featherbed.

"Separate bedrooms, of course," she said, and then mentally slapped her forehead.

I sound like such a dope.

"Of course." His smile made him look like the cat that swallowed the canary.

Damned if he couldn't read her thoughts.

"Does your family live in the area?" Laine drained the last of her wine.

"My mom and dad live in a canned retirement village in Florida. They have a summer place here in Seaglass Bay." Sam went on to explain his father was a retired doctor. "I tried a stint in medical school, but I didn't like it. I loved Seaglass Bay, even as development encroached on the open spaces. I figured landscape architecture was a way to preserve the natural beauty."

"But, you're an EMT too. Aren't you?"

"Why? You think I removed your jeans under false pretenses?"

"The thought crossed my mind."

"I wish I had to perform CPR too," he said with a shit-eating grin. "Yes, I'm an EMT. I'd rather save plants, but I don't mind saving a person now and then." He reached out to graze her cheek with his fingers.

Laine shivered.

LATER THAT evening, when they got back to her cottage, she surprised herself by inviting him in for coffee. He surprised her back by taking her in his arms, right there in the driveway. His lips brushed down her face until they found her mouth. His lips grazed hers, at first the barest touch, as gentle as a summer breeze. But the kiss grew steadily stronger, until their lips merged in passion.

Sam wrapped his arms around her shoulders, making her feel warm and safe. As she kissed with eyes closed, Laine let herself sink into feeling the lush heat of the moment. She savored the tingle electrifying her body as she melted into his arms.

After he brushed an unruly strand from her eyes, he kissed the nape of her neck.

If anything drove her wild, neck nibbling did. She pulled away before he could go any further. Ear licking usually followed neck nibbling. And after ear licking, *Oy!*, she didn't even want to go there.

"I've wanted to do that all evening."

"Double wow. Okay, time for you to go."

"But I haven't even gone in the house yet. We haven't had coffee."

"Extenuating circumstances."

"Does that mean you liked the kiss?"

"Good night."

BEFORE HE climbed back into his car she called, "I liked it."

Laine could see his wide grin from the doorway.

As soon as he drove a safe distance away, she stepped inside. She sank onto the couch, fanning herself with her hand.

The kiss was a weird moment brought on by wine, a strained ankle, and the fact that I needed to be kissed badly. I mean I badly needed a kiss. I'm okay now. I'm fine.

Laine eyed the coffeemaker. "I know what you're thinking. I couldn't let him in. I would have attacked him while you were percolating." A dog or cat would be much more understanding.

Eight.

Sunday

LAINE SPENT most of the next day at her desk at the BNC designing children's programs. A sandwich at lunch turned out to be her only break. After finally finishing at four-thirty, she flipped through the pile of mail. As she thumbed through *Newsweek*, her eye caught a photo towards the back.

The caption congratulated F.F. Pearson, the department store and real estate mogul, and heiress Samantha Colt Brownstone on their recent engagement.

The smiling Pearson looked familiar. She'd seen that regal bearing before. Ah yes, the mystery man from her walk on the proposed bike path.

LAINE HURRIED home after work and concocted a fruit salad with the usual fruits plus dried cranberries and pomegranate seeds to make it special. She drove to Sofie's house, thinking about Pearson. What was his connection to David Emson if he wasn't buying a house? A mogul and a real estate developer. Hmmm.

Darkness had descended by the time she reached Sofie's farmhouse. November slowly squeezed the days shorter, but Laine didn't mind. The darkness provided a sense of coziness and reassurance.

Laine smiled, thinking about the long evenings in the trailer with Aunt Rose when they played Boggle and Scrabble. Sometimes Aunt Rose had even let her win.

Soon Laine, ensconced in Sofie's warm kitchen, ate a hearty kale soup chock full of linguiça, the spicy Portuguese sausage.

"Umm," Laine murmured, "I love kale soup."

"Are you Portuguese too?"

"My mother was Jewish and my dad was Portuguese. Ever have chopped liver with sweet bread and chorizo? Kale soup with matzo balls?"

"I can't say I have, although anything tastes good with chorizo. Many Portuguese families around here have Sephardic Jewish ancestors. My family probably has Jewish roots somewhere in the past. We've always had a tradition of drinking kosher wine on Christmas."

"I read about that. The first Jews to come to Newport were from Barbados and had Spanish and Portuguese ancestry. The cultures do have a lot in common. Like bread, for instance. Both cultures have so much bread. I think my parents fell in love with each other's carbs."

"No kidding. I'm one hundred percent Portuguese. When I go to my folks' house for dinner, it's carbo-load central. They fill my plate with rice, fried potatoes, and bread. Then we have rice pudding for dessert."

Laine sighed. "I know the feeling. My dad used to ask if I wanted bread, even with ice cream. It got to be a joke. Every topic had bread involved. 'You feeling tired? You got all A's? Have a little bread with that.'"

"Used to?"

Laine gave Sofie the Cliff Notes version of her parents' deaths and being adopted by Aunt Rose.

Sofie's eyes filled with sympathy. "I'm sorry."

"Thanks. It sucks, but wait till you meet Aunt Rose. She's amazing."

"I can't wait." Laine felt grateful that Sofie picked up her cue and moved on to other subjects.

As she sipped her Portuguese wine, Laine found herself spilling her guts about her old flame, Toby. Sofie proved an avid and sympathetic listener.

When Sofie refilled their glasses, Laine proposed a toast. "To my first friend in Seaglass Bay. I'm into firsts, so thank you."

"Here's to new friends." Sofie raised her glass. "I'm glad our paths crossed."

"Speaking of paths, want to hear something weird?"

"Always." Sofie moved her chair closer to Laine.

"I saw F.F. Pearson talking to David Emson when I walked in the woods the other day."

"No kidding. The great and mighty F.F. Pearson? Are you sure you recognized him?"

"Pretty sure. I saw his picture on a magazine cover. I went for a hike and I saw them walking around Emson Estates. I wonder if he's interested one of the house lots."

"That would be a hoot."

"I don't know about that." Laine didn't think most Seaglass Bayers would find it funny, especially if they were as protective of their privacy as one Sam Holliston.

"I hope he's not considering building a department store in Seaglass Bay," Laine said.

"No kidding. The Seaglass Bay town council would never let that happen. Not in a million years."

"Good." Laine stood and insisted on doing the dishes. Sofie readily agreed, and excused herself to give her mother a call.

"She called me this afternoon, and if I don't call her back she thinks I've been kidnapped—or even worse, that I've eloped."

As Laine washed the plates, she marveled, not for the first time, how much more fun she had washing dishes for someone else. As she placed the last dish in the drainer, a knock at the door startled her.

"Can you get that?" Sofie called. "I'm still on the phone."

Laine opened the door. The man standing on the stair looked familiar. It took her a moment to place him.

"Oh, hi. Hank, right? I didn't recognize you without your uniform." She waved the EMT into the kitchen.

"Lots of people don't know me without the uniform."

"Sit down, Hank," Sofie told him, coming into the room. "Laine doesn't bite."

Hank stepped into the kitchen and folded himself into one of the kitchen chairs with elaborate care. As he gazed at Sofie, his usually foggy look transformed into sunny affection.

What is going on here?

"This is my friend Hank. He's here to fix my plumbing."

Is that what you call it? I wish someone would fix my plumbing. It's time to exit stage left.

"Can I make dinner for you one evening next week?" Laine asked. "Next time you can do all the talking."

"That sounds great."

Laine said a hurried goodbye and hotfooted it out of there. Fiona had said something cruel about Sofie going with a married man. Could Hank be the married man? Well, Laine decided whatever it was, Sofie had a perfectly reasonable explanation.

As she drove, Laine marveled at how Sofie had already become a friend. Judging by the way Sofie and Hank looked at each other, there was plenty of friendship going on there too.

Laine liked to think of herself as curious, but not critical. Having an affair with a married man would be the last thing she'd do. But if that's what Sofie wanted, she wouldn't judge. She ended her inner discussion by listening to some of her dad's favorite tunes by Joni Mitchell and James Taylor.

Laine turned her imagination to planning a dinner for Sofie. One problem stuck out right away. She didn't have much of a recipe repertoire. When Aunt Rose tried to give her cooking lessons, she had balked, feeling like she could never be as good a cook as Aunt Rose.

I wish I'd let her teach me a few things when I had the chance. All I know how to prepare is canned soup, salads, baked potatoes, and grilled cheese sandwiches. Oh, and a passable omelet. But, I'm a whiz with the microwave.

I'll think of something. What I lack in skill, I can make up in creativity. And my dial-for-takeout finger works just fine.

BY THE TIME she arrived home, an almost-full moon rose above the horizon. A rosy glow tinted the underbelly of gray clouds.

Feeling full and content, she sat at the computer and planned children's programs. Designing a course to augment school systems' science curriculums, was an enjoyable challenge. The planning stage was a bitch, with no way around it. Once it got going, it'd be easier. But for now, she didn't mind working overtime at home, especially since her desk faced the ocean. She could just see the waves slowly fading into darkness.

Later, her head sank to the keyboard and she dozed off. She woke an hour later, dragged herself to bed and pulled up the blankets.

Nine.

Monday

〰〰〰〰〰〰〰〰〰〰〰〰〰〰〰〰〰〰〰〰〰〰〰〰〰

A T WORK the next morning, Tim surprised Laine with a lunch invitation.

"The Seaglass Café is a real experience. Make sure you're hungry."

"No problem on that score." Laine had finished breakfast three long hours ago, and her tummy rumbled every fifteen minutes or so.

As she worked at her desk and the clock inched towards noon she wondered about Tim's motives. Did Tim have any interest in her romantically? Nope, she didn't feel that vibe; even though she'd caught him staring at her cleavage once. Did he have a more nefarious reason? Maybe Tim was in cahoots with Brooke and Fiona in a BNC scandal. After wining and dining her, he would make her talk. He'd tie her to a chair and put her in a darkened room until she surrendered.

Wait a minute. I don't know anything, unless Tim wants secrets of the piping plover count from my last nature center job. Geez, I better not share these thoughts with anyone. I'll be locked up for having conspiracy theory delusions. He probably wants to bond with a friendly fellow female colleague. Fellow female? Now that sounds like an oxymoron. Laine turned her efforts to the computer and the next chance she got to check the time it was close to noon.

After packing up, she drove the short scenic ride to the Seaglass Café. Laine arrived before Tim. She stood outside for a moment to take in the ambience.

Nets, buoys, shells and twinkling lights wreathed the restaurant, nestled between two docks at the marina. A fisherman sat on an outside lobster pot bench drinking coffee. Mermaids could appear at any moment, ready to party. The word "quaint" in the dictionary should refer to the Seaglass Café.

Inside, she chose a table for two made from lobster pots. Tim arrived just after she sat down.

"Hi, you told me to be hungry, but I went a step further. I'm famished," she told him by way of greeting.

"Perfect."

From menus the size of window shades they both ordered the kitchen sink salad. The salad came in a bowl designed to look like a kitchen sink.

"My God," Laine exclaimed. "I thought you were kidding about the portions. They are the size of small countries."

"Nope, I may have even under exaggerated."

"Cute bowls." Laine dug in. A spinach leaf slid off her fork and onto her lap. Slipping her hand into her lap, she picked it up and brought it to her mouth.

Tim obviously made her feel more comfortable than Fiona and Brooke, at least while eating.

After a Beachglass Beer, Tim opened up even more. He leaned across the lobster pot table and told her that his father's business, a protective eyewear company, would soon go bust.

"He needed to be innovative and move with the times. But instead, he insisted on making safety glasses the same way he always did. Now the more modern companies are taking over. The dinosaur is left in the dust." Tim gritted his teeth.

"Gee, that's too bad. You sound angry."

"Yup, I'm pretty pissed off. I begged him to modernize his manufacturing. Now I have to sell my boat. And my jeep." He spat out the words. "I can't believe how badly my dad screwed up his business. He wouldn't listen to anyone."

"Do you have to sell your racing bike too?"

"What? No. I get to keep it. Consolation prize. I need some way to get to school and work. I wonder if I can buy snow tires for my bike."

Laine tried to reassure him, but how sorry could she feel for someone so self-absorbed? What a spoiled brat.

"At least you have parents, Tim, even if they mess up once in a while."

Tim looked at her as if she hailed from Mars.

"My parents died in a car crash when I was thirteen."

Tim had the grace to look sheepish.

"Hey man, I'm sorry. I didn't know."

"That's okay," she said, even though it wasn't. "I'll get the check since you've fallen on such hard times."

"Oh, no, you don't." Tim roused himself from his self-pity party. "I invited you. I want to pay. I'm being a jerk."

"We all go there." Then he told Laine what a difference her work made at the center, which put a smile on her face and ended the lunch on a more positive note.

As Laine left the boatyard, she noticed a FOR SALE sign prominently displayed on one of the sailboats. Tim's boat? It had to be. She'd recognize that red stripe on the hull anywhere. This boat had featured in her first—what should she call it?—capsism . . . capsize event. She stopped the car and stared. She might not know much about sailing, but the sleek lines, the teak molding, made Tim's boat a classic beauty.

Pretty fancy shmancy for a grad student. I didn't even own a toaster in college. Should I park and take a closer look?

She glanced at the dash clock.

No. Better stop dilly-dallying. Time to meet Stanton Coles.

A SHORT DRIVE brought Laine to her destination. Stanton Coles's house, constructed of mostly glass, looked out over beach grass, rose bushes, a rocky beach, and the ocean.

Aunt Rose's adage, "people who live in glass houses shouldn't throw stones," came to mind. What about that joke from college? Oh yeah, people in grass houses shouldn't get stoned. A call to Aunt Rose later tonight seemed appropriate, if only for the pleasure of hearing her reminder to wear a wool sweater and earmuffs at all times.

Her knock at the door was promptly answered by a handsome man who looked to be in his late fifties.

Stanton's full head of silver hair sat like a wooly cap on his thin, craggy face. His features, though nothing special separately, fit together in an attractive package. As he bustled about welcoming her in, he looked trim and fit in his black cords and royal blue sweater.

After hellos, he offered her a bottle of local root beer. While he fetched it from the kitchen, Laine took in the large room surrounded by glass windows. Who needed pictures of the ocean when every window showcased a real seascape. "Great view," she said when he reappeared with two glasses filled with ice and root beer. Laine hoped he knew she meant the ocean and not his fit body.

"Thanks. If you come upstairs and look across the road, you'll see part of the BNC land."

Laine followed him up a circular stairway to another row of floor-to-ceiling windows. He handed her a pair of binoculars.

"There's the top of the BNC building. Over to your right, you can see Emson Estates. Soon Emson's crew will start building on the big plots of land."

"I hear you're on the bike path committee. I walked part of the proposed route the other day."

Stanton nodded. "It's a lot of work, but it's worth it. I can see a section of the path from here. Let me show you." He adjusted her binoculars.

Laine peered through and could make out the Windham Landing sign and a winding ribbon of path peeking through the trees.

Wow, this guy's got a bird's-eye view of sections of Emson Estates, the bike path, and BNC.

"On my walk the other day I thought I saw Mr. Emson talking to F.F. Pearson. I wonder if he's interested in a house lot."

Stanton looked startled. "*The* F.F. Pearson? No, you must be mistaken."

Really? Now what makes you think that?

AFTER THE TOUR, they walked back downstairs; the sheer richness of the sunset through the windows caught their attention.

The sky flashed a lush orange, melting to purple behind the Elizabeth Islands.

She let out a small gasp. "It's so intense, like fireworks."

"I know. No matter how many times I've seen the sunset, it still takes me by surprise."

They stood together and watched as the colorful panorama faded into almost ordinary twilight. Sharing something so lovely gave her a strange feeling of intimacy towards Stanton. Seaglass Bay was filled with magic. Events had brought her closer to people all over the place.

"You can stargaze right from your living room."

"I'm quite the amateur astronomer. I've got a small telescope upstairs."

"I love to stargaze. My favorite star is Sirius. Can you see it from here?"

"On a clear night you can see Sirius if you look through the telescope. We'll do that next time you visit."

THEY STOOD for another moment gazing out at the approaching darkness.

"Did you do your own planting?" she asked as she sat back down on the couch. An obsessive interest in landscaping had plagued her since she met Sam.

"I don't do anything. It's just natural beachfront. I have dune grass, beach peas, and white and pink roses that make the rosehips—*Rosa rugosas*. You can still see some wizened rosehips on the bushes. My next-door neighbor spends all his time creating a rock garden, coaxing plants to grow. All summer long, he and his wife prune and spray. Me, I let everything grow wild, and that means I have time to enjoy birding, beaching, swimming and sailing."

IN THE LIVING ROOM, Stanton took the rocking chair and Laine settled on the sofa. Laine asked him about his birding interests. Stanton explained that birding and photography kept him busy since his early retirement from the banking industry. He made detailed notes and watercolors of his observations. As proof, he showed her a sketchbook filled with lively bird studies. Handwritten notes accompanied each sketch.

"These are wonderful! I like your attention to detail. How did you get interested in our feathered friends?"

Stanton grinned. "I had a pet parrot growing up in the city. It was the only pet the super would let us have in the apartment building. I taught him how to say some pretty interesting words. Then in sixth grade I did a science report on hummingbirds. I was hooked. I love to travel, and enjoying birds from different parts of the world adds another dimension to my trips. I usually give a presentation once a month at the BNC."

"That's fantastic. Would you consider giving a bird sketching class for kids?"

"Absolutely. And maybe we can make pinecone bird-feeders. We can work out the details later. By the way, in February I'm traveling to Belize with a birding group. I could show photos and films at the BNC when I get back."

"That's great. But I don't want to take up all your time."

"I'm retired and I'm single. Time is one thing I've got plenty of."

Stanton must've taken very early retirement.

As if reading her thoughts, Stanton explained: after twenty-some odd years of banking, he'd been able to retire comfortably.

Maybe I should tell Sofie about Stanton. He certainly checks all the handsome older man boxes. And his living quarters suggest he could give someone a comfortable lifestyle. Sofie could live a life of leisure. Ha. Sofie will always live life on her own terms. But still, maybe they'd have fun together. OKay, time to get back to detecting.

"Emson Estates will practically be in your backyard. Does that bother you?"

Stanton shrugged. "You can't stop progress. I will miss my privacy, though. There will be a lot more traffic on the road. On the other hand, a gated community of large tasteful estates certainly won't be an eyesore and will increase my property value."

The cars going by would be BMWs, Porsches, Jags, and limos.

"I wonder how Brooke feels about a gated community abutting the BNC."

Stanton frowned. "That's a good question. I don't know Brooke well enough to know what she's thinking. She came to several of the bike path meetings, and I think she attended my Birds of Brazil presentation. We say hello and talk business, that's about it."

"Since you're on the bike path committee, maybe you can explain something to me. I read the grant regulations and the final bike path plans need to be sent to the state in two weeks."

"That's true." Stanton looked at her expectantly.

"It doesn't seem like anybody's working on the plans."

He shrugged. "I'm sure a group is working behind the scenes. After you're here for a while, you'll see Brooke is a very competent director."

Behind the scenes, huh? Way behind.

Laine drove home, with a smile playing across her mouth as she regained her perspective. *He's cool but too old for me.* Still, he possessed a certain vitality many guys her age lacked. Was he the lady-killer Fiona made him out to be? Laine didn't think so. He uttered no repertoire of sleek phrases and longing looks to devastate her defenses, to get her to succumb to his hidden agenda of lusty advances. Hey, what was she anyway—chopped liver?

Laine laughed aloud. Fiona got another one wrong.

In a few short hours, she would meet Sam at Serena's.

She began to feel the warm tingle of anticipation. Time dragged on, and she blamed her mounting excitement on a bad case of heartburn. *Better write that down as another symptom to tell Dr. Cremble.*

AFTER HER EARLY SUPPER, she let the fire peter out so the cottage wouldn't burn down in her absence. Her anticipation grew stronger, even though seven o'clock remained an hour away.

Laine experienced social jitters when she was about to meet a slew of new people. But as soon as she straightened her shoulders and said her first hello the butterflies always disappeared.

Laine had to face facts: Sam was her real reason for going to Serena's. Conflicting images flashed through her head, each vying for top billing.

First, the Sam who yelled at her to get off his property. Second, the Sam who carried her to his houseboat and sliced through her pants. She couldn't leave out the third Sam who brought her lunch. Most of all, the best Sam whose kisses made her feel aroused and alive.

In her mind's eye, she pictured Sam. Tousled brown curls framed a rugged, sensitive face. His dark eyes looked as if they'd seen it all and were still ready to come back for more. What gave him that hangdog air? That sadness that made every woman from here to Florida want to kiss it better?

Oy, she couldn't wait to see him again.

Laine splashed cold water on her face from the tiny bathroom sink. The place was so small, she half expected the seven dwarves to come home from a tough day at the mines, wanting stew. Well, they'd have to wait. She had a date. Not exactly a real date, but sort of a date, nonetheless.

Ransacking her closet for something to wear, she shook her head in disgust at her now pitiful collection of clothes. As soon as she made some money, she'd go on a shopping spree at the Diamond Bay Mill Outlet. She was sick of jeans and that old black sweater.

Wait a minute. What about the outfit Aunt Rose gave me last Christmas-Hanukkah? I was so bummed out about Toby that I tossed it in a bag and forgot about it.

Laine rummaged around in the clothes trunk until finally she found the blue bag. Pulling out a lime and turquoise fuzzy sweater and black jeans, she tried them on. They fit perfectly. She had enough time to polish her nails and scrunch gel in her hair before going out into the night.

"How do I look?" Laine twirled for the plant. "Do I look sexy? Nod yes or I won't water you."

The plant waved in the breeze of Laine's twirl.

Ten.

Laine drove the short distance to the club and parked her car in the lot. As she pulled open the heavy door, her nerves jangled with anticipation. *Look out, Serena's; here I come!*

As soon as she stepped inside, Sam's voice rang out loud and clear.

He stood in a corner with a group of musicians. His faded blue jeans and his dark curls tumbling over the collar of his black shirt made him extra sexy. He sang an old Bob Dylan song as he strummed his guitar, then segued into the Hank Williams tune, "I'm So Lonesome, I Could Cry."

November's theme song. It's not going to get to me, though. I am woman, hear me roar; that's me.

Laine sidled up to the bar and munched a few bar snacks; appropriately fish-shaped crackers. Sam and the gang began playing a rousing rendition of "The San Francisco Bay Blues." When the bartender appeared, she ordered a Stormy Night— dark rum, ginger beer, and lime juice. Her first swallow tasted both sweet and peppery. It warmed her throat.

Laine clapped appreciatively after the band played their last note. Sam's eyes swept the room and landed on her face. When their eyes locked, the peppery warmth of the drink surged through the rest of her body.

Sam beckoned her with a smile and a wave. She made her way between the crowded tables and stood beside him.

"That's one of my favorite songs."

"Yeah? I thought your taste would run to popular music."

"It does. I also like Vivaldi and Carly Simon. I even like country music. The lyrics are great, like 'All My Exes Live in Texas.'"

Sam laughed, exposing a dimple in his left cheek. "Let me introduce you to the gang. This is Doc Silvia and these are the Clay brothers, Steve and Rick. They own a lobster boat."

The guys all joked about Sam being on a date, and Laine's protestations only made it worse.

As the night wore on, Laine noticed doctors, professors, and lawyers chumming up with carpenters, farmers, and fishermen. More than friendly, they made plans for boating, or drinks, or golf. Sam's words proved right—Seaglass Bay was a real melting pot.

Sam appeared by her side and after a few minutes of chit chat asker if she could sing.

"Not unless you have a shower handy. Why?"

"I want somebody to sing 'Blue Kentucky Girl' while I strum. Could you do that for me?"

One time in college, after singing "Swing Low Sweet Chariot" in the shower, she had stepped out to the sound of applause. Her suite mates insisted she had a deep, rich voice. Aunt Rose told her she took after her dad.

"I'll try. My dad was a musician. Maybe a bit of his talent trickled down to me."

Sam had the lyrics written in bold letters, readable even in the dim light. He leaned forward to place the music on the stand in front of her. He stood so close; his body radiated heat and a pine forest scent.

Pavlov's dogs had nothing on her as the hairs prickled up and down her neck. A longing rose within her for his arm to brush against hers.

"You ready?"

"Ready for what? Oh, that. Sure. Don't introduce me. I'll just start singing."

At first she sang softly, then louder as she gained confidence. When she finished singing, the ring of musicians applauded.

"C'mon, use the microphone so everybody else can hear you," Sam coaxed.

"All right." Laine took a swig of her Stormy Night.

Steve Clay joined in at first, but stopped as her strong, deep voice took over. A sudden silence held the dusky room in its grip, and at the end of the song the audience burst into loud applause.

"Encore, encore," Doc Silvia called.

"Go Laine! Go Laine!" Mike chanted.

"Sing another song with us," coaxed Sam. "Please." His begging face looked so appealing; she'd do the chicken dance naked in front of the crowd if he asked. *No*, she corrected herself, *I am an independent woman and can think for myself. Okay, so maybe I would insist on wearing panties while I danced.*

"That's all for today." *Maybe you'll hear me when I'm in the shower. Yeah, right.*

"You have a great voice," Sam told her. "Your dad definitely must've passed his talent to you."

"Thanks." Laine's face flushed at the compliment. "He was a gifted musician."

Sam placed his hand on the small of her back. "Can I get you another drink?"

Why did his every touch feel like a lover's caress? She closed her eyes. Her back was now the most erogenous zone of her body—in the top three, anyway.

"Do you want a drink?" Sam repeated, louder this time.

Laine opened her eyes and turned towards him. "I'd love one, but don't you need to stay with the band?"

"They won't even notice I'm gone." He called to let the guys know he was on break. Nobody even looked up.

"They obviously can't do without me." He directed her to a booth. "My fifteen minutes of fame has come and gone."

The bartender came by to take their drink orders.

"Beachglass Beer," Sam told the bartender. "It's the local brew," he explained to Laine.

"I'll try one too," Then she sat in reverent silence for a moment.

"Yoo-hoo, anybody home?"

"Sorry. This is the first time I ever sang in public. I'm into firsts," she added.

Sam smiled. "I'll have to remember that."

The bartender brought their beers. Sam raised his glass.

"Here's to your first time singing in public. I hope there will be many more." They clinked glasses. He took a hearty swallow, and Laine a tentative sip.

"Um, that's good. I'm not a big beer fan, but this is smooth."

Sam beamed as if he had brewed it himself. "Seaglass Bay produces its own wine, beer, cheese, blueberries, and boats. If an earthquake separates Seaglass Bay from the rest of the world, we could survive all by ourselves."

"I feel safer already."

When Sam smiled, her nether regions tingled.

"Boy it's warm in here. They really crank the heat up. Next time I'll wear a T-shirt."

Sam's smile was a little too knowing, as if he understood the real cause of her flushed face.

"You said your dad was a musician. What did he play?"

"Guitar. He played folk music."

"Cool." At the moment, Laine didn't feel like explaining that her dad was the well-known folk singer, Seth Roth, cut down in his prime by a drunk driver. She turned her eyes to the dance floor and away from the intensity of Sam's gaze. The pulse of music and movement mesmerized her.

"Want to dance?" Sam asked.

She nodded. Why not? It was ages since she'd danced. "It has to be a slow dance. I'm still a bit wobbly on my ankle."

"That's fine with me." His eyes met hers and held them.

A sudden thrill of anxiety ran through her body at the thought of slow dancing with Sam. She imagined his strong arms around her, her body pressed against his as they swept around the dance floor.

The next song was a fast one.

"Damn," Sam said, already looking around the room for a different partner. "There's Steve Clay's wife, Dana. Mind if I dance this one with her?"

"Sure, go ahead." She settled back to watch.

Sam moved like an energy ball, flashing like lightning around the dance floor. Free and uninhibited, his steps might have looked silly performed by another guy, but Sam danced like a pro. He seemed so different from the down-to-earth Sam she'd seen so far. He'd turned out a multi-faceted guy. At least she'd never be bored knowing him.

"I don't think you even broke a sweat on that one," she told Sam when he returned to the table.

"You should see me do the limbo. I've won contests."

The band played an old Sinatra tune. Sam took her hand and guided her to the crowded dance floor. She and Sam glided across the floor in effortless perfection. The dance floor melted away as she closed her eyes and felt his arms around her and his warm breath tickling her neck. All she needed was the fairy godmother to poof her outfit into a ball gown. While she was deciding between a strapless sapphire blue and a cap sleeve pink, the song ended. Opening her eyes made pumpkin time seem very near.

No, damn it, she couldn't fall for this man. She'd fallen for Toby and still hadn't gotten back on her feet. Even though the picture of Toby in bed with another woman left an indelible mark, the crux of the matter had been his ultimate betrayal. She, whose friends always praised her intuitive powers, had turned out to be just another dupe. It wouldn't happen again.

"Is something wrong?" Sam sounded concerned as she broke away from him, a frown on her face.

"I'm just tired is all. I'm ready to go home."

"I'll walk you to your car." They grabbed their jackets and stepped outside amidst a flurry of goodbyes. Everyone seemed to know and like Sam.

When they reached her car, Laine opened her driver's side door and turned to say good night. Sam put his arms around her. She started to pull away; then changed her mind. The hug, warm and tender, was the kind of hug she could get lost in. Time stopped as she burrowed deeper into his arms.

"Oh, Laine," he whispered into her hair. "You make me want to forget all about my past."

Laine wanted to reassure him with her arms and gentle words; wanted to ask him what the heck he meant by his past. Why all the stupid secrecy? Didn't he know she had ways to make him talk? A *Hawaii Five-0* track ring startled her and she quickly pulled away from the embrace.

"I hate these things," Sam muttered, as he pulled the cellular phone from his belt clip. "I'm on EMT call." He listened for a few seconds.

"Okay, I'm on my way."

Sam hooked the phone back on his belt. "There's a situation at Grover's Cove. A group of shit-faced teens thought they'd get an early start on our Polar Bear swim. Water and alcohol definitely do not mix in this case."

"What's a Polar Bear swim?" *And what about your past?*

"Every New Year's morning Serena sponsors an ocean dip. Anybody who swims gets invited to a free buffet. Bye, Laine, see you soon."

But what about your past?

Sam sped off into the night.

LAINE SAT in her car and said a quick prayer the teens would be okay. Tonight was far too cold for a swim. She, personally, would much rather have Sam's warm arms wrapped around her.

I'm wide awake now. She pulled out of the lot. I can get some work done when I get home. Then I can sleep in tomorrow morning. Good plan, except for one little detail: my folder is sitting on my desk at the BNC.

Wait a minute; I have a key to the office.

Laine felt inside her purse until her hand closed around a plastic key ring. She pulled it out. She pulled out of the lot and drove the few miles to the BNC.

AS LAINE PULLED her car into the BNC lot, she saw lights in the windows of the building. Maybe Brooke worked late. Laine felt a chill up her spine. She wouldn't put it past Brooke to have secret meetings. Laine knocked, and then waited, watching her cold breath dissipate into night air. No answer. Brooke had probably left lights on by mistake, or for safety reasons.

Laine used her key. The key wouldn't turn until the third try. As Laine slowly opened the door, instinct warned her to remain quiet. She moved, without making a sound, to her desk. She retrieved the folder, and made her way to the front door, again without a sound.

A voice from the dark hallway stopped her. Her hand froze on the doorknob.

"Brooke, pet, listen to me," a man said. "It's the only way."

"I don't want to do it, Davie," a familiar voice replied. "It's not going the way it's supposed to."

Laine exhaled. The woman was like Brooke, and not some murderer after all.

"You have to do it," the man said. "We have beaucoup bucks riding on this. You can't back out now because of a complication. Put on your big girl pants, love."

"I don't want him involved," Brooke said. "He's a wild card. You promised it would just be the three of us."

"Hey, I don't like it either, but now he's part of the deal. You've got to see that."

"I don't like it."

Without warning, the door opened and they emerged from the hallway and stared at Laine. The man dropped Brooke's arm.

Brooke found her voice first. "What are you doing here?" Brooke demanded. Her cheeks were beet red and her lettuce hair had lost some of its crispness. She resembled a salad bar after a long day.

"I stopped by to pick up my paperwork." Laine tried for a casual tone in contrast to the six-piece band playing in her chest. "I was on my way out. Goodbye then."

"Good night," Brooke said, composure creeping back into her voice.

Laine turned and walked out the door, ignoring the creepiness of the situation. She hurried to her car. As she drove away, she took a few steadying breaths and tried to remember what she had overheard. Where were their cars? Laine's had been the only one in the lot. They must have parked around the back, but why bother? What were they hiding?

Brooke hadn't introduced her companion to Laine. Rude, though Laine needed no introduction. Davie's florid face belonged to David Emson.

LATER THAT NIGHT, lying in bed, she tried to think. Emson and Brooke supposedly hated each other, according to Fiona of the barbed tongue. So why the heck had they met in a clandestine manner? David had called Brooke "pet" and "love." Not exactly the language of enemies.

Laine had to smile. David had chutzpah, or balls, to use "Brooke" and "pet" in the same sentence. He might think rattlesnakes resembled kittens. Maybe he and Brooke could be in some kind of money scheme together. After all, Emson had talked about "beaucoup bucks."

Laine sat up in bed. What was going on at the BNC? What did Brooke mean by *the three of us*, and who was the wild card? Maybe it was Brooke, Emson, and Fiona. She thought until her brain hurt, but she couldn't come up with anything more.

When she fell asleep she dreamed she stood at the edge of a big hole. She took a step forward then fell all the way to the bottom, like Alice in Wonderland. Only there was a bed at the bottom, and when she finally landed, she was right on top of Sam. He was naked, and he was warm and soft and hard and . . . *Oh my God.* Laine woke with a start. *Oh great. Now I'm having wild sex dreams. I really better make that appointment with Dr. Cremble. I could be low on calcium or some other vitamin.*

Eleven.

Tuesday

A T 5:30 A.M. Laine gave up trying to sleep and opened the folder she'd gotten from the BNC; her reason for last night's adventure. As she copied her noted to her laptop, she kept stopping to wonder about her unexpected meeting with Brooke and Emson. What shenanigans were they planning in a secret meeting at the BNC? And why meet at the BNC when other more secret, out-of-the-way places were available?

After a scant breakfast, her lack of appetite caused by her stomac churning from last night's adventure, Laine drove to work, her mind still buzzing with questions. Weren't Emson and Brooke bitter enemies? Apparently not. How would Brooke explain herself?

At the BNC, the mystery grew even deeper. Brooke had sequestered Tim in her office.

"Do not disturb," Fiona warned, "on pain of death."

Laine thought Fiona came on a bit too strong. Certainly they wouldn't do more than maim her. Too bad "on pain of maim" didn't have the same ring to it. She shrugged and started working.

Brooke usually gave her free rein to design children's programs, so Laine didn't need much coaching. Still, she wished Brooke showed more interest in her programs. So far, Laine had planned a whale watch, a puppet workshop, a poster contest, and a bird drawing lesson featuring Stanton. Not bad for such a short time. Not bad at all.

Now she immersed herself in learning the intricacies of designing the kids' camp. The task turned out far more complex than she had imagined. Her duties included everything from acquiring camp insurance to hiring counselors. She settled down at the computer.

A few minutes later, Laine looked up when Brooke's door opened.

Tim bounded out like a cheerful puppy. Behind him, Brooke stood in the doorway. The dark circles under her eyes made her look like a prizefighter, and not the winner. Her jeans, however, remained freshly pressed, as always.

How does she do it? Maybe she sleeps on the ironing board. Gives board meeting a whole new meaning.

"Laine, I'd like to speak to you." Brooke gestured Laine into her office. "Come in and sit down, please." She closed the door.

Laine sat, her legs trembling with anticipation. Yikes; it brought back memories of getting called into the principal's office after getting in trouble at posture class.

"I want to explain about the other night," Brooke said without preamble. "When Seaglass Bayers get worked up about the issues, it's my job to listen to them. You saw me with an irate BNC member. It's part of my job to calm members down so we can work effectively for change."

Calm him down? Huh? Brooke had looked like the one who needed to be shot with a tranquilizer gun.

"Who was that man?" Laine tried to make her voice light. "He looked familiar."

"Oh just an outspoken Seaglass Bayer," Brooke said. "I can't even remember his name at the moment. Anyway, I'm sorry I was abrupt with you."

"It's okay. Things happen."

Shit happens and this sounds like a crock of shit.

What a lame excuse. Maybe Brooke's exhaustion prevented her from rising to the occasion. She looked like she needed a gallon of her Dragon's Brew tea. It'd been a busy night, after all. But why lie about meeting with David Emson? What was Brooke trying so ineptly to hide?

"Good." Brooke regained some of her brisk demeanor. "I looked over your emails, and your projects are right on schedule. Keep up the good work."

"Thank you."

What are you hiding, woman? What will I have to do to find out?

LAINE WENT straight from work to the market and practically bought out the snack food section. Aunt Rose had warned her against food shopping while in the throes of hunger pangs, and now she knew why. Her stomach rumbled as she pulled into her driveway and climbed out of the car.

I bought a load of stuff I don't need. I got a hunk of chocolate cheesecake from the hunk behind the deli counter. I don't need that baguette or sorbet or bag of potato chips either. But I will enjoy all of it. No one can think straight without junk food.

It sure got dark early these days. Kind of ominous, actually. Like the calm before a storm.

Before opening the trunk, Laine glanced up at the sky.

Clouds obscured a yellow moon. Shadows of pine branches splashed across the yard.

One of these nights she'd stay up till midnight to look out at her favorite star, Sirius.

A weary Laine gathered her groceries. Her arms full, she shut the hatch with her elbow. The resounding slam echoed in the darkness.

Laine walked towards her cottage, barely able to see, arms loaded. As she reached the door, the clouds gently peeled away from the moon and bathed the yard in silvery light. She stopped to watch, thinking for a frivolous moment she could drop her bags, kick off her shoes and dance in the moonlight.

A sudden sharp noise made her turn back towards the car. "Who is it?" Her voice trembled with fear. Her hands tightened on the grocery bags. "Hello? Anybody there?"

Complete silence. Then a rustling in the bushes. She wanted to run through the door, escape inside to warmth and safety. But she stood rooted to the spot, her curiosity at war with her fear.

An owl cried in the distance, and a coyote yelped from the other side of the field.

Laine breathed a deep sigh of relief. *I'm so paranoid. I'm only hearing animal sounds.* A chuckle escaped her; amazed at her own timidity. She could bike across Vermont alone, but one little night noise turned her into a trembling idiot.

Laine let herself into the darkened house and plopped her belongings on the kitchen table.

I read too many mystery novels. It's less stressful to read them than live them, that's for sure.

She stood at the table and wolfed down a turkey sandwich and the entire wedge of cheesecake. Then licked her plate and her fingers. The joy of living alone.

Someday my metabolism is going to change. Then I'll be in huge trouble, with the emphasis on huge.

Her chores planned for before bed could wait until morning. She'd eaten too much food to consider work. Bed would feel wonderful tonight.

It did.

Thursday

I N THE MORNING, after a repentantly simple breakfast bar and a mug of mint tea, Laine headed for the door, arms laden with briefcase and lunch. She opened the door, stopped to rebalance her stuff, and screamed.

"No!" Her belongings tumbled from her arms to the ground.

At the doorstep lay a wild rabbit, dead, mauled and bloodied.

A surge of lightheadedness hit. Laine steadied herself against the doorframe and took several deep breaths. Though she needed to get to work, she couldn't leave the poor creature lying there. Backing into the cottage until she hit the sink, she found a trowel under it, and pulled an old towel from the ragbag. Trying not to look too closely at the tiny corpse, she covered it with the towel, slipped the trowel underneath it, and carried it to the backyard.

It's those damned coyotes. But why would they display the rabbit on my doorstep? Could it have been someone trying to scare her?

If so they succeeded, at least in grossing her out.

Laine dug a shallow grave next to the ginkgo tree. After lowering the rabbit into the grave she smoothed the dirt in place.

What a way to start the day. Much worse for the rabbit though, poor thing.

WHEN SHE ARRIVED at work, late of course, she made the mistake of telling Fiona about her morning.

"You can stew it up for supper, kiddo," Fiona said. "Rabbits make good eating."

"What a gross comment. Do not ever call me kiddo again," she surprised herself by snapping back. "Ever."

"Touchy, touchy."

LAINE AVOIDED FIONA for the rest of the day. Another uneventful workday. Laine couldn't understand it. Shouldn't there be hustle and bustle over the bike path? Arriving home, she took out her watercolors and painted swirls and whirls on wet paper. Color therapy. A perfect activity after a long day. *This orange blob represents Fiona. Angry. Stupid.*

Her ringing cell phone pulled her out of her self-pity party. Sam. She'd put his name in her contacts.

"Hello," she gasped. The way he affected her bordered on her reverting back to an adolescent.

"Hi, it's Sam. You sound out of breath. Was it something I said?"

"Ha ha."

"It's going to be at least fifty degrees tomorrow. Let's go rollerblading."

Laine prodded her ankle. No pain, much better. She deserved a bit of fun every once in a while.

When she didn't speak right away, Sam added, "You said you wanted to learn to rollerblade. Remember?"

"I did?"

"Maybe not outright, but you implied."

"I don't have skates."

"My cousin Jenna left her blades last time she visited. They're your size."

"How do you know my size?"

"Chalk it up to my EMT training."

"Ha. Foot fetish training, more likely."

"I saw your bare feet, remember? I have a good eye."

"What size am I, then?"

"Seven and a half."

"That's impressive, but I bet you looked inside one of my shoes."

"I did not. Look, do you want to try rollerblading or not?"

"Okay, but I probably still need to go easy on my ankle."

"Pick you up at nine."

Laine said goodbye and hung up the phone.

"He's just a friend," she said to the asparagus fern.

Wagging a finger at the coffee pot, she added, "Don't look at me like that."

Twelve.

Friday

HE NEXT MORNING Laine woke up and took extra care with her hair and clothes. Looking into the mirror, she considered the appropriateness of the low-cut slinky red jersey for rollerblading. Did some kind of rollerblade dress code exist? Nothing wrong with looking good for a date. While waiting, she practiced a few yoga relaxation moves.

When Sam's truck pulled into the driveway, she grabbed a heavy sweatshirt and pulled it over her shirt. So much for the sexy look.

From the doorway, Laine watched Sam climb out of the truck. Her eyes swept over him and stopped at his legs.

Oy, he's wearing shorts. This is against the Geneva Convention.

Laine couldn't take her eyes off his muscular legs with their well-defined calves. Even his knees looked cute enough to bite.

"I know. Hairy, aren't they?"

Laine's face flushed. "I can't believe we have such a nice day for this." She tried to modulate her voice to a casual tone, but it started as a squeak and ended as a croak.

Sam led her to his truck. "I want you to meet an old buddy of mine."

Laine grinned at the sight of the black dog.

"This is Dolphin, my Labrador retriever. Dolphin, I'd like you to meet Laine."

The dog reared up on hind legs and slobbered all over her face.

"He hasn't been drinking water out of the toilet lately, has he?"

"Absolutely not. I think we've been insulted," he told Dolphin.

Laine eyed the large cooler in the back of the truck.

"I raided my fridge, brought a few munchies."

"It looks like enough to feed an army."

"It is. C'mon, we'll go to a quiet, newly paved road."

As THEY DROVE, she asked about the emergency call at Grover's Cove. "Were the kids okay?"

Sam snorted. "They were fine. Leave it to Heather Emson to instigate skinny-dipping in November."

"Any relation to David Emson?"

"His daughter. She's rebellious and spoiled. Got to hand it to her, though. As soon as they were caught she 'fessed up to being the ringleader. Took responsibility for her actions."

"Sounds like you like her."

"I'll admit it; I've got a soft spot for the teens. There's not much for them to do here."

"Unlike New Hampshire, where we could sit around and watch loons all day."

They laughed, and then Laine told him about Emson and F.F. Pearson meeting on Emson Estates.

Sam's smile changed to a glower. "He's got to be really interested to come out here and look at property. It'll be the end of another bit of paradise. We better enjoy it while it's still unspoiled."

"What's David Emson like?" Laine asked.

"Don't ruin a perfect day. He'd do anything to make a buck. If he could break up all of Seaglass Bay into quarter-inch parcels and sell it, he'd be right on it. Emson has a fight with the conservation and planning boards at least once a week. The guy is a whore, in my humble opinion."

Sam pulled over on a narrow, paved side road. "Let's forget about all the F.F. Pearsons and David Emsons of the world and have fun."

"You got it."

They climbed out of the truck and donned kneepads, elbow pads, and helmets. Laine sat on the ground and fiddled with the skate clasps.

"How am I going to learn to skate if I can't even get them on?" she groused.

"Let me help. It's easy once you get the hang of it."

As he leaned over and buckled her skates, she had a flash of her father tying her sneakers at a much younger age. But instead of squeezing out the memories like she often did, she let herself drift back in time. She lost herself in the past for a moment, packed the treasured memory away, and then stood up, ready to skate.

Laine skated slowly beside Sam, with Dolphin leading the way.

"Uh-oh. Is that a hill I see up ahead?" The modest, gradual hill looked like Mount Washington. She hung back.

"I just remembered an appointment for a root canal in an hour. I have to hurry home."

"Ha, ha. C'mon, Laine, you can do it. This is more like a pimple than a hill."

"Mount Blackhead." She gave a nervous hiccough laugh. Sam took hold of her hand, and a surge of warmth radiated up her arm. They skated side by side and reached the bottom with no trouble at all.

"You're right. That's easy stuff." The wind and excitement had flushed her cheeks. "Let's try that hill over there." She pointed to a side lane sloping down into a private beach parking lot. "Can we go in there?"

Sam nodded. "People only use it in the summer. Did you know the population of Seaglass Bay decreases by five thousand once Labor Day rolls around?"

Laine shook her head.

"You sure you're ready for this?"

She nodded. "I want to try it all by myself."

"Okay." He started down the hill. "I'll wait at the bottom; you can skate right into my arms."

"Keep dreaming." Laine took off down the hill, feeling free as the winter seagulls. When it was time to apply the brakes, she put one foot in front of the other. She slowed, but not enough. Sam loomed ahead.

"Gangway." She hit him full force, toppling them both onto the sand. Garbling an apology, she became uncomfortably aware she had landed square on top of him. Her nose crunched into his neck and her breasts felt mashed flat on his chest. His—oh my God, something hard in the crotch area pressed against her.

"Don't worry about it. This is one of my favorite positions."

I can tell. "Dirty old man." He wrapped his arms around her and pulled her closer. She could feel the outline of his taut body. Laine did not resist.

"I resent being called old. You seem determined to keep crashing into me. Is this a mating ritual in your culture?"

"Ha, ha, very funny." She wrestled to pull away.

"Hey, is that any way to treat your rescuer?" Sam said in mock offense. "The least you can do is give me a kiss, Laine."

Laine puckered her lips to give him a light kiss, but he responded with a lip-lock, taking her breath away.

"That's enough skating." She disentangled from him and began taking off her skates. "I think I'll go home and take a cold shower." *And call Doc Cremble about all these weird symptoms I've been having: lightheadedness, palpitations, and sweating to name a few.*

"What about the picnic?"

"Oh yeah, I forgot. I am kind of hungry."

"Me too." He gave her a wolfish grin.

"Behave yourself, Mr. Holliston." She waggled her finger at him.

"All right, if I must. You sure you're okay?"

"I can't get hurt, with all these heavy-duty knee and ankle pads."

"And I thought it was all voluptuous you."

Laine laughed. She didn't know about voluptuous. No hips and no butt; her body went straight up and down except for her full breasts. Being the first one in sixth-grade gym class to wear a bra had made her feel embarrassed, not curvaceous. She finally made it past those grade school inadequacies and now enjoyed her body for being healthy and strong.

While she and Dolphin found a flat rock for picnicking, Sam skated to the truck to retrieve the food.

He returned with the large cooler. "I don't know what I packed in here. I threw in the contents of my fridge."

"Talk about a smorgasbord." Laine surveyed the contents.

Sam pulled out cheese, pickles, olives, mustard, jam, cold cuts, bread, raw veggies, and . . . a raw potato.

"What the heck is the potato for?"

Sam lifted his hands in mock surprise. "I told you I raided my fridge. The potato was an accident."

"Who puts potatoes in the fridge?"

"I usually put the potato inside my bathing suit. Makes me look like a manly man."

"Does the potato go in the front or the back?"

He raised his expressive brows in mock surprise. "No wonder I strike out with the ladies."

Laine laughed so hard she thought she would wet her pants. What a goofball.

THEY MADE GIGANTIC Dagwood sandwiches filled with pickles and cold cuts. Dolphin wolfed down an entire salami sandwich in one gulp.

As Laine played catch-the-potato with Sam and the dog, she thought about how perfect this day had gone so far. Then, Dolphin took a bite out of the potato, his way of saying enough already.

Laine peeled off her vest and sweatshirt, revealing her slinky jersey. Dolphin curled up beside her and she patted his head.

"He likes you." Sam stared at her red top. "I like you too."

Laine smiled. A little cleavage went a long way, apparently even with canines.

She stretched out next to Sam on the flat, sun-drenched rock. They lay on their backs, close together but not quite touching.

In the sun, Sam's dark hair glittered with red highlights.

"I was surprised you knew the words to 'My Blue Girl,'" he said, his voice lazy with sun.

Laine thought for a moment. How much did she want to tell him? Lying on the rock in the sun, her comfort zone had lifted so high she could say almost anything. Almost, but not quite.

"My father cut an album of folk tunes right before he died. 'My Blue Girl' was one of them."

"Sorry again about your dad. What was his name?"

"You probably never heard of him—Seth Roth."

"You're kidding! Seth Roth?"

"Don't tell me you recognize the name."

"I'm a big fan. I went to one of his concerts in upstate New York when I was sixteen years old."

Excitement rushed through Laine. "Was it the one at Cornell?"

"Yes, that's the one."

"I was there too."

They both sat silently, remembering the summer day years ago. The same concert! And now the fates had brought them together again.

For what exactly, I have no idea. Well, I have a bit of an idea, but I'm trying not to go there.

Laine told Sam how she used to sing along while her father strummed the guitar. Sam told her how much he had admired her father's stage personality.

"He was so down-to-earth. He acted like the audience was giving him a gift, letting him play."

Laine nodded, her eyes filling with tears. "That's how he felt." She hadn't talked about her dad with anyone but Aunt Rose for years. Now she pictured him with his black curly hair and green eyes, sitting on the back stoop with his guitar, picking out a tune. Her mom chiding him because his dinner would get cold.

"Your last name is Camara, not Roth."

"That was my mother's last name. I had a Jewish father and a Portuguese mother. Ever have Portuguese sausage on a bagel?"

He raised his eyebrows. "I can't say I have. How come you've got your mother's last name?"

"Mom kept her name after they got married. She didn't want to be Ruth Roth."

"That is quite a mouthful."

"Try saying it five times fast. She was in labor for twenty-three hours giving birth to me. When I finally came out, she looked at my dad and said, 'It's Elaina Camara.' And that was that."

"Your full name is Elaina?"

"Yes, after my father's sister. Everyone's called me Laine forever. I only got called Elaina when I was in big trouble. I haven't talked about my parents in a long time and I'm missing them right now."

"Let's change the subject, then," Sam suggested in a gentle tone. "We can talk about anything you like."

He placed his hand on hers and warmth radiated up her arm. He stroked her hand.

"Okay. So what made you leave Boston for the country life?"

"I needed a change of scene."

Sam's arm swept to include the rocks, the sand, and the water. "You definitely got that. But how come you wanted a change?"

Laine told him the bare bones of the Toby story. Ending with, "That's completely over. It just bothers me that I was such a dupe."

"Yeah, I know what you mean." Sam sighed with feeling.

"Did something like that happen to you?" Laine tried not to sound too eager. *C'mon, tell me. Keeping this stuff to yourself causes cancer.*

"Yeah," he drew the word out. "It was a long time ago. No use crying over spilt milk."

My God, Aunt Rose would have a field day with these maxims. *Tell me or I'll have to beat it out of you.* But he seemed to have nothing more to say, and she let him keep his secrets.

EVEN IN THE TRUCK on the way home she showed remarkable restraint, asking no questions. They rode in silence, lost in their own thoughts.

"I guess I better get some work done," she told him when he pulled into her driveway. She meant to lean over and give him a quick kiss on the cheek.

Instead, he turned and kissed her fully on the lips. His kiss was long, slow and probing. It would leave a stone hungry for more. A rush of warmth spread through her body.

Thank God I'm sitting down. Please don't kiss my ear. A person can only take so much.

Sam chose that moment to graze her ear with his lips.

He is psychic. Or maybe I am. Or maybe I said it out loud.

She turned away so his lips grazed her hair.

Laine turned to look at him. The hungry look in his eyes completely replaced the hangdog kiss-it-better expression. He obviously meant business. Laine lost track of seconds, minutes, maybe even days as Sam nibbled her ear. A bark from Dolphin made her pull away.

"Got to go."

"What about your other ear? I wasn't finished. You'll be lopsided for the rest of the day."

"That's a chance I'm willing to take." She slid out of the truck, giving Dolphin a quick pat of farewell.

"See you soon, Laine." His eyes never left her as she walked away.

She walked with a lopsided gait to show how his attentions had left her off-balance with one neglected ear.

"You're taking a chance with one ear undone," he called. "Hey it's your life." He drove away still calling to her.

STILL SMILING, Laine tried to settle into work mode, which turned into a Herculean feat with the tang of Sam's lips still on her mouth. In the end, she forced herself to concentrate on her camp brochure. She wanted to get information out early. Never too soon for parents to decide where to send the little darlings next summer.

Whenever she glanced up from her computer, the beauty right outside her window struck her anew.

The backyard with its salt-stunted pines led to the golden marsh grass, to end at the rock-strewn bay. Stones lay scattered in every direction, like a giant's game of marbles.

And she couldn't forget her *Ginkgo biloba* tree in all its glory. The leaves had turned a bright yellow.

At suppertime she took a break. After her enormous lunch she didn't have room for more than a cup of tea, but she needed to stretch and take her mind away from work. Without conscious thought, she opened the newest edition of the *Seaside Gazette*.

An ad for defense classes practically jumped out at her. The classes took place one morning each week.

No time like the present, as Aunt Rose always said.

Online, she signed up for her first self-defense course ever. Raising her teacup in a silent toast, she sipped, and contemplated how much exercise Seaglass Bay provided. Walking, jogging, and rollerblading. Now, she'd added self-defense to the list.

She got Sofie on the phone, and it didn't take much convincing to get her on board for self-defense classes.

Replacing the receiver, Laine considered counting kissing as an exercise. She'd read somewhere kissing burned a calorie a minute and boosted the immune system. So, an hour of kissing could burn sixty calories and ward off colds for the next five years.

LAINE SETTLED back to work on advertising projects. Every so often she glanced out towards the dark waves and thought about Sam.

What would he do for the rest of the day? Would he go on a hot date? Laine had noticed enough women drooling in his direction at Serena's. Or, would he sit in his cozy houseboat staring out at the sea? She shut her eyes and imagined him kissing her lips, and the rest of her body, until desire and frustration made it impossible to keep working.

She decided it was the perfect time to haul her ass to bed. Tomorrow's activities included the birding program with Stanton Coles at the BNC, and she needed her rest. Tomorrow would bring its own surprises.

Thirteen.

Saturday

WIRED WITH ANTICIPATION, Laine parked her car in the BNC lot and hurried toward the building.

A glut of kids milled about by the door, and the noise level soared with excitement as Laine wove her way through the children.

Stanton Coles arrived in time to help with crowd control. Laine counted twenty-five children attending her first activity. They led the children down the red trail towards the water.

Hoping the birds would show up in droves today, her shoulders relaxed at the sight of the seagulls circling the shore and the two swans hanging out at the island.

The children took turns peering through the binoculars as birds soared over the river.

They Stanton with questions, and he answered every one. He shared interesting facts about the birds and showed them a family of eiders through the binoculars.

"They make eiderdown pillows from the eider duck," he told them.

Two boys tried to climb his back when he bent down to pick up a feather. He got them off without too much fuss and gave each of them a "magic" feather.

"The kids love you," Laine told him.

"Thanks." Stanton stretched his shoulders. "I'll need a massage therapist when I'm through."

120   *Linda Richter*

At the end of the walk, making sure the children held the rope railing, Laine and Stanton herded their tired charges up the steps. Back inside, the children enjoyed cocoa with mini marshmallows.

Afterward, Laine went from table to table, cleaning cocoa spills and talking with the children. For the final activity, she helped them make pinecone birdfeeders.

The children spread peanut butter on their pinecones and dipped them in birdseed. The finished cones looked good enough to eat, and one little boy, Dustin, actually tried one. Soon though, the parents came and retrieved their kids.

With the children gone and the mess cleaned up, Laine somehow made it home and collapsed on the couch for what she thought would be a quick power nap.

Two hours later Laine woke up refreshed and ready to patrol the beach. Her walks had become her therapy, her meditation. The fresh salt air sparked a light inside of her; the lush odor of pine and nearby water energized and soothed her. Deep in her heart, she had to admit she embraced stolen fantasies of Sam along the way. Although she loved the solitariness of the beach, she wished he walked beside her, sharing feelings and thoughts.

That night, in preparation for her next morning's self-defense lesson, she watched *Karate Kid* and practiced high kicks and quick punches. In the process, she managed to split her pants and kick over a chair, but nothing could dampen her enthusiasm.

Sunday

The next morning, Laine reached the community center barely in time for class.

Inside, Sofie already performed warm-up exercises. She looked resplendent in a leopard spandex leotard.

The twenty women of all ages, shapes, and sizes jumped around in the gym. The teacher, Jillian, a large woman with solid muscle, looked about thirty-five. She joked to the class, "I work out all day and eat all night."

"I like her already," Sofie whispered. "She speaks my linguini."

Jillian started them off with several yoga stretches. Then she began teaching self-defense techniques.

Laine and Sofie paired up. For one exercise, Sofie wrapped her hands around Laine's throat.

"Not too tight!" Laine yelped.

"Sorry."

Jillian showed Laine how to bring both her arms up from inside Sofie's grasp. Sofie's grip slipped free, and Laine brought her arms down with a dual chop to both sides of Sofie's neck.

"Hey, I'm a friend, remember?"

The follow-through looked even more dramatic.

"Now watch carefully." Jillian brought the heel of her hand under Sofie's nose until it touched.

"Right here . . . Do that with some force, and you'll knock them into tomorrow. Then knee the guy in the balls to finish him off just right."

Sofie and Laine observed with nods of appreciation.

"One more thing: If you do that, don't stand around waiting for applause. Run like hell and get help. If you lose the element of surprise, you won't get it back again."

They went back to practicing. Over and over again, they repeated their moves under Jillian's watchful eye.

"I don't know when we're going to use this stuff," Sofie said. "We live in such a safe, boring, little town."

"You never know."

AFTER THE SELF-DEFENSE WORKOUT, the students cooled down with deep-breathing exercises. Laine lay on her mat, watching the watery November light filter through the window.

Go away, she mentally told the pesky little scenario playing in her head. She had to admit it was fun, picturing Sam rubbing coconut oil into her skin on a tropical beach. Sam's hands caressed every part of her body.

Taking a deep breath, Laine tried to move to a more spiritual place. A golden path with lush trees on each side appeared as she relaxed into her breathing. Next thing she knew, Jillian's soothing voice called her back to the present.

AFTER CLASS Laine suggested coffee at the Seaglass Café. "My treat."

"Don't get your wallet out too fast. I want scones and bacon and a mushroom omelet. The best thing about these stretch pants is how far they stretch."

Sofie is so refreshing and open. I'm so glad I met her.

WHILE SITTING IN THE CAFÉ, Sofie asked, her mouth full of omelet, "Is your love life improving any?"

I said her honesty is refreshing, might as well tell her.

"There is a man I have some chemistry with," she admitted. "We've kissed." *Boy have we kissed.*

"Sam?"

"Is it that obvious?" *Talk about ruining the element of surprise.*

Sofie laughed. "You don't know many other guys around here yet. Anyway, he stopped by yesterday and told me the same thing about you. He didn't call you a man, of course, but the rest is verbatim."

Laine's heart pounded. "What did you tell him?"

"I told him to get you into bed, the sooner the better."

Laine choked on her corn muffin, spewing a fine spray of crumbs over the table. When she composed herself, she asked Sofie about Hank. *Payback is a bitch.*

Sofie explained Hank's wife suffered from a rare auto-immune disease.

"He really did fix my plumbing the other night. He's a good friend."

One look at Laine's face had Sofie asking if she'd heard differently. Laine reported Fiona's accusations about the married man.

"That bitch," Sofie cursed, loud enough for the inhabitants of the next table to turn their heads. "The only way she can smell like a rose is to make the rest of us stink like weeds."

"My aunt Rose certainly is here in spirit. She has sayings for every, and I do mean every, occasion."

"Hope I get to meet Aunt Rose someday," Sofie said, as they walked out to their cars.

"We'd have to drive to New Hampshire. Aunt Rose doesn't like to travel."

"A road trip? Count me in."

Laine stopped at home to change her clothes and then drove to work. At the office she had plenty of paperwork to catch up on.

Fiona warmed up enough from time to time to offer heartfelt criticism of some random subject. At coffee break, the criticism hit a direct target.

"I hear you've been seen around town with a certain someone," Fiona said after she sank her teeth into a particularly puffy honey-glazed donut.

Laine, wondering if the donut had been injected with collagen, stopped short at Fiona's comment.

"Take it from a friend, he wines and dines all the new women who come to town."

"I hardly call rollerblading wining and dining."

"I bet he asked you to sing with him at Serena's," Fiona said, a sly arch to her black brows. "He does that to all his new women. Makes them feel special." Fiona took a huge bite of donut; then tossed her head, letting her hair do the undulating ripple thing.

Oh yeah, I bet none of them brought the house down.

Laine scooted back to her desk before Fiona finished chewing. She shouldn't take Fiona's remarks to heart. Sam could ask Miss America to sing if he wanted to. She wouldn't make it her concern.

So why did she feel a knot in her belly? Because, she considered herself special to him, that's why. But if Fiona was correct—no, of course Fiona wasn't correct. She liked to find buttons, and press them hard.

SEVERAL HOURS later, Laine had answered every important email, and had a newsletter and brochure design ready. With deep relief, she forwarded them to Brooke for approval.

Well, maybe approval was too strong a word when it came to Brooke.

Brooke didn't look unhappy—at least not yet—with Laine's finished results.

With her work complete, and to celebrate, she headed to Corner Kitchen for a gourmet sandwich for supper. But first, she needed to detour to the apothecary to buy vitamins.

A man stood at the counter talking to the pharmacist. He turned and their eyes met. David Emson. Laine stood rooted to the spot.

"Hello. I don't think we were properly introduced. I'm David."

Friendly booming voice. Round face and cold eyes of an indeterminate color—maybe dishwater.

"Nice to meet you. I'm . . . Laine." *Oy it sounds like I forgot my name.*

"Got a few minutes to grab a cup of coffee at Corner Kitchen? I like to get to know the Bay Nature employees."

God no.

"Sure." *Assertiveness Training 101.*

They walked two doors down to the Corner Kitchen. David had a commanding presence and a self-possessed air about him. Laine could see why some women—not her—would find him attractive. At the café, David picked a booth in the back. Not a good sign. The waitress arrived right away, saving Laine from having to make conversation. Better let him do the talking.

David ordered high test coffee. Black. Laine ordered a mocha cappuccino.

David smiled or smirked; it could go either way. "I figured you for a cappuccino kind of gal." The way he said it didn't sound like a compliment. "I'm glad you agreed to have coffee with me. After all, my land abuts the BNC property. We're neighbors, when you think about it."

Laine tried for a natural smile. "Your property is beautiful. At least what I've seen of it."

The waitress arrived and placed two steaming mugs on the table. The waitress smiled at David. "Hello Mr. Emson. Hope your coffee is strong enough."

"I'm sure it will be, Kate."

Laine took a tentative sip of her hot drink. Not too hot; exactly right.

David nodded towards the retreating waitress. "Friend of my daughter, Heather. I know almost everyone in this town. As I said, you're my neighbor."

He took a large mouthful of coffee. "Now be a good neighbor and stop meddling in my business."

"Wha . . . what are you talking about?"

"You know perfectly well what I'm talking about. I caught you spying on me in the woods. I know what you are up to."

"I wasn't spying. I went for a walk in the woods. I'm not up to anything."

David took another large mouthful of coffee, swished it around his mouth like mouthwash, and swallowed.

"As far as I know, I walked on a public path. I heard noise and stopped to check it out. I saw you talking to another man. I continued walking. End of story."

"You mean to tell me you were there by accident right at that particular moment? I don't believe that one for a second."

Laine tried to remember some suggestions from the book she read about dealing with difficult people. *Talk calmly and slowly.*

"I got out of work early. I decided to check out the path. I heard voices and peeked through the bushes. I saw you talking to F.F. Pearson. I kept on walking."

"Did you hear what we were talking about?"

"No."

"Well, you better keep your nose out of my affairs, or else. I don't take kindly to people who get in my way."

"Are you threatening me?" So much for calm.

"Let's call it a friendly warning." He gave what was meant as a wink but came out as a squinty scowl. He drained the last of his coffee, threw a ten on the table and sauntered out of the café.

Nice meeting you, too. Who does he think he is, threatening me like that? And who does he think I am; that I would be intimidated by his threats? If anything, I'm more determined than ever to solve the mystery. He is kind of scary, though. He didn't correct me when I mentioned F.F. Pearson.

Laine gulped down the rest of her drink, hurried to her car and drove towards home. *Damn, I forgot to grab a sandwich. Better stop and get something to eat at Dude's Place, it's the nearest restaurant and coffee shop to my cottage. Don't want to starve before I figure out this BNC mess.*

The minute she walked into Dude's Place, she spied Sam sitting at the first booth. She ran her hand through her hair, wishing she had a comb handy. Crap, she wished for an entire beauty parlor.

The wait person chose that moment to walk by, just as Laine's elbow was at coffee cup height. Luckily, the wait person was an acrobat. The tray rattled, coffee sloshed, but nothing fell.

"I'm sorry."

"Don't you worry about it." The wait person winked at her as if she knew what caused this sudden clumsiness.

Why does Sam always make me feel this way? I haven't felt this gawkward since seventh grade when that hunk Dave Mattos said hello to me.

Gawkward was a term she'd coined at her first dance.

"I'm so graceful," she joked, trying to cover her nervousness and annoyance. Yeah, she felt annoyed. She hadn't thought about him in days, well, at least a couple of hours. Now here he sat, ensuring he'd be on her mind for most of the night.

Sam gave her his best hangdog expression. "C'mon, I'll buy you a burger." His dark curls tumbled over the collar of his denim shirt.

Laine melted enough to smile. *He can't help it if he's sexy.* She slid into his booth. *Maybe I should give him a break.*

The wait person came to take their orders. "Laine, Tillie. Tillie, Laine," Sam said, by way of introduction. "Tillie owns this fine establishment."

"I know who Laine is. I heard her sing at Serena's. How you doing, Laine?"

"You're speaking to a Seaglass Bay newk. That's what we call newcomers," he added in response to Laine's puzzled expression.

"I make an exception for her because she can sing. You got a voice like an angel."

"Thank you very much."

"No, thank you," Tillie said.

Laine ordered a turkey club and a cup of tea.

"I'll try the veggie burger," Sam told Tillie.

Laine blinked and raised her eyebrows. Dude's made veggie burgers but not decaf coffee?

Sam took in her look of surprise. "There's more than meets the eye in Seaglass Bay. It's a town of farmers, fishermen, lawyers, and artists. We're all one big blend. You never know how it's going to mix up."

"I'll try the veggie burger too, then."

"Are you okay? You look a little rattled."

"I am." Laine took several deep breaths. She told Sam about having coffee with David Emson.

Sam clenched and unclenched his hands while she talked. He looked like he would jump from his chair any minute.

"That bastard," he said when she finished. "He has no right to bully you. He ever bothers you again, you let me know."

Laine agreed. She could handle herself but no need to say so.

"Most of us in town know if Emson ever asks us to go for coffee it's best to say no and make a run for it."

"I'll remember that from now on."

When she dug into a plateful of Cajun French fries and a thick, juicy veggie burger, her face lit with pleasure. "I'll never make assumptions again."

"Because that just makes an ass out of you. Um, do you always make moaning noises when you eat? Sounds like you're having great sex."

Laine grimaced in embarrassment. "I only moan when I'm eating someone delicious. I mean something," she amended, feeling her face flame as Sam laughed. "I mean food."

Please God, if you love me, let the floor open and swallow me up.

"Don't take advantage of my foot-in-mouth disease." Laine's face got redder by the minute. "Hopefully, Doc Cremble knows how to treat this."

"I won't." Sam tried to arrange his grin into a more serious expression.

"What else have you been doing?"

"Working hard. Getting those children's programs up and running is taking a lot of time. I'm surprised they never had kids' activities before."

"You've got to remember Brooke's not big on kids. Never has been. Good thing she doesn't have any."

Laine could believe it. "It's hard to picture Brooke as a kid. Maybe she was born a mini adult."

Sam laughed. "Possible. She did go prematurely gray in her late twenties."

Laine swallowed her last bite. "Delicious."

AFTER FINISHING their meal, they walked out together. Everyone they passed stopped to say hello to Sam.

When they got to his truck, she said, "Sam, you're like the unofficial mayor of Seaglass Bay."

Sam chuckled. "I've lived here all my life, so I know almost everybody. I also landscape half the houses and businesses in Seaglass Bay. They want to stay on my good side so I won't plant ragweed in their yards."

"I doubt that's the reason. I'd like to see some of your landscape designs."

"You got it. I'll show you some day when I have more time. Want a ride home?"

"No thanks, I'm going to walk." Some days she had less willpower than others. She suspected if she got into the truck with him today, she'd be compelled to stroke his clean-shaven chin and gently kiss his sensual lips. Then what would happen?

She pictured the headlines: "Woman Arrested for Stroking and Kissing Sam Holliston."

Every woman in town would sympathize, except for Fiona.

"Can you sing again tonight at Serena's? Everyone's talking about your voice."

"Okay, sure."

"See you tonight at Serena's."

She stood there even after Sam's truck disappeared down the road.

Fourteen.

Sunday

LAINE STARED at the computer. She wanted to write, but not flyers for kids' programs. Her fingers hesitated to start; then gathered momentum until they flew over the keys. She'd entered another world, oblivious of time.

She wrote about sitting in the front row at her father's concert. Much to her surprise, her dad had called her onstage to harmonize with him on his hit single, "When She Dazzles." She had sung with her dad in front of thousands of fans. On the ride home they had chatted about everything from boys to music to the environment.

Too tired to write another word, she read over her pages. At last, at least in her estimation, she had a passable story about her dad and his concert in upstate New York. She hadn't told Sam, but that concert had ended up the last event she ever attended with both her parents.

Talking to Sam about my dad got me started on this. Incredible. I never wrote about either of my parents, until now. I've wanted to do this for years.

Laine's eyes filled with tears. She let them flow unchecked. Laine knew she'd never get over her parents' deaths, and the pain and longing would recycle over and over again. But this time, when she stopped crying, a sweet sense of relief filled her soul.

Enough with the tears. It was almost eight, time to go to Serena's. She put on her black shaggy sweater, jeans, and cowboy boots. Silver earrings, bangles, hair gel and a pick through her short shiny hair completed the ensemble. She told herself she dressed for herself. It had nothing to do with Sam. Not much, anyway.

WHEN SHE PULLED into Serena's parking lot, a thrill of anxiety ran through her. Cars filled the lot. If she walked through the door, she'd have to sing in front of at least seventy-five people. She sat in her car, considering running home to safety.

"Good evening." She glanced up; the Clay brothers stood beside her car, waiting to escort her inside. Too late to turn back now.

"I hope you know the words to 'Me and Bobby McGee.'" Steve held the door open for her.

"I do, as a matter of fact." Dad had taught her well, and she had a good memory for lyrics.

"Great. We have a slight problem. Juli, who usually sings with me, is home in bed with the flu. I know you plan to sing a couple of songs. Think you could do a few more?"

"How many is a few more?"

"Twenty." Steve gave her a sheepish smile.

Laine ran her fingers through her short hair. She had cut it in the first place to signify she'd become a new, brave, independent Laine. In this new light, she answered, with only the slightest tremor of fear, "I'll do it."

"That's the spirit. Let me get you something from the bar."

Laine straightened her posture as confidence surged through her. Steve brought her a glass of wine. She sipped it as she followed him to the circle where Sam stood with a group of musicians.

Several members of the group turned towards her, curious. The rest remained too busy tuning up to notice anyone, least of all a singer with pre-performance jitters.

Her dad always got jitters before a performance, and he always did a great job.

Before she had time to think much further, Sam asked her to sing "Me and Bobby McGee." She nodded. She knew that song by heart.

Inside her head, Aunt Rose's voice told her to stand tall, not small.

Laine squared her shoulders and took a deep breath. Then she sang her heart out with the gutsy voice the song demanded. After all, she could relate to the lyrics. She'd been busted flat, maybe not in Baton Rouge, but with the same kind of longing in her heart. Her voice filled every pore of the smoky room, stilling the usual loud conversation. One by one, people stopped talking to listen. Some even shushed those nearby and wagged warning fingers to quiet them. When the song ended, the audience responded with a moment of awed silence, and then broke into hearty and heartfelt applause.

Laine smiled and bowed. Lightheaded, she gasped to catch her breath. She sank down into a chair.

Wow, what a rush! This must be how Dad felt after his performances.

Laine remembered she'd felt this way once before, when she'd harmonized with him for the song at Cornell.

AN EARNEST-LOOKING MAN hurried over and introduced himself as the high school music teacher, Drake Fielding.

He filled her ears with great praise, clasping her hand and pumping it with gusto. She had the right stuff, he told her. She just needed voice training to pull it all together. He offered her free lessons.

"You don't need much, but it would be a pleasure to work with a voice like yours. You've got some talent, young lady."

Laine accepted his offer with a rush of gratitude. "Thanks Mr. Fielding. As long as you don't mind waiting until I get used to my new life here in Seaglass Bay. I want to be able to focus on my lessons."

He pressed a business card into her hand, and extracted a promise she call him as soon as possible. "Please call me Field. Everybody does."

Laine's break over, she took her place again with the musicians. She caught sight of Sofie in the audience. Sofie grinned and gave her a thumbs-up. A fan already.

"Got any suggestions?" Steve asked her.

"Do you all know 'Summertime'?"

"Sure do."

"I'll sing a bluesy version." As she sang, "Summertime and the livin' is easy," she marveled at how comfortable she already felt with the crowd. As Laine relaxed, her deep, honeyed voice built up steam, and a hush again fell over the audience.

"So hush little baby, don't you cry."

Sam leaned toward her with a grin, and his voice tickled her ear. "They've never shut up to listen like this before. You are magic."

Laine sang her heart out, stopping only when her voice began to feel raspy and raw around midnight. After bowing to a final applause, she sought out Sofie's corner table.

"You were fantastic," Sofie said.

At that moment, a man with a beard and mop of shaggy hair grabbed the third chair and sat. Sofie introduced him as Muddy Waters.

Laine got a glimpse of a handsome face under the mop of hair.

"You were great," Muddy told Laine, turning away from her toward Sofie. "Sofie, can you come for supper tomorrow night? I've got a new action film I want you to watch."

"I'll be there at six. Now scram, we're talking about men."

"I don't mind a little girl talk. I like to understand what women think about men."

"Very noble of you, but we're talking about things that start with men, like menopause, mental illness, and menstruation."

"Guess I'll be going then." Laine burst out laughing as Muddy grimaced and disappeared into the crowd.

Next, Mike the EMT stopped at their table.

"You're good," he told Laine. Then he turned his attention to Sofie.

"Hey Sofie, some of us guys are going to play pool Friday night. Can you come?"

"Sure. Meet you there at eight. Now scram. Go hone your flirting skills."

"Yes, your highness."

"Jeesh," Laine said. "You've got every man in Seaglass Bay after you."

"No, they just think I'm one of the guys. I play a mean game of pool. And if I need a cuddle, Muddy Waters is always available."

"Is that his real name?"

"Actually, his real name is Bill Muddle. I guess it's an old Yankee family name. Muddy is a fisherman, so his nickname works. He owns two lobster boats and makes a great fish dinner."

"He seems to really like you. And he's cute, too."

Sofie made a face. "Naw, he's an old friend. We got diaper rash together."

They talked for several more minutes, until Sofie explained she had to start working on another model.

"So late?"

"The muse has called. I must obey." She rose and left.

LAINE LEFT fifteen minutes later. She'd parked her car at the very edge of the dark lot.

Usually she could hear the wind and the sloshing of the waves, but the night seemed weirdly silent.

Did I remember to lock the car doors? It's important to lock the doors because someone could hide in the backseat.

Why think about this creepy stuff now?

She let out a breath when she finally reached her car.

As Laine started to unlock the door, a figure sprang towards her out of the shadows. Startled, she yelped, "Help," and then high tailed it back towards Serena's.

Ahead of her, the bar door slammed open and the voices of the Clay brothers rose in merry bar-leaving tones.

Thank God. She flung herself into Steve's arms.

"Whoa, what's going on? I like you too, but . . ."

Laine took several ragged breaths. "Someone tried to grab me when I got to my car."

Steve turned on his flashlight and walked around, sweeping its beam throughout the lot. "I don't see anything. We must have scared him off."

"Are you okay?" Rick asked.

Laine nodded. "I think so. It surprised me."

Sam joined them in the parking lot. "Hey, what's going on?"

Laine started to babble, blurting out the story in an almost coherent fashion. "I've got to sit down, my legs feel like rubber."

"Let's get you into my truck. I'll turn the heat on and you can sit nice and cozy until the police arrive. They'll take your statement and then patrol the area at regular intervals tonight, make sure nobody is hanging around."

Sam used his cell to call 911; then turned back to Rick and Steve. "I told Serena she needs more lighting out here. Maybe a police report will motivate her."

"We're in luck; it's Witty," Rick said as a police car pulled up next to them.

"Witty?"

"Sergeant Witkowsky. He plays poker with us."

"Hey, Witty," Sam said as the officer rolled down the window of his car.

"This better be urgent. I was in the middle of important paperwork."

"Playing poker online again? This is important. Some guy jumped out at Laine in the parking lot."

"Where is she?"

"I'm right here." Laine came up beside him.

"Why don't we get this straightened out inside Serena's, where it's warm and there are those nice little fish crackers?" Witkowski suggested.

"There's still a crowd in there. If Serena finds out we brought a uniform inside, she'll kill us. Maybe even ban us for a couple of weeks."

"You're right. What was I thinking? Let me pull my cruiser into a space. C'mon, Laine, climb in back. You can answer questions comfortably there."

"Did you notice anything?" Sergeant Witkowsky asked after she explained the situation.

Laine squeezed her eyes shut to think. "The person wore a dark-colored ski jacket."

"Anything else?" Witkowsky scribbled notes.

Laine shook her head. "It was pitch black out there. I think I surprised them trying to slash my tire. I saw the flash of a knife."

"Did you notice any other details? Height, weight?"

Laine shook her head. "Not that I can remember. They disappeared so quickly into the shadows. It must've been someone who knows the area. They headed towards the beach."

"That sure narrows it down," the sergeant muttered. "Let me take a look at your car."

Laine handed him her keys. Witkowski clambered out of the cruiser, spent several minutes crouched beside Laine's car, opened and closed each door, and ambled back to where she waited.

"Nobody got inside the car. But the left front tire is slashed. Have any idea who'd want to do something like that to you?"

Laine shook her head in slow motion. She harkened back to her weird encounter with David Emson. He had warned her to stay away. "Someone who doesn't like newcomers, maybe?"

"Who knows?" Witkowsky spent a few minutes interviewing the Clay brothers, then left.

Sam refused to let Laine call Triple A. He changed her tire using the headlights from his truck.

"Thanks for being a sport and letting me get rid of some testosterone," Sam said when he finished. "I guess I need to play He Man every once in a while."

"I have a need to be She Woman on occasion, so I understand. Next time I'll try to get a flat on the edge of a cliff in icy twenty below weather. Then your testosterone will really get a workout. But right now, I have to go home. I'm exhausted."

"Want me to stay over? I'm worried about you. I could sleep on the lumpy, uncomfortable couch."

Laine laughed. "No thanks. But I would appreciate you following me home and checking the house."

"Sure, I'll check for boogie men and make sure the house is secure. I'll also program my emergency number on your cell. And Laine, next time you go to Serena's, would you mind giving me a call and I'll come over and pick you up?"

"Okay, thanks." She looked down at her trembling hands and knew she had to take his offer seriously.

AT THE COTTAGE, she sat shivering in the car while Sam went inside the house. He returned to the porch.

"All clear." He held open the front door for Laine.

"No monsters under the bed. You could use a new lock on the front door. Okay if I come back tomorrow and install one?"

Laine nodded, blinking back tears. "Thanks. I really appreciate all you're doing for me."

Laine wanted to show her gratitude with a warm goodbye kiss.

It turned out to be a great kiss, filled with promise of much more to come. Even with her mantra—*I am celibate, I am celibate, I am celibate*—she couldn't stop kissing him. When she couldn't take any more, she pulled back and sent him on his merry way.

As she watched his truck pull out of her driveway, she intoned her new mantra: "I am horny. I will not go crazy."

Later, as Laine lay in bed, alone, safely sandwiched between flannel sheets, she wondered who wanted to scare her.

It took a very long time to fall asleep.

Fifteen.

Monday

~~~~~~~~~~~~

S AM PULLED IN the driveway as Laine stretched on the porch, warming up for her jog and beach patrol. *Oh Lord. Why now? I'm sleep deprived; I've got raccoon circles under my eyes. And worst of all, I have a stress zit on my chin.*

He bounded out of the truck, much too cheerful. "I'm here to put new locks on your door. Are you okay?"

That's right, new locks. He did say something about that last night. Be nice, Laine. He's here to help.

"Much better. Thanks."

Instead of going out on beach patrol, she watched Sam work. Nice ass. Nice arms. Nice how his hair curled just the right amount at the nape of his neck. Watching him was far less productive than beach patrol, but far more entertaining.

While Sam worked, he talked. "I was worried about you after last night. That was weird. You sure it wasn't someone who wanted to talk to you?" He put a key into the new lock, turned it, jerked at the knob. Solid. Well done. He nodded, kept talking. "Seaglass Bay has always been so crime free."

Laine shook her head. "Most people who want to talk to me don't slash my tire."

"Maybe they thought your car belonged to someone else."

"Maybe."

He took her face in his hands and tilted it until their eyes met. "I would hate to think anyone would deliberately try to hurt you." His hands felt warm and his voice was a low growl. Man version of a purr.

Her gut twisted and the sensation continued beyond.

"If I ever . . ." He stopped.

"If you ever what?" Laine moved in closer.

Sam dropped his hands, stepped back and averted his eyes. "Nothing."

He unlocked the door, pushed it open. "There you go. Safe again."

"Thanks, Sam. I appreciate the new lock. What do I owe you?"

"Not money, that's for sure. But how about you come for a ride and see my landscaping?"

"I'd love to, but I have to do beach patrol."

"Ha. There's nothing much on the beach today except a couple of seagulls. You said you'd be interested in taking a look at what I do. My day job."

"Sofie gave your landscaping five stars."

"She did?"

"Yes."

"That's what I pay her for. Come see for yourself. What else did she say about me?"

"She said you were difficult, stubborn, and could do anything you put your mind to."

He made a sound between a laugh and a snort. "That's my Sofie. She said the two of you really hit it off."

Ooh goody, they talked about me.

He eyed her closely, taking in the circles under her eyes. "Not losing sleep over me, I hope." His teasing words didn't quite hide a note of concern.

"How did you know? You must be psychic." Thank God he really didn't have the sixth sense. If he did, he'd pick up on some pretty erotic fantasies and dreams. "I'm still a bit freaked over what happened last night."

"I think you can relax now. Serena promised to have outdoor lighting installed this week, and Seaglass Bay's finest promised to keep patrolling the area."

"Thanks, Sam." Laine squeezed his hand. "Yes, of course I want to see your work."

WHILE THEY DROVE, Laine said, "I liked Sofie the minute I saw her."

"You couldn't find a better friend. She helped me through some pretty tough times." He pulled into a driveway and turned off the engine.

Laine wondered what those tough times were and if she would ever find out. She didn't mean to seem nosy, of course, just concerned.

"Here's one of my landscape designs. No one's home, but they won't mind us taking a peek in the backyard. Remember, it looks shabby this time of year as compared to spring or summer."

Whatever she expected didn't hold a candle to the magical world awaiting her.

"You create these spaces? This is incredible."

Stones set into the hillside made layered plateaus for flower plantings. A slate walkway surrounded a small pond with a brass fountain in its center.

"In the spring you can watch frogs jumping on the lily pads."

Beyond the pond, a stone path led to a gleaming set of white French doors. A tall handcrafted wooden trellis leaned against the house. Clematis and morning glories would scramble up the wall in summer.

"Glorious. It's beautiful, Sam," Laine whispered.

"Thank you. They've got apple trees and blueberry bushes. I'll make sure they give you some bloobs this summer. They have more than they can use."

"Bloobs?"

"Yeah, blueberries, what did you think I meant?"

"Never mind. How did you have time to do all this, plus all your other work?"

"I designed it and laid the stonework. Hank takes care of the rest."

"The EMT?"

"Yeah, that's only a part-time job. He gives me a good thirty hours a week. And you should see his green thumb."

The sight of a whimsical horse caught Laine's attention. The body created from rough-sawn pieces of wood, juxtaposed with the painstakingly carved mane and face. The mixture of spontaneity and careful design startled and excited her.

Sam smiled. "You like my sawhorse?"

"I love it. I love the whole garden. It's open and peaceful and exciting at the same time. This is land art."

Sam grinned. "Land art?"

"I don't know the right words to explain it. Don't laugh."

"I'm not laughing at you. Land art is a great way to describe my work. I like the way you move your hands when you talk."

"Well, okay then."

"I'm selling my sawhorses on the internet," he told her with pride. "I got quite a few orders. It should keep me out of trouble this winter."

That's good, because I could be tempted to get into a mess of trouble with you.

"We better get going," he sighed. "I need a cup of coffee. But someday soon I'll show you my own garden. I think you'll like it."

"Your house must be incredible."

He shrugged. "Someday I'll design a garden with a special someone. Herbs, a fountain, ornamental grasses—the works. For now, my garden is fairly simple. It's big though, and teeming with veggies in the summer." His dark eyes held hers for a moment; then he took her small hand in his large, tanned one and helped her into the truck.

THEY DROVE to Dude's Place in silence. Laine couldn't speak, afraid to voice her inner thoughts. The woman who would someday design a magical house and garden with Sam would be lucky, that's for sure.

A few minutes later, they sat at a booth in Dude's Place. Laine sipped a steaming mug of cocoa. Sam drained a cup of high-test.

"Coffee with Emson and Serena's parking lot aren't the only strange things that happened to me." She told him about the dead bunny and her run-in with Brooke and Emson. "There are weird happenings at the BNC."

"Are you serious?"

"Yes. I think someone is trying to frighten me."

"What could be strange about a nature center? C'mon, lighten up. I'm sure they were having one of their little arguments."

"But he called her pet."

"You must have misheard. They hate each other. Maybe he said something else."

She tightened her shoulders in exasperation. "What about 'beaucoup bucks'? You think he was talking about ducks?"

"Now there's a perfectly reasonable explanation. After all, they do talk about ducks at nature centers."

"I promise you, my hearing is perfect. Also, I have a nose for trouble." She went on to tell him about the mysteries she had solved in college. "I even discovered which professor was misusing grant money. I saved the college a lot of dough."

"You have an adorable nose. But nothing's going on here, I guarantee it."

Laine sighed. *Guarantee, my butt.* Life held no guarantees. This conversation with Sam hadn't gone as planned.

"So Nancy Drew, what do you say we share a piece of chocolate cake?"

"You wouldn't be patronizing me, would you?"

"I'm sorry. I guess I can be opinionated."

"You guess?"

He gave her a sheepish grin. "I've known these people forever. They aren't perfect; I mean everyone has issues and skeletons in their closets. But these are solid people. I can't help thinking you're stringing random incidents together."

Laine gave him a sweet smile. "I'm going to prove you wrong. Now let's change the subject and have that piece of cake."

Tillie came by to refill their cups and take their cake order. She stayed to chat for several minutes.

After she left, Sam said, "She really likes you. I've never seen her take to a newk before."

"I'm flattered."

Linda Richter

"Laine, I know Brooke and Fiona aren't exactly warm and fuzzy. I know from personal experience Fiona is a bitch. But I've known them all my life, and believe me nothing is going on."

"Please, let's agree to disagree and change the subject."

Tillie brought the flourless chocolate cake and two forks. They dug in.

"Did you really like my landscaping?" Sam asked when they had devoured the last morsel.

Sam's voice, usually strong, sounded so vulnerable, so in need of her approval. Her heart teetered on the verge of melting another twenty degrees. Part of her wanted to run away, never giving an answer.

"I love it."

Sam immediately rewarded her with a boyish, sexy grin.

"You've made my day."

Maybe Sam didn't believe her suspicions about the BNC. But she knew someone who would.

After Sam dropped her off, she called Sofie and asked for an hour of her time.

"Sure, as long as you don't mind if I sew while you talk. I'm putting the finishing touches on a leatherback turtle."

At Sofie's, Laine sat in a rocking chair looking as if it came over on the *Mayflower*. "Don't tell me you collect antiques too."

"I dabble," Sofie admitted. "Now tell."

While Sofie stitched the leather turtle, Laine filled her in on recent events. "And don't tell me that's not weird."

Sofie looked up from her sewing. "It's very weird. Emson and Brooke can hardly stand to be in the same room together. You said they called each other pet and Davie. Usually they call each other jerk and idiot."

"What about my run-in with Emson?"

Sofie shuddered. "No kidding. I can't believe you agreed to go for coffee with him."

"Sam acted like I was delusional when I told him. It bothered me because I've got good instincts. I wish he would believe me."

Sofie raised her brows. "Sam's a guy. He's got his head up his ass. Now, what do you think is going on? And what are we going to do about it?"

A HALF HOUR LATER, with the leatherback turtle finished, Laine and Sofie had a plan. Laine couldn't wait to Google Pearson. She would also write down anything striking her as odd at the BNC. Sofie would question people who knew Emson.

"Because you know how to schmooze, girl. Maybe we can find out what's happening with him and Brooke."

LAINE ZOOMED OFF full of energy and enthusiasm, and glad she'd talked to Sofie. She headed down Morris Road, a winding, narrow road skirting the deer habitat. The sun-dappled trees splashed lacy shadows on the road. Laine opened the window to let the wind blow in her face. She remembered her childhood dog, Hero, who always stuck her head out the window when she rode in the car. Today, Laine imagined herself reincarnated as Hero, with the wind whipping her hair back.

Laine tapped the brake as she turned the bend at Cedar Crossing. The next mile or so, a straight run, had Laine leaning on the gas pedal to enjoy the ride.

At Edwards Farm, the road snaked sharply left. She neared the bend in the road and stepped on the brake. The pedal, loose and mushy beneath her foot, sank without much resistance. The car slowed slightly as it reached the bend. Laine pressed the brake pedal harder until it touched the floor.

Nothing happened.

Laine kept pumping the brakes. If she pumped until her foot fell off, it wouldn't matter. She had no brakes.

Her car veered around the curve, tires squealing. Laine hugged the wheel with her hands, the white-knuckle express. The car took on a life of its own; she turned left, it pulled right. All she could do was hang on for dear life. The car swerved around the corner on two wheels and catapulted on. The road sloped gently downhill, but the ride remained as non-gentle as you could get as Laine's speed accelerated each second. She nearly collided with a battered pickup truck. The old horn honked as she spun out past the truck, brushing the edge of the road.

Laine battled with the steering wheel as the car swerved, vibrating, into the soft shoulder. Like fighting the tumble cycle of an old dryer, she jerked the car back onto the road. She headed left, aiming for a pile of huge, plastic-covered hay bales. In the next moment, too close to keep her sanity, another car swung around the curve and headed right for her.

Oh, shit, I am going to die! My life isn't even flashing before my eyes. Maybe because I haven't had much of a life yet.

Turning off into the hay bales looked like her only chance. She missed the front bumper of the other car by scant inches, and her car pummeled into the hay with a loud thud.

Her head lurched forward and hit the steering wheel. The world turned dark.

OUT OF THE DARKNESS, from somewhere close by a voice said, "Hey, are you all right, lady?" A young man's voice.

She forced her eyes open, and his anxious features came into focus.

"I was afraid I was gonna hit you. You came right at me when I made the corner."

"Don't call me lady." Her voice came out as a croak. A siren sounded in the distance. Who'd caused the trouble? Oh yeah, she'd done it. Oh crap! The kid must have called the ambulance from his cell, because Hank and Mike lifted her, with a gentleness that surprised her, out of the car and onto a stretcher.

We've got to stop meeting like this, she tried to say, but no sounds came out. She could see the words in a bubble above her head.

The ten-minute ambulance ride seemed to take forever.

AT THE HOSPITAL, images stayed fuzzy and she mumbled like she had a mouth full of marbles. "Lost control," she muttered as they wheeled her into emergency. "No brakes. They tried to kill me."

"No one tried to kill you," Hank soothed. "You had an accident."

AN HOUR LATER, the emergency room doctor diagnosed concussion, scrapes, bruises and shock. She wanted Laine to stay overnight for observation.

That suited Laine fine, because she didn't want to move. She had more mental acuity now, but her body ached from head to toe. She settled as comfortably as she could in her hospital bed and sipped apple juice as Sam burst through the door.

He took one look at her and stammered several unintelligible words.

"Hey, I thought I was supposed to be the one in shock," she said. "You must've found out Mike looked up my skirt when he put me in the ambulance."

"Don't even joke. Are you okay? What happened? Is anything broken?" He sat at the edge of the bed, his brow furrowed in concern.

"Be gentle. Nothing broken, but everything aches."

Laine told him the story, leaving out her suspicions someone had tampered with her car. After the response she got from Hank, she didn't want Sam to think her a paranoid fool. Sam held an "Andy of Mayberry" idea of a perfect Seaglass Bay, and she didn't want to be the one to change it. Not yet.

"Anyway, I feel lucky to be alive."

"Jesus, you could have been killed. You've got to be more careful. First your ankle, now this."

"You're cranky. You're worried about me."

"I'm concerned. Okay, yes, I fucking panicked. I almost had a heart attack. You're driving me crazy. You're so accident prone."

I am not accident prone. No one has ever called me super careful, but they never called me accident prone either. How am I supposed to prove my track record to people who I just met? When Aunt Rose visits she'll vouch for me.

Before she could protest, a nurse interrupted and shooed Sam away. "She needs her rest."

LAINE SPENT the rest of her hospital stay sleeping and eating hospital food. But her mind kept going back to the fact her brakes had failed. Who wanted to hurt her?

Sixteen.

Tuesday

THE NEXT MORNING, Sofie rescued Laine from the hospital and drove her to the mechanic's where her car had been towed after the accident.

"This is getting freaky. Maybe you should come and stay with me. Or go on vacation for a while."

Laine shook her head. "Thanks, but I'll be okay. Someone is trying to scare me, not kill me. If they are trying to kill me they're doing a terrible job." She tried for a smile.

"Someone cut your brakes."

"We don't know that for sure."

"Yeah, right. Please be careful, okay?"

"I need a little time to find out what's going on. I'll be cautious, I promise."

"Okay. What does Sam say?"

Laine pursed her lips in disgust. "That my imagination is running wild. He says nothing like this could happen in our perfect Seaglass Bay."

"That's bull, Laine. Sam of all people knows what can happen in a small town like this."

Laine really wanted to ask Sofie what she meant. But right now, the car needed her attention. "Bye, Sofie. Thanks for the ride."

Laine entered the garage and found the mechanic munching corn chips and talking on the phone. When he saw her, he got off the phone and gestured toward her car.

"Looks like you broke the brake line here." He pointed. "Snapped right off."

"I had those checked a few months ago. What could cause the brake line to snap like that?"

"Oh, any one of a number of things. Brakes can be tricky, if you know what I mean. They can go—like that!" He snapped his fingers. "Accidents happen."

Especially to me lately. Did this accident happen without human help? Or did someone want to scare me enough so I would leave Seaglass Bay and never return? Or like Sofie said, kill me?

"Could someone have cut them?"

The mechanic peered at her more closely. "Sure. Someone could have cut them. But why would anybody do that to a pretty little lady like you?"

Why indeed?

"It's all fixed." The mechanic handed her a bill. "You enjoy working at the BNC?"

"Yes, and I love Seaglass Bay." *Especially if whoever's harassing me would stop.* In this small town, people knew each other's business. But not their secrets. Skeletons in the closets filled the homes of Seaglass Bay. The time had come to confront a few of them.

Laine paid the mechanic's reasonable sum. She wondered if Sam had had a word with the mechanic.

Behind the wheel again she nestled into the seat, although she wondered if she would feel compelled to look under her car every morning to insure her brake lines remained intact. Maybe she'd have to buy a car lift.

Laine drove to the police station and asked for Sergeant Witkowski. In less than a minute, he opened the door of his office and waved her in.

"Look what the cat dragged in. Have a seat. Want some coffee? How about a doughnut?" He opened a Barry's Bakery box and waved it in front of her.

"You okay?"

Laine nodded. "I appreciate you coming to see me in the hospital."

She picked a jelly donut, to be polite. She took another to be friendly. Who was she trying to kid? Barry's made the best donuts on the East Coast.

As she sipped at a cup of strong lukewarm coffee she told him everything about the failed brakes and the dead rabbit. "Add in the incident at Serena's, and I think someone's trying to scare me."

"Who would want to scare you?" Witkowski selected a cream filled donut. "Can you name any names?"

Shit, how could she answer that question without sounding paranoid? "It could be somebody at the BNC."

Witty guffawed.

Laine always wondered what a guffaw sounded like. Now she knew.

"You're kidding me, right?" Witty wiped doughnut crumbs from his chin. "I mean there has never been a whisper of anything even remotely suspicious connected with the BNC."

Doesn't that in itself seem suspicious?

Laine swallowed a surge of anger at how people stereotyped evil intent. Upstanding members of the community could slash tires too.

"Look, Sofie Pacheco says you're good people and you're smart. We'll send a patrol car by the cottage at regular intervals. That's the most we can do right now. We've got a record of your complaint, and be sure to let us know if anything else happens." Witkowski turned his back to open the door.

Laine allowed herself an uncharitable thought about Witty's completely flat ass.

Better get back to the BNC and make up some of her hours.

As she drove to the BNC, her mind returned to the sergeant. Tall, thin as a reed. Delicate fingers drumming on the table. Pianist's fingers. Mop of shiny black hair. Nice guy. Attractive in a lean and hungry way. Personally, she liked guys with more meat on their bones.

Aunt Rose used to joke she liked them short and chubby. Laine's father had been height impaired and stocky.

Sam's frame was tall and muscular. Enough flesh on the bones to make him cuddly, solid. Shoulders almost big enough to need a wide load sign.

"That's the way, uh-huh uh-huh, I like it," she sang out loud as she pulled into the BNC parking lot. *Time to get back to work, and get my mind off men and murder.*

There were no other cars in the lot. Laine walked to the back of the building to check for other cars. She didn't want to interrupt another secret meeting. Whew, the coast was clear. She'd have time to do a little personal research.

At her computer, she decided to search for F.F. Pearson online. Nosy people appreciated the internet more than its inventors would ever know. She typed in his name and instantly hit pay dirt.

Pages and pages about Pearson's own Horatio Alger rags to riches story made up the listing.

Born May 11, 1960, Schenectady, New York

Father died five years ago

Mother, Emily, resided in an assisted living facility in Newport, Rhode Island.

Laine skimmed the rest of the information. She learned Pearson embraced an entrepreneurial spirit from an early age to become the fifth richest man in the country.

She slowed down when she came to the section about Samantha Colt Brownstone. Pearson's fiancée came from an old Boston family. She designed high-end wedding dresses.

Hmmm. Laine kept reading.

F.F. Pearson and Samantha met while skiing in Vale the winter before. The list of celebrities at their engagement party could have wallpapered a large ballroom.

Another site talked about Pearson's real estate vision. Having learned much about F. F. Pearson and his fiancée, but not getting much work done, Laine decided to call it a day.

Brooke came into the office as Laine put on her jacket. "What happened? I heard you had an accident."

No asking me how I'm feeling. At least I know it's the real Brooke and not an imposter. Laine gave a condensed version of her accident, then watched Brooke's reaction.

Had the color drained from Brooke's skillfully made-up face, or had Laine's imagination supplied the details?

"That's awful," Brooke sputtered. She muttered something and stalked into her office, slamming the door in her wake.

Laine shook her head. Brooke seemed really upset. *Didn't know she liked me that much.*

AFTER PLAYING several hours of catch-up, Laine drove home without incident. After starting the fire and making a simple supper, she tried to concentrate on a mystery book but kept getting distracted by the thought running around her head: *Why would someone want to cut my brakes?* With the question still unresolved, she took a hot bath to ease her aching muscles and went to bed.

Then darkness slipped in like a gentle breeze and draped warm arms over her. She slept.

Seventeen.

Wednesday

~~~~~~

THE NEXT MORNING at Dude's Place, Sam sauntered in as Laine took her first bite of corn muffin with scallions and cheddar cheese. The wind had ruffled his curls and made his cheeks rosy.

"Summer's definitely over," he said to no one in particular, rubbing his hands together.

"Honey, fall's almost over," Tillie called from behind the counter.

"Should warm up later, though." Sam glanced around the room, his eyes coming to rest on Laine.

"Hey there, mind if I join you?"

Laine nodded and he slipped into the opposite side of the booth.

"What are you, Seaglass Bay's weatherperson?"

Sam chuckled. "I'd be right as often as they are. Hey, how are you feeling from your bumps and bruises?"

"Still a little stiff. But much better, thanks."

"Good, glad to hear it. That corn muffin looks tasty." He glanced at a menu, flipped it shut. "I'm working at the houseboat today, but I need coffee to fortify me first."

"The houseboat? Isn't it too cold today?"

"I've got a small woodstove. It warms the place up in about fifteen minutes. I'll be there all day. If you're not busy, come over later and watch the sunset with me from the deck. I'll rub your back; you must still be sore."

His invitation sounded way too good to pass up. "What time is sunset?"

"If you show up at four fifteen, we'll have plenty of time to get settled on the deck."

"Sounds great. See you then."

"Better yet, why don't you follow me to the houseboat now," Sam suggested. "Then you'll know how to drive through the back way."

AFTER HOLDING BACK the desire to lick the corn muffin crumbs from her plate, Laine rose to leave. Sam extended a hand to help her from the booth. He held the door for her and she thanked him with a smile.

Laine waited in her car for him to drive out of the lot. Her pulse raced at the thought of watching the sunset with Sam. Maybe they would toast its autumnal beauty with a bottle of wine. Maybe they wouldn't have time for a toast. A sudden sense of heat surged through her despite the brisk November air.

Sam waved to her as he pulled into the street. She followed him for about a mile up the road, the same road she lived on.

He turned through a small break in a split-rail fence and onto a narrow dirt lane. They followed the crooked path past fields, through tangled brush and bittersweet vines, and over a small wooden bridge. The lane ended in a shell driveway.

To the left, Sam's houseboat bobbed on gentle waves. Beyond the houseboat, seagulls flocked around a small island.

Laine climbed out of her car and stretched. "I love these old country roads."

"Me too. So now you can't use the excuse you don't know the way. See you here at four fifteen."

"Sounds perfect."

Laine climbed back in her car and drove to work, savoring the sweet edge of anticipation.

The workday seemed to stretch interminably long. She had just enough time to rush home for a shower.

In her bathroom, after a vigorous session with the exfoliating salt scrub, she dried off and slipped into a skirt and sweater. A fresh application of lipstick, and she felt ready to roll.

She pulled into Sam's driveway at four fifteen.

But before getting out, she had a million things to do. First, she checked her lipstick in the mirror. Second, she lifted her skirt to make sure there weren't any runs in her black tights. Then, she checked her nails to make sure her polish wasn't chipped. Oh yeah, she didn't have any polish on, but her hands trembled. Definitely a case of the jitters.

Probably that cup of green tea, which has a small percentage of caffeine. I'm probably just sensitive to the stuff. Another thing I'll have to check with Doc Cremble.

A rap on the car window made her jump.

"Ouch!" she exclaimed as she hit her head on the ceiling. She opened the door and stepped out, rubbing her head.

"You okay?" Sam asked, concerned.

"I'm fine. Just a small bump."

"I could rub it better. I'm an EMT, remember." He lightly massaged her head with his fingertips. "You sat there so long I thought you were glued to the car seat."

"No, just making last-minute adjustments."

"You look well-adjusted to me." Sam moved his eyebrows up and down in a Groucho Marx imitation.

Laine laughed and immediately calmed down a couple of notches.

Sam took her arm and guided her down the dock and into the houseboat. The sliders opened to a small deck facing the inlet.

They sat beside each other on blue deck chairs and watched the red sun do its slow sinking act beyond the horizon in comfortable silence. He put his arm around her. Then he put his hand on the top of her head and massaged her scalp in slow circles.

"I wish my hair was long again so I could really feel your fingers running through it."

"How long was it? When did you cut it?"

"It was almost down to my waist. I chopped it off before I moved here."

"There's got to be a story connected with that. Wanna share?"

She did. "I always wore my hair long. I think I was born with long hair. I got sick of it in ninth grade, but I couldn't cut it. People always complimented my hair. I was afraid that if I chopped it off, maybe they wouldn't like me as much. But at least once a week I dreamed about cutting my hair. Short hair became a symbol of freedom and independence. My hair was heavy, and gave me headaches.

"About a week before I arrived in Seaglass Bay, I ambled, without a destination, around Boston. I came to a hair salon with a sign saying 'Walk-ins welcome.' Right away, I knew what I had to do. I thought about how long it would take to grow back, how unprotected I'd feel without it. I was numb all over, but I managed to tell the hairdresser to cut my hair. While she snipped, I sat there with my eyes shut. I didn't even look in the mirror. My instincts told me to trust her, and when she finished, I opened my eyes and stared into the mirror. My hair was exactly the style I'd picked from a magazine but never shown anyone. Cropped in the front, with longer wisps in the back—like it is now. I loved it right away. I laughed and I cried, and she laughed and cried with me. I took my leftover tresses and donated item to Locks of Love, where they make wigs for cancer patients. Then I came here and started a new life. End of story."

Sam whistled. "Sounds like only the beginning." He ruffled her curls with his hand. "I like your hair short. I wish I could have seen it long, though."

"I have some old pictures at home. I'll show you sometime."

"You're shivering." Sam wrapped a satin comforter around them. They sat and watched the pink sky fade into gray. Dusk brought a chill even the comforter couldn't banish.

"Let's go inside." He took her hand and led her into the houseboat.

The stove made the cabin as warm as toast, but she still shivered.

Sam lit three tall, cinnamon-scented candles. The spicy smell added an exotic quality to the growing dusk. He put the kettle on for tea, and then slid in next to her on the couch. After a moment of silence, they looked at each other and burst out laughing.

"Are you thinking what I'm thinking?"

Laine nodded.

"We're sitting on the infamous couch where you cut off my jeans."

Only this time was far more exciting. Their bodies were inches apart, yet she sensed his flesh as though it pressed into her. He smelled strongly of pine forest, woodstove, and salt spray. She leaned towards him, and Sam pulled her closer.

"Are you wearing your joke panties?"

"None of your beeswax." His hand grazed her breast. The lazy sensuality implied luxury.

"I could make it my business." He ran his fingers through the layers of her hair. "So silky," he murmured into her ear. "Give me your hairbrush."

"Huh?" She reached into her purse and handed him her brush.

He brushed her short tresses, then put the brush down and massaged her neck and shoulders with gentle strokes.

Laine sighed. How often had she sat in a negligee and wished for a man tender enough to want to brush her long tresses? Now here she sat with short hair and a man who did just that.

"You don't seem like a hair brushing kind of guy. More like a 'pull a woman by the hair and drag her to the cave' guy."

"I'm multifaceted. I'll show you the cave later."

Aunt Rose always said, never look a gift horse in the mouth. Why was that, anyway? Oh yes, because then you could tell how old the horse was by the condition of its teeth. And if it was old, you might not want it.

I want this all right.

"Ummm." Heightened awareness filled her with a lazy sensuality.

When the teakettle whistled, Sam made no move to get up.

"I'll get it." Laine stood to turn off the burner.

Sam pulled her back onto the couch and kissed her lips with a surprising tenderness. She responded to his kisses while the kettle screamed unheeded. When the whistling hit the annoying stage, she pulled away and shut off the stove.

"You want tea?"

Sam came up behind her and reached around her waist;

his strong arms clasped her. "I want you." His voice sounded husky.

"Why?" She had to know.

"I want you because of the way you sing, the way you talk about your father. I want you because of the sexy moaning sounds you make when you eat. And call me shallow, but in case you haven't noticed, you're gorgeous."

Laine's jaw dropped.

Gorgeous? He thinks I'm gorgeous? Holy crap!

"Your eyes blaze with spirit." He paused to look at her.

He undressed her with his eyes. They penetrated her skin and bones, to her very marrow.

"Believe me; I've tried not to care for you. Something happened to me once, and I vowed I would never get close to a woman again."

"It must have been something awful." She tried to sound concerned, and not overly curious. But the need to know gnawed at her gut.

"Forget it; it's old stuff." His jaw tightened. He shook his head as if to fling off the memories.

"What about your old stuff? You haven't exactly been swooning over me."

She sighed. *If you only knew. We can't both be the strong, silent type. One of us has to be the strong, talkative type. That's right; it takes strength to speak your mind and your heart.* Wondering if she could pull it off without spilling, she deftly poured hot water into two earthenware mugs.

"What kind of tea do you have?" She didn't expect much of a selection.

"Check the cupboard above your head."

She did, and found a tea lover's treasure trove.

He's constantly surprising me.

She opted for ginger lemon, and Sam chose green tea.

Carrying the cups to the couch, she tried to banish the feeling of playing house.

"Okay, tell me why you aren't begging me to make love to you." He smiled with dimples on high beam but his tone sounded steady and serious.

So she told him more about Toby, how he had wined, dined, and cheated on her.

"I was gullible enough to fall for a real jerk," she admitted. "I didn't heed any of the signs. My instincts are good, except with men. My early warning system is broken."

With a gentleness that belied his strength, Sam took her face in his hands. "Is that how you feel around me, like you should be warned?"

His warm, sweet breath caressed her face.

"Listen," Sam took his hands from her face so he could use them to gesture. "I don't want to be that guy. I can't promise you much right now, but I will try so damned hard not to hurt you."

Her face stayed warm from his hands. His eyes probed deep into her eyes and the passion again flared between them.

"And whenever you want to stop, you say so."

Laine trusted him, or at least she wanted to. "Maybe we should have a safe word in case I want you to stop," she half teased.

"You mean like Milwaukee?"

"Or zucchini. I think I like that better."

"Okay, zucchini it is. Now where were we?"

He pressed his lips against hers again, this time with more passion, and his surprisingly gentle hands drove her wild.

Laine pulled back and stared at his shirt, unbuttoned to reveal a curly tangle of chest hair. The desire to undress him, to let him carry her to bed, and then carry her to wherever their passion led them, filled her to the brim. Her heart vibrated with a thrill of fear. She couldn't do it yet. Maybe he'd end up the one, but she had to know him better. Sam wouldn't become another mistake. Once more she kissed him, trying to express her desire with her lips.

"Zucchini," she said as she pushed away and stood up with an effort. She smoothed back her hair and glanced at the clock.

"It's getting late. We both have work in the morning."

The silence in the room became almost palpable as Sam searched her eyes with his. She wanted to hide from his stare, feeling as if he'd glimpsed all her secret places.

He nodded slowly and stood up. "You're absolutely right," he said, his voice thick as molasses. "Thanks for coming."

Laine had a wild desire to tell him she wanted to come, very much, but choked off a hysterical laugh. This evening might end like a bad play.

Sam took her hand, kissed it, and led her to her car.

AFTER SITTING in her car staring at the night for several long minutes, Laine drove halfway down the dirt road, and then stopped the car.

"Sam, oh Sam," she moaned as she sat in the darkness. *I want you more than I've wanted anything in a long time. Why pretend otherwise?*

Laine turned the car around and drove back.

He stood in the doorway. Even through the shadows, his expression looked hopeful.

She stepped towards him. "I forgot my scarf."

"Oh." His face fell.

His disappointment, fueled by her own desire, lit a fire she could not ignore. "And I forgot you."

He gave a sharp intake of breath.

She took his hand and led him into the bedroom. There the wild-hearted musician's daughter took over. She often tried to hide this side of her personality, but Sam brought it out in her.

"Laine, are you sure?"

"I'm not sure of anything. Shh." She put a finger to his lips. Fire consumed her now, her body an ache of longing.

Sam stared at her in surprise and wonder, and then pulled off her clothes with a fierce pent-up passion. When he got to her panties, he moaned. She didn't need any writing on these thongs. The sheer black lace said it all. He pulled her panties off.

"Are you sure?" Sam whipped off his clothes without waiting for an answer.

Laine didn't know. She only knew it had to happen; it would happen, tonight. She nodded and smiled.

Sam lost all hesitation as he lifted her into his strong arms and placed her on the bed. He climbed on top of her, but she playfully rolled him over, and ended up on top. They stared at each other, drunken with desire as she lowered herself onto his perfect body. Making herself sink slowly, she shivered with delight at the first feel of him inside her. When she lay completely on top of him, he filled her every pore.

They became a tangle of movement. He rolled over on top; then suddenly they moved together as one. She stared into his hypnotic brown eyes and then they both gasped for breath and clutched each other, and her last thought before she gave herself up completely was, *This is it. I can't turn back.*

LAINE WOKE a couple of hours later with her head resting on his chest.

He smiled down at her, ruffling her tangle of curls.

"You're still awake," she murmured. "I thought it was the guy who passed out."

"I must be getting in touch with my feminine side. I wanted to watch you sleep."

"Did I snore or drool?"

"I did notice some drooling action."

She traced her fingers over his lips. "Will you still respect me in the morning?" Laine fluttered her lashes.

"Respect you? You have my deepest admiration for all time. You are some woman!"

"Once I came back, I never said zucchini."

"I know."

"It's now my favorite vegetable."

"Mine too."

An hour later, Laine drove home, floating in a haze of sweet satisfaction.

Once home, she plopped into bed and fell asleep still smelling Sam's woodsy scent.

Eighteen.

Thursday

~~~~~~

LAINE WOKE UP surprisingly refreshed after only four hours of sleep. She hummed while toasting a bagel to eat with her fruit. The bright sunlight kept her buoyed all the way to self-defense class.

AT HER SELF-DEFENSE CLASS, learning how to poke eyes and the correct way to knee groins turned out to be hard work. A good thing guys had groins, so you could really hurt them if need be.

"I could use a cup of coffee and a pumpkin scone right about now," she told Sofie as they hobbled to their cars.

FIFTEEN MINUTES LATER, they sat at the Seaglass Café, soaking up the seaside charm and wolfing down junie-cakes, the café's version of johnnycakes.

"How are these different from johnnycakes?" Laine couldn't help talking, even with her mouth full.

"Johnnycakes are made with cornmeal and water," Sofie said. "Juniecakes are made with cornmeal, apple cider, and dried cranberries."

"Yum."

"Your bruises are almost gone."

"Thanks for the arnica oil and the epsom salts. They really helped. You're the unofficial Seaglass Bay natural healer."

"Don't forget assistant sleuth. I'm sure I'm going to use

those self-defense techniques a lot." Sofie sipped a mocha latte.

"Do I detect a note of sarcasm? I rather enjoyed myself."

"You look entirely too happy. It must be more than aggressive fighting techniques. The dreamy look in your eyes wouldn't have anything to do with Sam Holliston, would it?"

"You're psychic. Laine laughed, a strange squeaky sound. "I must admit, we did have one night of intense passion, unlike any I've ever experienced. Other than that, we're just friends."

They both laughed.

"No wonder you're so hungry, you hussy. I found out some info, by the way. Muddy's sister, Clare, works for Emson. I asked Muddy to ask Clare, and as you suspected, Pearson bought one of the largest house lots."

"Excellent. I'm glad we have that confirmed."

"Cost him like five million dollars. Chump change for that guy. A writer for that show starring a moose used to live here. Oh, and a famous boxer lives on Main Street. Manny the Mangler, I think his name is. Nothing like this, though. He'll be our first major celebrity."

Laine made a face. She liked it when people said, "You live where?"

"I almost forgot. According to Clare, Emson had wet dreams about selling to a celebrity, and this sale fell into his lap. Clare said she thought he'd be whooping with joy, but instead he's been on edge. She can't figure it out."

"That's interesting. Did Clare say how Emson got so lucky?"

"As a matter of fact, she did. Pearson and his fiancée took a drive to Newport. He detoured off Route 195 for some chow and ended up at the Seaglass Café. Emson just happened to be at the next table stuffing his big moon face."

"I can't imagine Pearson on a road trip. I picture him hopping on his private plane and giving his pilot the coordinates."

"Apparently he had a brand new Jaguar XK to try out. They were on their way to visit Pearson's mother in Newport."

"Maybe they had trouble with the navigational system. And if Pearson is like every other man I've ever met, he probably hates to stop to ask directions."

"No kidding," Sofie said. "But wait, there's more. Last week Clare returned early from lunch and sat reading at her desk. Ten minutes before she's supposed to be back, guess who pops out of Emson's office?"

"Who?"

"Brooke," Sofie said. "She jumps two feet when she sees Clare and then bolts out of the office."

"Cool, calm, collected Brooke is losing her cool."

Sofie leaned closer, "Clare said Emson slammed the door to his office and didn't come out for two hours."

"Pearson doesn't just move into a town, he practically reinvents it!" Laine told Sofie about her internet findings.

"This is his pattern: He discovers a lovely backwater and develops an exclusive gated community. The town becomes prosperous and touristy. He puts these little towns on the map. Nobody ever heard of Catman's Cove in Rhode Island until Pearson got hold of it. Now it's almost as busy as Newport."

"No kidding. He must make enemies taking small towns with character and making them into movie sets."

Laine shrugged. "He gets mixed reviews. Property values go up and businesses flourish. On the other hand, if he invests in Emson Estates, Seaglass Bay will lose some of its charm."

"That's going to cause problems," Sofie said, "especially for people like Muddy and Sam who have lived here forever. They don't like change. It took years for townies to accept a bike path."

"I can't see Pearson or other potential buyers wanting a bike path skirting their property. But if they were going to stop the bike path wouldn't they have done it already?"

"Maybe Brooke is secretly part owner of the estates. She wouldn't want anyone to know she's participating in developing the town."

"That's a good theory. It explains why they're meeting. And why Brooke has expensive photos in her office. But we're missing a vital piece of information. The bike path has been approved, and Pearson owns the land. So what exactly are they up to?"

Sofie leaned forward. "We should find out."

"Hell, yeah. We definitely should."

LATER, when she sat working at her computer, doubts about Sam began to plague her.

What did last night mean? Maybe a one-night stand. Two people getting their rocks off.

A wry smile came to her lips as she stared out at the rocks on the beach.

Give it a rest. You had fun. You liked it. Okay, you loved it.

Nineteen.

Friday

~~~~~~

A T WORK the next day, Brooke's mood seemed even more taciturn than usual. She walked past Laine's desk several times without a word or even a glance.

Laine decided to tackle the problem head-on. "Brooke, can I talk to you?"

Brooke spoke without turning around. "Come into my office."

Laine straightened her shoulders and followed Brooke to her desk. Brooke sat and gestured to a chair, but Laine remained standing.

"Brooke, are you unhappy with my work?" Laine blasted right to the point.

Brooke's face registered surprise. "No, your work is fine. Whatever gave you that idea?"

Hmmm, let me think. Only about a million reasons. "I haven't gotten much positive feedback on my proposals and projects." *Or any feedback, for that matter.*

"I see. Well, I've been extremely busy lately on some special projects. The BNC is experiencing budget problems; jobs might need to be cut. But your work is fine. And if you focus completely on your specific jobs, you'll get a substantial raise. I'm glad you asked, and glad I could clear that up."

Yeah, clear as mud. That budget cut stuff sounds like nonsense.

You have to cut jobs, but if I stick to my job I'll get a raise? There are only three paid people here. You are certainly not going to fire yourself. I guess you suspect me of putting my nose where it doesn't belong. That is not going to stop. This all sounds like a huge load of bull shit.

As Laine returned to the shelter of her own desk, Fiona's voice broke into her inner rant.

"That's exactly what I told the *Gazette*."

Laine peered around her partition; Fiona had her ear glued to the phone.

"Yes, our plans are on permanent hold," Fiona continued. "That's all I can tell you. Have a nice day." Fiona plunked the phone down with an exasperated sigh. "Damn thing's been ringing off the hook."

"Anything wrong?"

"Everything is wrong. Didn't Brooke tell you?" Fiona snapped. "I saw you come out of her office."

"Tell me what?" Laine waited while Fiona perfected her annoyed sigh.

"The bike path plans are cancelled."

"Huh?" Laine did a double take as she tried to process Fiona's words. "Brooke didn't tell me. No bike path? You're kidding."

"Do I look like I'm kidding?" Fiona leveled Laine with her steely gaze.

Nope, no joking there. She looked as if she could devour a baby gorilla.

"Why? It can't be finances. The BNC got a state grant."

"I'm ready for a break." Fiona yawned. She fished a chocolate bar out of an enormous handbag. "If I don't eat something every couple of hours, my blood sugar dips too low."

I'll bet you don't even have blood. Laine's mind raced. Brooke cancelled the bike path at the last minute. How could she justify her actions? Why didn't Brooke say something to her?

Fiona sighed again, apparently exhausted by the stress of her phone conversation, or by low blood sugar.

"Be a dear and get me some coffee, kiddo. I don't want to get up."

"If I do, will you tell me what's going on?" *This ought to be good.*

"I might."

If I don't want her to tell me something she'll do it anyway. Now I'm begging for info, she'll think about it. I'll bet if I put rat poison in her coffee, the jury would side with me.

AT THE COFFEE MACHINE, she poured coffee into Fiona's "Born to be a Bitch" mug, sans rat poison, and carried it to Fiona's desk. She had to admire this woman, for standing right up with the bitch thing. Maybe a dear sweet person existed somewhere on the inside.

Maybe pigs could fly.

"Okay." Laine put the coffee down. "Now please tell me."

"If I must. Tim checked the ponds on the bike path."

"I thought he did that already."

Fiona shrugged. "Well, I guess he did a recheck of the check."

"And?"

"He found a connected pond loaded with pond trout. I guess they're on the endangered list. Brooke had no choice but to withdraw our proposal."

Aha. Another piece of the puzzle slid together.

"I don't understand," she said, even though she had a pretty good idea. "Couldn't they make last-minute adjustments? The committee worked so hard."

At that moment, Brooke poked her head out of the office. "Fiona, as soon as you're done socializing, please print those letters." The door slammed with a deafening thump.

"Brooke sounds pretty stressed."

"She is. She's on her fifth cup of Dragon's Brew and she's breathing fire. The bike path committee is pitching fits about withdrawing the plans."

"I can imagine."

"Brooke's tough as nails. She can handle it."

I'll bet. Brooke probably has a metal heart. You'd break your teeth on it if you took a bite. Plus enough green caffeine in her system to jumpstart a tank. Interesting how Fiona sticks up for Brooke, yet drags everyone else through the mud. Wonder why.

Laine drummed her fingers on her desk. What in hell was going on around here?

A FEW HOURS LATER, still trying to make sense of all she had learned, Laine drove home. In her living room, as she lit a fire and prepared a chef's salad, she wondered about Tim and the bike path. To distract herself, she grabbed the latest tough woman mystery and tried to read while she ate, but her mind kept whirling.

Why hadn't Tim found the pond trout sooner? It's not like they called them hidden pond trout. Was Tim in on it? Was he the wild card?

And then, of course, the inscrutable Brooke, a woman who did whatever she wanted. No one would question the highly respected Brooke. The regal, well-pressed air of hers told the world she was irreproachable. Looks sure were deceiving.

Laine threw her book down in disgust. She couldn't concentrate, even though tough woman detective seemed about to seduce sensitive cop. She could call Sam and ask him to come over to talk. But she knew how it would turn out. Besides, he had a phone. His dialing finger looked in good shape. He could call Laine anytime.

Laine called Sofie to fill her in on the day's news.

"No kidding, that totally sucks," Sofie said when Laine finished her tale. "I'm angry the town can't even get it together for a bike path. Pretty sad when they pass up all that state money."

"Not them. Brooke and Emson."

"This does fit right into our suspicions."

"I think so too. Let's talk tomorrow and come up with a plan."

Twenty.

Saturday

~~~~~~

I N THE MORNING, Laine woke to a slate gray day. Some cloud covers looked cozy, but this one veered more toward oppressive. In Boston, her senses had been deadened to the elements. Often, she didn't track the weather, not caring what happened outside. Rain, snow, or even golf ball-sized hail didn't interest her. Now, she rated cloudy days on a scale of light to doomsday.

To counteract the clouds, she would make herself a comfort breakfast of scrambled eggs, home fries, English muffin, and ginger tea. Experimenting with her home fries recipe, she came up with a doozy: dice a quarter of a red onion, a clove of garlic, and half a red pepper; sauté in olive oil; add three diced red potatoes; season with kosher salt, pepper, and marjoram. At the last minute, she added a generous sprinkling of golden turmeric, an inspiration of exceptional import.

Pleased with her creation, she wolfed down the entire pan of fries. Maybe next time she'd add a touch of horse-radish. Excitement welled up inside her. Aunt Rose wouldn't believe how far she'd improved in the cooking department.

Laine's morning activities included watering her asparagus ferns, washing the floors, mending her old jeans, and returning emails and phone calls. By the time she finished, the time for a pre-beach grilled cheese sandwich and a cup of tea had come.

Before her walk, she opened Aunt Rose's box of sayings. Today's saying: "Bite off more than you can chew, then chew it well."

She'd remember it next time she bit into a slice of chocolate cheesecake.

ON HER WALK, Laine moseyed along the path, retrieving trash. Further along the shoreline, a large rock stood out from the rest.

How odd. I could swear that stone wasn't there yesterday.

Upon closer inspection, it turned out to be a beached harbor seal instead of a boulder. Her heart racing, she approached with caution. Seals usually managed to swim back to deeper waters in a few hours. Even so, she should check to make sure the creature still breathed. Good thing passersby would be scarce this late in the season. Still, she needed to stand guard, or sit guard. Laine settled on a rock, staring alternately at the seal and out to sea.

A year ago, if a crystal ball showed me babysitting a seal, I wouldn't have believed it.

"Hey there." Sam's voice startled her from her reverie. She looked up and watched him amble over. Long legs encased in jeans just tight enough to remind her that she knew what his tighty-whiteys looked like. He handed her a sweatshirt and a mug of coffee.

"I thought you might need this."

She stood and pulled the sweatshirt over her head. "How come you're always here when I have emergencies?"

"That's what we EMTs do. I caught sight of the seal with my binoculars."

"Snooping," she teased.

"It's not snooping, it's a hobby. You looked good but you looked cold. I could practically see your nipples from the houseboat."

"Oh puhleeze." Laine couldn't help laughing. What a goof. She took a sip of hot coffee. "I hope it's decaf."

"It is. What would happen if it was caffeinated?"

"I would sprout dark hairs on my chest and howl at the moon." Her quip caused Sam to bark with laughter.

"I'd like to see that."

"Be quiet. The seal will think you're trying to mate."

"The seal would be right on. What are you doing later?"

"In your dreams," she teased. *And mine.*

Sam sat next to her on the rock. Even in the raw breeze, heat emanated from his body. Sexy and comforting at the same time. She wanted to run from Sam, and at the same time devour him whole.

Like I did the other night.

Sam broke the silence. "About us," he began.

Here it comes. He's going to tell me it was heat of the moment, gonads gone crazy.

"It was fantastic, that's what I wanted to tell you."

Laine's heart opened to a startled surge of happiness.

I love it when I'm wrong. Thank you, fairy godmother.

"It wasn't bad," she said. "It's the best I've had in a year."

"The only you've had in a year. Or so I've heard."

She grinned as she took her last sip of now lukewarm coffee.

"I meant to call," Sam said. "I was really busy. Oh hell, the dog ate my homework."

"What are you talking about?"

Sam gave her a rueful smile. "As a kid, whenever I started making excuses for myself, my mother would ask me if the dog ate my homework."

Laine looked at him with expectation.

"I missed you. I worried that you didn't want to…" He chose that moment to take her face in his hands and kiss her.

The harbor seal chose that same moment to drag its body to the ocean and dive into the water.

Laine pulled away at the sound of the splash.

"The seal is officially un-beached," Sam said. "Maybe our kiss reminded him he had a love seal somewhere.

Hopefully it's a tight seal."

"Double groan." Laine scrunched up her face. "Why do I put up with you? I'm glad the seal is now un-beached. My fingers were starting to go numb."

"You should've said something. I could have warmed them using EMT techniques."

"I'll bet. What were you going to say before you kissed me?"

"Nothing really. No biggie."

Argggh. She had to fall for a coy boy. *Doesn't he know openness is sexy? Guess he forgot to read that relationship skills book.* She glanced at her watch. "I've got to run. Sofie is coming for dinner tonight and I haven't even shopped yet."

"I haven't seen Sofie in a while."

"Uh-huh."

"Well, I guess I'll go home and eat a bowl of cold, stale cereal all by myself."

I will not invite him to dinner. I will not invite him to dinner. Nothing wrong with playing a little hard to get. Because we had sex once doesn't mean we're a couple. I will not invite him to dinner.

"Okay, be there at six," she said with a flip of her wrist. So much for positive affirmations.

"How about I pick you up in about fifteen minutes and take you shopping?"

"Sure." Her play-hard-to-get genes came from a gnat.

Back at the cottage, she called Sofie to tell her the change of plans. "Sam's coming and I thought I'd invite Stanton Coles. Make a real party."

"Stanton Coles? I've heard of him, but don't know him personally."

"He's a single, handsome, older man. What could be bad?"

"You've got my attention."

When she called Stanton, he readily accepted. Now all she had to do was buy food and cook.

Later, when she and Sam arrived at the grocery store, Sam pushed the cart down the aisles as they picked out delicacies for dinner. Laine could think of nothing more sensual than food shopping with Sam—well, almost nothing. As they stood close together to choose a fresh baked baguette, Laine wondered why couples didn't have wild sex right there in the bread aisle.

Laine chose goat cheese, avocados, artichoke hearts, and baby lettuce. The supermarket had such a large gourmet section; dinner would be a success for sure. As soon as she found out the market sold homemade pizza dough, she scratched her earlier omelet idea. Dinner would consist of calzones with turkey breast, mozzarella cheese, and garlic pesto.

"Parsley?" Sam offered her a bouquet of curled, rough-edge leaves.

"Yes, perfect." As she took the parsley, tingly warmth suffused her. Afternoon delight hadn't been invented for nothing. Body temperatures reached their highest between 5:00 and 7:00 p.m., and hers had definitely reached its peak. She hurried to the checkout counter. If she seduced Sam in frozen foods, they'd ban her from the store forever.

On the way home, she took a deep, steadying breath. If going to the grocery store with Sam had invoked such strong desires, she could imagine how the hardware store would affect her, with those power tools and all.

As they unloaded and unpacked the groceries, Laine marveled at how they worked like a real team. They moved like Fred and Ginger as they emptied bags and opened fridge and cabinets.

After unloading, Laine poured them each a Beachglass Beer, and put Sam to work chopping and dicing. Stanton arrived at the tail end of preparations with a pan full of brownies.

"They smell heavenly," Laine told him. "Maybe I should try one as an appetizer." She bit into the chewy chocolate and groaned. Usually more of a *Thelma and Louise* kind of gal, a chocolate bar in the fridge could last a few days if she played it right with tiny bites. But these brownies tasted too good. She ate the whole thing in two bites. She moaned again and reached for another.

"Don't mind her," Sam said. "She makes weird noises when she eats."

Stanton laughed. "My secret ingredient is raspberry liquor."

Laine put the calzones in the oven, and opened the door when she heard a knock.

Sofie stepped in and handed Laine a bouquet of yellow chrysanthemums. She shrugged out of her black wool coat to reveal a slinky black dress and black boots.

"You look great!" Laine exclaimed.

"Thanks."

Laine introduced Sofie to Stanton and by the way he looked at Sofie, Laine could tell he also thought she looked great. Laine trotted off to find a vase and check on dinner. Spicy Italian deli smells oozed from the oven.

"Dinner's almost ready. Sit wherever you want."

She felt warm arms around her waist and turned her head as Sam kissed her cheek.

"I was hoping it was you."

"I poured our guests each a Beachglass beer and I'm here to help serve."

"If you don't stop rubbing up against me, dinner will have to be postponed indefinitely."

"Tempting." Sam gave her one last squeeze. "Those calzones smell too good."

SEVERAL TIMES during dinner, Laine noticed Stanton staring at Sofie. The talk stayed comfortable, made even smoother by the local brewery beer. Sam told everyone about their adventure with the harbor seal. Sofie talked with her hands as she described her soft sculptures to Stanton. Laine alternately served food and ate like a pig.

"A penny for your thoughts," Sam whispered to Laine.

"I was thinking how much Seaglass Bay's starting to feel like home." *And how much I want to take you to bed again. And about the BNC, which I won't mention, because you'll think I'm obsessed. Or crazy.*

"Did you hear about the bike path?" Stanton asked. "Brooke abandoned the project at the eleventh hour. I couldn't talk her out of it. Apparently we can apply for the grant next year." He winced. "All those boring meetings I suffered through for naught."

"It's strange they didn't find the pond trout sooner," Laine said.

"They were pretty hidden. Tim had to portage the canoe through marsh and waterways."

"What's portage?" Sofie asked. "It sounds like a hot breakfast cereal."

"It means he had to drag or carry the canoe from one waterway to the next," Stanton said.

"Tim sure went to a lot of trouble to find those fish," Laine said.

Sam held up his hands. "I'm sure there's a reasonable explanation. Maybe he's a big fan of rare pond trout. You guys watch too many crimes series."

LATER, after they fought over the last crumb of Stanton's killer brownies, Sofie said her goodbyes. Stanton collected his jacket and hat.

"You don't have to go. Stay for another cup of coffee."

"No thanks," Stanton said. "I had a great time, but I need to get up early tomorrow morning."

"I'm off to work," Sofie said. "The muse strikes again."

After they left, Sam said, "Wonder why they were in such a hurry to get out of here?"

"Come see." Laine stared out the picture window. The outside light illuminated Sofie and Stanton chatting next to Sofie's car. "Maybe she's going to get lucky."

"Would you like to get lucky tonight, Laine?" Sam's serious look made Laine hoot with laughter.

"That did not make me feel wanted." He wrapped his arms around her.

"I have to do dishes." She shoved a dishtowel into his hand. "You can dry."

As they washed the dishes, Sam brushed gently against her every chance he could. Who would imagine dish drying could be an erotic experience?

"You need to cool off." Laine flicked soapy water at him. "Here's a sponge, you can take care of the counters."

"Counters be damned." Sam swept her into his arms and carried her to her purple bedroom.

Easing her down onto the bed, he murmured, "Should we have some discourse to get emotionally connected? I try to be a sensitive guy."

"Maybe we should have intercourse to get connected. I try to be a sensitive gal."

Oy, I can't believe I said that.

Sam kissed her forehead, her eyes and her lips.

Her words had Sam all hot and bothered if his body pressed against hers was any indication. She sighed.

"I was beginning to think you preferred chocolate over me," Sam said.

"Hmmm, chocolate is rich, sweet and good for you. Plus, it doesn't talk back. Tough call." She pulled him closer. "Is there some kind of gravitational pull this close to the water? I seem to fall into your arms an awful lot, lately."

"I could tell more if you took off your clothes. Clothes inhibit the gravitational pull test."

"Really? I hate to impede an experiment. I will if you will."

Sam turned to undo his belt buckle. "Race you."

But Laine was already completely naked. "Slowpoke."

"Some women like it slow." He took her in his arms.

"Not me." She wriggled around beneath him. Every time he tried to hit home, she dodged to the right or left. Laine grew increasingly aroused as they wrestled. Finally, she could take it no longer.

"Poor baby. Having trouble getting it in?" Even as she spoke, he slid inside her, hard and wonderful.

After they'd climaxed, Laine sighed with contentment, and then burst out laughing. She told Sam about her morning saying.

"I'm supposed to bite off more than I can chew, then chew it."

Sam made a protective cup with his hands as Laine tried to grab him. "Leave the little guy alone. You can't take those sayings literally."

When she and Sam played together, she tapped into an inner Laine. A Laine more open and free than she'd been in years, maybe ever. Her previous meager experiences with romance had been earnest and serious. This new way of loving—playful, down-to-earth— fit her style much better.

SOON AFTER Sam's truck rumbled out of the driveway, Sofie texted to thank her for dinner and report that she had made a dinner date with Stanton.

Laine texted back:

Great news. He meets all your qualifications. A shopping trip to celebrate tomorrow at The Diamond Mill Outlet?

Sofie texted back:

Two thumbs up. I'll buy something sexy to wow him. LOL.

Laine texted back: *All your clothes are sexy already.*

Laine had a grin on her face as she hopped into bed. She thought about the recent turn of events. Boston *had* trillions of single guys. But she hadn't met anyone, except disastrous Toby. It had been a long, dry, without-guy spell. Now, out in the boonies where people warned her she'd be dating livestock, to her surprise, single guys ran rampant.

Twenty-One.

Sunday

~~~~~~~~~~~~~~~~~~~~~~

THE NEXT MORNING Laine drove to Sofie's and sat in a rocking chair in her cozy kitchen. Sofie handed her a mug of hot cocoa topped with tiny colored marshmallows.

"You really do have quite a maternal side," Laine told her. "You're like a wild domestic goddess. You can play pool and poker with the boys and then whip up a batch of chocolate chip cookies."

"I even make beach plum jelly. But don't spread my secret around. It'll ruin my reputation as a woman of action."

"You remind me of my mother, with your creative food touches. She used to make Suzies for lunch. They were little girls with tuna bodies, toast arms, and carrot stick legs." Laine smiled at the memory of her mother trying to find ways to make her eat lunch. Now Laine spent many waking moments in eager anticipation of her next meal. *Go figure.*

"Sam doesn't believe us about the bike path. I think when the subject comes up, he mentally covers his ears and sings to block out the noise."

"He doesn't want to get involved with anything having to do with Fiona. There's bad blood between them. That's my take on it, anyway."

"What happened between them?"

Sofie looked at the clock. "Look at the time. We better leave now if we want to catch the bargains."

I wonder why she doesn't want to tell me. It can't be that bad. Besides, I'll find out one way or another.

After they climbed into the old pickup truck, Laine asked if she could drive. "It looks like fun."

Sofie nodded and handed her the keys.

"I am woman. Hear me roar," Laine said.

A short time later, she pulled the truck into the mill outlet parking lot, parked, switched off the engine, and handed Sofie the keys. "Thanks for letting me drive." A shit-eating grin plastered on her face. "I might want to be a truck driver when I grow up."

THE DIAMOND MILL, a three-story brick mill building, had been used to make thread. It now housed a series of ten outlet shops. The largest one sold discount doors, windows, and even furniture.

In the back corner, Laine found a stack of used stained glass windows. The salesclerk explained they had come from an estate in Fall River.

"My grandmother had a stained glass bathroom window," Laine told Sofie. "I used to stay in the bathroom for the longest time. My parents thought I suffered from constipation, but I was just watching the world through the colored glass. I have to buy one of these."

Laine finally settled on a green and blue peacock design in a rectangular frame.

"This window was over the door of the carriage house," the clerk told her. "The glass is at least a hundred and fifty years old."

"C'mon," Sofie urged, after they put Laine's treasure in the truck. "We've got a lot more shopping to do."

THE BOOKSTORE enthralled Laine, especially the selection of discounted art books. Maybe she should get back to painting. She kept most of her nature scenes in a portfolio under the bed, except for the ones on the bedroom wall.

After perusing the selection, she bought a book on watercolor techniques and a tough woman mystery, both for a mere pittance. She told Sofie she felt guilty, as if she'd stolen the books.

"No kidding. Maybe we should go home."

"I don't feel that guilty. Besides, I'm just getting warmed up."

AT THE CLOTHING OUTLET, they grabbed handfuls of off-rack designer clothes and retreated to the dressing rooms.

"The prices here are cheaper than a yard sale." Laine brought piles of clothes to the register. "This store is one big clearance rack."

"Clearance Rack is my first cousin." Sofie's picks included sexy leopard prints, fringe, fur, and leather. "The usual country girl garb."

Liane held up her favorite pick: a black dress and black clingy skirt made from an unidentifiable new fabric.

"I better not get close to an open flame in this skirt. I might spontaneously combust."

"Wow. Sam will combust when he sees you in it."

THEY STOPPED for lunch at a small Lebanese restaurant where they munched on spinach pie and pita chips.

"Are you feeling okay?" Sofie asked.

"Definitely okay. Why do you ask?"

"We're almost to the baklava and you haven't mentioned the BNC."

Laine smiled. Sofie's positive energy had acted like a soothing balm. She had actually forgotten about the bike path for a couple of hours.

"Thanks for reminding me. I wish we had more proof Brooke sabotaged the bike path grant."

"What do you mean more proof? We don't have any, in case you haven't noticed."

"Don't remind me while I'm eating."

"We could always hack into Brooke's computer. My sister Lucy is a computer genius. I'm sure she'd help us."

Laine considered Sofie's offer. It sounded illegal and dangerous.

"I like the idea. Let's do it."

On their way home Laine remained quiet, mulling over her conversation with Sofie. They needed to break into Brooke's computer. After all, the good of Seaglass Bay depended on them. And aboveboard methods had produced no results. A tiny bit of crime wouldn't cause that much trouble, anyway. Time to broaden her horizons. And maybe while in prison, she'd receive the community service award.

Laine spent that evening working at her computer. At school in Boston, she could stay up all night writing. Here, the ocean sounds and smells permeated the cottage and lulled her into la-la land. Tonight, the onset of sniffles and a scratchy throat made staying awake even harder than usual. When the computer screen turned to a blur, she decided it was time for bed. She took a dose of cold medicine and soon fell asleep.

In her dream, there was a drumming circle gathering in her living room. She could hear the bongo drums, could smell the jasmine incense. Someone shook a tambourine. The snare drum sounded like footsteps.

An alarm sounded in her head and woke her from her noisy dream. Had she heard footsteps? She strained to listen. She'd heard footsteps all right.

Stay calm. Don't panic. She sat up and surveyed the room for a weapon. Moonlight glinted on her dad's vintage guitar. No, she couldn't use the treasured heirloom as a bat. But when the footsteps moved closer to her bedroom door, she realized if one of them was going to get smashed to bits, she'd rather it be the guitar. Dad would rather she saved herself than save his guitar. She eased out of bed.

Stay calm. Breathe deep.

The cool floor brought life to her feet. Tiptoeing to the guitar, her heart pounding like a steel drum, she lifted the guitar and held it over her shoulder like a baseball bat. Weapon in hand, heart in throat, she tiptoed towards the kitchen; the noise had come from that direction.

Swell, the intruder stopped to make a sandwich before he killed her. Why did she think it was a man? She hated to be prejudiced at a time like this. It could just as easily be a woman.

She could call 911. But no, she'd put her cell phone next to the fridge to recharge, right beside the regular phone.

Note to self: Keep the phone in the bedroom tomorrow night and every night. It's not like the fridge would ever call 911.

The shadow of the intruder stood near the sink, facing the window.

Damn. I wish I knew what part of the head I could hit to maim him. I really don't want to kill anybody.

Laine tiptoed closer, then, mustering her courage, rushed forward. Wielding the guitar high, she brought it down hard. At that moment, the figure spun around and grabbed the guitar, but not before the wood thunked into a head. The figure yelped as Laine's fingers found the light switch.

"Oh my God, it's you!" she cried as she recognized her intruder. "What the hell are you doing here?"

"Ouch. Getting a throbbing headache for starters," Sam moaned, gingerly touching his head.

"I could have ruined my dad's guitar. I almost had a heart attack."

"You could have killed me."

"I'm sorry, I really am, but you shouldn't sneak up on people like that."

"If I recall, you snuck up on me."

"Never mind that now. Let's get you to the couch. It's my turn to get you some ice." She opened the freezer and found a pint of Ben & Jerry's.

"How is your head?"

Sam rubbed his noggin. "Sore. How's the guitar?"

Laine gave it a quick check under the light. "Pretty good. Not even any blood on it."

"Luckily I've got a pretty hard head. Holy crap, hit over the head with Saul Roth's classical guitar. It's almost an honor."

"Sounds like you might have brain damage. This ice cream should do the trick." She held the container against his head. "By the way, do you mind my asking what you're doing here, in the middle of the night?"

"It's only ten o'clock. You didn't show up at Serena's like you said you would. I stopped to make sure you were okay. I knocked and knocked, and finally I climbed through a window. I was looking for the light switch when you attacked me. Sorry about that. Guess I got worried."

"Oops. I got the sniffles and forgot all about Serena's. The cold medicine must've knocked me out. Sorry." She pressed the ice cream to his head and held it there. "You better stay the night so I can keep an eye on you and make sure you don't have a concussion. I think I have a pair of jammies you could borrow."

"Jammies my ass." He pushed the ice cream carton away and took her in his arms.

QUITE SOME TIME LATER, she decided Sam definitely did not have a concussion. She lay in bed thinking about him. *I like that he worries about me. That is a plausible reason for being here isn't it? I'm so suspicious.*

"Do you want some ice cream?" Laine asked Sam. "It must be refrozen by now." All she got in answer was a snore.

Oh yeah, men pass out after sex. That's why they're the weaker sex.

Twenty-Two.

Monday

L AINE ARRIVED at the BNC early the next morning, her cold miraculously cured. Creative energy pulsed through her veins. Today, her afterschool program began: "Bird Art" with Stanton Coles. Laine hummed while she tended to last-minute details.

Brooke created the big surprise of the morning: an invitation to lunch. Laine couldn't refuse, much as she'd prefer to spend her lunch hour alone, sketching the cedar and scrub pine trees behind the BNC. To be honest, she'd rather clean a sewer than have lunch with Brooke. But Brooke, the boss, had issued the invitation, so to lunch, *with Brooke*, she went.

At the Corner Kitchen, Brooke led Laine to a small table near a wall.

I'm feeling perverse and I'm going to order something messy and unprofessional.

When the waitress appeared to take their order, Laine requested the barbecue special: ribs, coleslaw, and baked beans. *Good chance I'm dining with a criminal. May as well do it in style.*

"I know you were excited about the bike path," Brooke said. "Next year we'll have an airtight plan to send to the state. In this situation we are victims of unfortunate timing. But we have Tim to thank for saving an endangered species' habitat."

Laine couldn't imagine Brooke ever being the victim of anything.

"Is it possible to send a modified plan to the state? The architects could change the blueprint so the path detours around the pond."

"That's not an option. The state is strict about the due date. Submitting an entirely new plan takes weeks. I did ask of course, but the state refuses to accept new plans, even considering our situation." Brooke paused, her face a mask of sincerity. "I assure you, Laine, I'm as disappointed as you are. I'm not used to things going wrong like this."

That is probably the one true thing you've said since we sat down.

Their orders came and Laine concentrated on eating her delicious, sloppy lunch with gusto. When she finished, she thought she must look like a four-year-old after a catsup fight.

Brooke excused herself to go to the restroom. Laine examined her barbecue sauce stains. *Why do I feel such perverse pleasure in being such a slob? Maybe because Brooke is the most outwardly fastidious person I know. Neat on the outside, but something messy happening on the inside.* Then again, there was a slight chance she could be wrong about Brooke. After all, Brooke's story about the bike path sounded plausible. Maybe her dark imagination working overtime had created the whole situation. Maybe Sam had the right idea and she should add delusional and paranoid to her list of symptoms for Doc Cremble. Maybe, maybe, maybe.

But Laine didn't think so.

Later, on her way back to work, she stopped to buy a *Seaglass Gazette.* The lead article blared—*Hidden pond trout found. Town loses grant; finds endangered species.*

A photo of Tim beside a picture of a pond trout had been positioned next to the article. "Amazing find," the article read.

Yeah, amazing is the word for it.

Laine sat in her car to read the story, then crumpled the paper with clenched fists and hurried into the office.

Tim sat, bent over the keyboard, his streaky hair flopping into his eyes.

"Hi Tim. I saw your picture in the paper. Tough luck about the bike path, isn't it?"

He swiveled around in his chair and his face looked properly somber. "It sucks."

"How did you happen to find the pond trout?"

"I was studying an old report mentioning the fish. Pond trout weren't endangered back when the report was written, so it wasn't a big deal at the time. But I thought I better check for myself, save everyone a lot of trouble after the fact."

"Wasn't it hard to get through the marshes?"

"Not for a resourceful guy like me. I took the BNC canoe. What's the big deal, anyway?" His voice took on a defensive edge.

"I'm sorry. I was so looking forward to the bike path. The whole thing seems odd."

"I don't think finding an endangered species is that weird. I guess I'm cranky because I worked through lunch."

"Oh, I almost forgot." She handed him a paper bag. "I brought this back for you."

Tim opened the bag. "Tuna on rye. How did you know my favorite?"

"I'm psychic. Plus, whenever I've seen you eat lunch, it's always tuna."

"Thanks. I'm starving." He bit into the sandwich. "Tastes great."

"Did you sell your sailboat yet? I have a friend who might be interested." She crossed her fingers behind her back.

Tim swallowed and forced a laugh. "Oh, didn't I tell you? My dad's business made a turnaround. I don't have to sell my boat after all."

"You're kidding. That's great news. How about your jeep?"

"What about my jeep?"

"Don't you have to sell that too?"

"Nope, not anymore. I get to keep my toys."

"Wonderful. How did your father turn around the business?"

"Huh?" Tim looked confused for a second.

"Oh that? I guess things always come back into style if you wait, just like Dad said."

"Congratulations. Say, I'd like to learn more about pond trout," Laine lied. "I don't even know what they look like."

"If you're so interested, ask Brooke. She knows a lot about them. Listen, I've got a bunch of work to do. Thanks again for the sandwich." He made a great show of returning his attention to his laptop.

Okay, I get the message. How very convenient. All of a sudden Tim's father's company pulled out of its slump. She couldn't wait to tell Sofie about this new development. And maybe, she should tell Sam too. Let him in. Try to trust him. If only he didn't have such a stubborn streak.

Right now Laine had other, more urgent concerns. The children's program started in half an hour, and if she didn't go to the bathroom before the kids arrived, she'd never get a chance. How did moms ever find time to pee?

DURING THE PRESENTATION, Stanton showed the children slides and sketches of owls. He told a story for each picture.

Laine helped them create owl designs with ripped tissue paper glued onto cellophane. When the kids held their finished creations up to the windows, Laine thought they looked like stained glass. Observing the happy faces, she knew she'd planned a successful program.

"I want to see your designs hanging in windows when I drive by your houses," she told them.

AFTER THE LAST mom drove off, Laine thanked Stanton. "The kids were smitten with you."

"You're welcome. I enjoy children, even though I don't have any."

They walked to their cars, the only two left in the lot. "I can't believe the bike path is cancelled. It would be so great for the kids. If I were Brooke, I'd..." Laine's voice wandered off.

"What would you do?" Stanton's grey eyes were serious.

"For one thing, I'd do everything to make sure the town got a bike path."

"I believe you. In fact, I personally am going to try to stay on your good side."

"The whole thing stinks."

"You know, sometimes things really are what they seem. The Brooke I know has always been a pillar of the community. The BNC is a dedicated organization. There's never been any question of wrongdoing."

"Okay." Laine felt stung by his gentle criticism.

"But pillars can fall," Stanton relented. "I promise I'll keep an open mind."

As she drove out of the BNC parking lot, something Stanton said nagged at the back of her brain, but she couldn't retrieve it. An overwhelming urge to see Aunt Rose swept over her. She needed the safe, warm trailer where she knew what to expect.

New Hampshire, too far away, made Sofie's house the next best choice.

Laine pulled over and used her cell phone. Sofie picked up right away. Of course Laine could come over. She'd get the wine glasses out.

Laine turned her car around.

On the short drive to Sofie's she suddenly remembered Stanton's words. *The Brooke* I *know.* But Stanton had made a point of telling Laine he didn't know Brooke very well. The Brooke I know—maybe he used a figure of speech. She had also heard him say he tried to talk Brooke out of cancelling the bike path. That suggested more than a hello-goodbye relationship. Why would he lie about it?

At Sofie's, Laine sipped merlot and told her about the children's program, lunch with Brooke and, of course, Tim's suspicious behavior.

"No kidding," Sofie said once Laine finally stopped chattering. "Tim comes out of Brooke's office looking happy, he happens to find an endangered species, and he's suddenly flush again. You'd better take him somewhere and pump him for information. Not literally, of course. And be sure to let him pay since he's got so much cash now. Make sure you show a lot of cleavage."

"Don't laugh. That's exactly what I had in mind."

"I'm kidding."

"I'm not."

"You better keep your hand on your cell phone and call me if anything seems the least bit off. I don't trust that guy. Promise me."

"I will. I'm touched by your concern."

"You're touched all right. Don't forget to call me."

Laine smiled as she planned.

Twenty-Three.

Tuesday

THE NEXT DAY after work, Laine called Sam and left a message on his machine with an impromptu invitation to dinner. Laine settled in to try baking her first meatloaf. Mashed potatoes and carrot slaw would create a real comfort meal. Sam's presence would make the meal a pièce de résistance. *If Sam can't make it, I'll have meatloaf sandwiches for the rest of the year.*

Sam called back a few minutes later proclaiming his utmost desire for meatloaf and her company. Meatloaf would have to be one of his favorite meals. She hoped hers turned out edible, or at least didn't cause any lasting tummy trauma.

Laine breathed in the spicy aromas from the oven as she whipped the potatoes. With the radio turned to her favorite world music show, she set the table. A dance song came on and she found it impossible not to kick up her feet to the Latin beat. On one of her twirls, Sam's face appeared at the picture window. She let out a half scream, half laugh, and opened the door.

"You Peeping Tom," she accused, still laughing. "You really are a snoop."

"Peeping Sam to you. I tried knocking, I really did." He set a bottle of wine and a bouquet of pink carnations on the table. "Don't stop now. Keep dancing."

She did as he asked, feeling his eyes on her every move. The song changed to a reggae tune, and Sam reached for her hands. He swayed to the beat while she followed his rhythm. Then she shook and shimmied, and he followed suit. They danced so seamlessly together, as if they'd practiced for weeks. Maybe true love felt this way. When the song ended, Sam gathered her in for a hug, starting off friendly and ending triple-x friendly. He let go with a sigh, but not before giving her three kisses on the back of her neck.

Laine let out a moan as a delicious shiver skated up and down her neck. *Screw dinner. Food is overrated.*

"The flowers are beautiful. I don't know if my meatloaf will do them justice." She tried for normalcy, but her voice came out with a croak.

While she arranged the flowers in a blue ceramic vase, Sam added a log to the fire and poured them each a glass of red wine.

Laine took the pan out of the oven, heaped two plates with mashed potatoes and meatloaf, and brought them to the table.

"This is incredible. You even baked rolls."

"I cheated. I bought them at the market and browned them in the oven."

"Well, they are perfectly brown."

"You flatter me, Rhett," she drawled. "The mashed potatoes are lumpy and the meatloaf is overdone."

"Exactly how I like them." He held his hand across his heart.

For several minutes, two hungry people digging into their food made the only noises. Silence usually made Laine uncomfortable unless she was alone. But this

Sam-silence held warmth and comfort. Plus it wasn't totally quiet, if one counted the sounds of chewing overdone meatloaf.

Did he realize how good they were together? She wanted to feel safe enough to open up to him; tell him all her deep dark secrets.

Yeah. It's like opening a can of corn with a can opener. Once you pop the vacuum, you can't seal it again.

After cleaning his plate, Sam sat back and patted his stomach. Or maybe he rubbed it better. "That was great, especially since you insist you don't know how to cook. Or have you been lying to me?"

"I would never lie to you." At least about food. "You sure you don't need an antacid or anything?"

"That was delicious. My stomach feels great."

What a guy.

LATER, Laine washed the dishes and Sam dried. Then they migrated over to the couch. Laine was about to broach the subject of the BNC, when Sam leaned over and lightly stroked the nape of her neck. Shivers sparkled down her spine, reminding her of childhood tickle games with friends. Only Sam looked way cuter than Suzy McGiver.

We're going on a treasure hunt, X marks the spot. Three steps up. Three steps down.

Then he flicked her neck with a delicate tongue, and let out a gentle breath.

And a pinch, and a squeeze and an old-fashioned breeze.

Nothing like that had ever happened in tickle games. She held her breath.

Maybe he'll kiss my ear. Oy, there he goes.

She let out her breath as he slowly pressed the tip of his tongue into her ear. Then he blew gently until she had goose bumps on her goose bumps. He pulled her from the couch to dance again, and they swayed in perfect rhythm. His hand, a warm pressure on her back, made the song seem like an excruciating wait for him to kiss her again.

As if in a trance, she let Sam pull her onto the couch. He kissed her as if he couldn't get enough of the way her lips tasted. Right when she thought she might die from lack of oxygen, he pulled away. He gazed into her eyes and then kissed her again. Their kiss grew more passionate until they finally came up for air, gasping for breath.

"You sure know how to kiss. I'll get dessert."

"I thought that was dessert."

"Wipe that smirk off your face."

As THEY ATE thick slices of Boston cream pie, Laine's thoughts strayed to the BNC.

Sam watched her with interest. "What are you thinking about?"

"I'm thinking about Boston cream pie. Did you know it officially originated in Boston in 1856 at the Parker House Hotel? It's the Massachusetts State dessert."

"That's fascinating, but I can't believe your pensive look is totally to do with pie."

"I was thinking about the BNC. I know for sure now there is something wrong there."

"Tell me about it."

Her exhale surprised her. She hadn't realized she was holding her breath.

"I think the story about the endangered pond trout is complete fabrication. I'm pretty sure Brooke made up the story to sabotage the bike path."

"Slow down. Start from the beginning."

"I told you. Emson and Fiona spoke in her office and David called her pet and he called her Davie. F.F. Pearson bought an Emson Estates lot for big bucks with a bike path about to go past his property. Now, presto, no bike path. Oh and Tim is in on it. First he was broke. He found endangered trout on the bike path and-and presto, he has money again."

"Whoa." Sam put his hands out in a stop motion. "What exactly are you implying?"

"I'm saying Emson, Brooke, and Tim sabotaged the bike path so it wouldn't go through. It's a scam. And Stanton Coles might have something to do with it too; I haven't figured out how yet."

"What exactly is the motive?" Sam's voice had turned ten degrees colder.

Laine huffed in frustration. "Money, that's what. Aren't you listening to what I'm telling you?"

"Those are strong accusations on very little proof." His voice had gone stiff and businesslike.

"What about Brooke's expensive office decorations? And listen to this: Suddenly Tim doesn't have to sell his sailboat or jeep. His father's business has made a miraculous recovery from bankruptcy."

"Are you implying Tim's father is in on this too?"

"Don't you see? They're paying Tim off. I have good intuition about these things, I really do."

"Look, you come into town and suddenly you're an expert on people I've known for years. You're making them sound like the environmental mafia."

"I'm at the BNC almost every day and I see things. I'm not blind."

"No, but you do have a very active imagination. Maybe you can put a spy camera in Brooke's office or have her followed by a private detective wearing a trench coat. C'mon, we've got way more important things to do than argue."

Laine's face flamed. Her hands trembled, probably because they itched to wring his neck. "You don't believe me?"

"No I don't. You're accusing four people of illegal activities. Brooke and Fiona aren't the warmest people on the planet, but I've known them all my life. The BNC is a well-respected organization, dedicated to the environment. Just because they found out last minute there are rare pond trout doesn't mean they're common criminals. These are pillars of the community you're accusing—well, besides Tim."

"I know, but this is different. And by the way, even pillars fall."

"Listen, I'll tell you what I think. I think you should leave the whole thing alone. It sounds like you're prying into the lives of innocent people. Save your great imagination for your children's programs."

His cavalier tone pressed her buttons big time. Her next words came out in a rush of hurt and anger. They surprised even her with their vehemence.

"Don't you *dare* patronize me." Laine's voice was loaded with icy indignation. "I don't need people who don't respect me."

"Hey, don't get upset just because I disagree with you. I thought friends could disagree. It's only my opinion." Sam reached for her shoulders, but she jerked away.

Oh, so he thought of them as friends. Swell.

"You aren't disagreeing. You're putting me down. Friends, or whatever you call us, are supposed to support each other." Laine's temples throbbed with tension. She couldn't believe she had to hear this crap from him.

He shook his head. "Not when they're acting crazy. I can't help you on this one, babe."

"Screw you!" Laine's voice sounded harsh. "I don't need your help. And don't 'babe' me."

"All right, if that's how you feel." He stood up. "But there's nothing wrong with the BNC, you can take my word for it. Brooke won Seaglass Bay Woman of the Year last year. She wins all kinds of awards for her environmental projects. You come along saying she's botching this one up on purpose. I don't think so. You're wasting your time. Go back to your job and stop causing trouble."

"How dare you tell me what to do!" She rarely got this angry. Her teeth clenched, her fists clenched, hell - everything clenched. "Fuck you."

"Hey, don't get hysterical. I don't want you to hurt innocent people. You could get hurt too. I care about you. I think you're looking for trouble, that's all."

"Now I'm a hysterical woman?" Laine's voice turned from indignation to rage. "Maybe the only trouble in my life is standing right across from me."

"If that's how you feel, I'll leave."

"That's a great idea. Don't let the door bite you in the ass on the way out."

Sam pulled the door open. His stormy eyes flashed. "Call me when you come to your senses. I really do care about you."

"That will be never."

Sam turned and headed into the night, slamming the door behind him.

The old Laine thought of calling him back and apologizing. But the new Laine would not turn back.

LAINE CLEANED the kitchen with a vengeance, muttering and swearing to herself while she scrubbed so hard she almost took the finish off her pots. Then she threw the clean pots and pans around the kitchen.

I can't believe that jerk had his tongue down my throat. I can't believe I slept with him. I am never, ever making meatloaf again.

"I hate him. I hate him, I hate him," she told the microwave.

She cleaned until she was bone-tired, and finally collapsed in an exhausted heap on the bed.

Twenty-Four.

Wednesday

~~~~~~~~~~~~~~~~~~~~~~~~~~

L AINE WOKE the next morning and stared out at the now bare ginkgo tree and the maple. On the maple, a few red leaves still clung to the branches. The others littered the ground like a somber mosaic.

She wanted to be a leaf falling gracefully, not one holding on far too long. Squeezing her eyes shut, she couldn't bear to look at the tree trunk, etched in dark velvet against the sky. It looked so vulnerable and alone, mimicking her inner turmoil. She shuddered, then crossed her arms over her chest and hugged herself. She would lie here for a few more minutes, then get up, let go of her dream of being a we with Sam, and get on with her life. After all, someone said the best revenge was living well.

The phone rang. She tried to say hello in a normal tone, but it came out a croak.

A concerned Sofie said, "What's wrong, Laine? Are you sick? Your voice sounds funny."

"Sam and I had a big fight." To Laine's embarrassment, she burst into tears.

"I'll be right there."

WHEN SOFIE ARRIVED ten minutes later, Laine's eyes were red rimmed, but her crying jag had ended.

Sofie engulfed her in a fierce hug. "What's going on?"

Laine told her everything. "His final words were to call when I came to my senses. But don't tell me to run after him because I won't."

"Men." Sofie snarled. "Of course, I know Sam is worried about you getting hurt. Anyone can see that."

"Maybe I need glasses."

"No kidding; that idiot is crazy about you. Why do you think he acted that way?"

"Let me guess. It's because he's an asshole."

Sofie frowned. "Listen, I know how stubborn Sam can be. I think it comes from an old fear. Let me tell you a story. I guess I should have told you before but I promised to keep my mouth shut. Not that it excuses what he did. I'd like to smack him around a bit."

"You'll have to get in line. But go ahead, tell me the story." Even in pain, her curiosity got the better of her.

"During college, Sam was engaged to a woman named Louisa Krenshaw. Sam was even more of a hunk in those days than he is now. Another woman with the hots for Sam did everything she could to snag him for herself. She even started rumors about Louisa."

"What kind of rumors?"

"Louisa was having an affair with two other students and one of the professors."

"Wow. Sam didn't fall for that, did he?"

Sofie nodded. "He left Louisa for the other woman. Louisa ended up killing herself."

"That's awful, horrible, terrible." Laine couldn't find words strong enough to describe the tragedy. "How did she die?" Her voice seemed to come from far away.

"She jumped off the Seaglass River Bridge on Fern Road and drowned."

Laine shuddered. "That's awful. How deep is the water there?"

"About nine feet. Maybe she hit her head on the rocks. Maybe she took drugs. I don't know the details. It happened in November, right around Thanksgiving. The water was cold."

"November is the month my parents died. We have that in common; November tragedies."

Sofie squeezed Laine's hand. "Sam thinks it's entirely his fault, even though Louisa had a history of depression. Men think it's all about them."

"Who was the other woman? Does she live in town? Do I know her?"

"Oh all right, I'll tell you. You won't believe it."

"Who? Who was it?" Laine held her breath.

"Fiona Glaze. Sam should have told you."

Laine's eyes widened in stunned silence.

"Hon, Fiona was gorgeous back then. She had the shiny long black hair and a killer bod. Unfortunately, her tongue was even sharper than it is now. Besides spreading the rumor, she said some nasty things right to Louisa's face."

"That's cruel." Laine hugged herself as if to ward off the images of the young, heartbroken Louisa.

"No kidding. I want you to understand Sam's behavior a little better. He's scared to get close to a woman, scared that something bad will happen, and he'll be to blame. Sure, he's had his share of relationships, but they don't last long. Since Louisa, he keeps women at a distance—that is, until you came along."

"What do you mean?"

"I've known Sam for a long time. He's never acted this way before. Whenever he mentions you, he acts like an excited puppy."

"Swell. Too bad he's not paper trained."

"Plus, he's told me things."

"What has he said?" Laine hugged herself, worrying.

"Never mind. I've said enough already."

No, you haven't said enough.

"I can't let a guy treat me with disrespect. I want a man who takes me seriously. I've read enough self-help books to be dangerous. I know I can't take away his fears and pain."

"No kidding. Look, I know how inflexible he can be. It's been a long time since he trusted a woman. But right now you have to trust yourself. And be real careful around the BNC bunch. I'm worried about you."

Laine sighed. "Thanks for believing in me. I won't forget this." She gave Sofie a warm hug.

She made it to the car without crying. Then she gave herself permission to bawl for five minutes.

Okay, self-indulgence over. Time to move on, at least take a few steps.

Twenty-Five.

Wednesday afternoon

PUTTING MORE ENERGY into solving what Laine now referred to, at least with Sofie, as the bike path debacle, turned out to be a good way to keep her mind off Sam. After lunch, she called Sofie and asked if her sister Lucy could help them hack into Brooke's email.

Sofie's sister lived in New Bedford, a half-hour ride from Seaglass Bay. Lucy owned a renovated house near the historic district in the old whaling city.

"Her major fault is she's an exercise fanatic. She wears shorts in January, if you can believe it. Not to show off her fantastic rock hard gams, but to be ready in case she gets an urge to exercise. Don't mention anything even remotely related to movement. Don't even say you're running an errand, or jogging your memory. She'll sign you up to go rock climbing or play basketball."

"That doesn't sound so terrible."

"Don't say I didn't warn you. She designs computer games for manic kids. When you meet her you'll understand."

IN DOWNTOWN NEW BEDFORD, Sofie parked in front of a yellow Victorian three-story house with red trim.

Laine gasped. "This place is amazing. Is that a real widow's walk up there?"

"Yep. A sea captain built this place. Now the historic district is a national park; many of the old homes like this are being restored."

The door opened and a voice called, "Were you going to come in anytime soon or just stay outside all day?"

"Hi to you too, Luce." Sofie mounted the stairs with Laine, and they entered an enclosed porch, complete with fan-backed wicker chairs.

Lucy stood under a chandelier the size of a sofa, in a foyer larger than Laine's living room. Maybe "stood" didn't describe Lucy enough. Rather, she bounced in place. Lucy had tamed the wild Pacheco tresses into a sleek ponytail. In her gray sweats and running shoes, she bounced, looking ready for action. Lucy greeted Laine in a fast staccato voice and asked if she wanted the grand tour.

Laine had, as far back as she could remember, always had a rush of excitement at stepping into someone else's home. And Lucy's house brought her back to the Victorian era. Aunt Rose was more of a seventies buff, so Laine knew more about lava lamps and tie-dye then she did about antiques. But these looked like real Victorian pieces.

Dark mahogany furniture carved in high relief with intricate flower and bird designs filled the living room. Crocheted cloths draped the back of the rosewood sofa.

This would be more interesting if thoughts of Sam weren't popping into my head every two seconds. Thing is, I have no control over these thoughts. If I try, they'll only get worse. I've got to let them run their course, like an old Beatles song I can't get out of my head. She's got a ticket to ride. She's got a ticket to ride, and she don't care.

"Are there any men out there who don't have to be in control every minute?" Laine asked apropos of nothing.

Sofie put her arm around Laine. "She's having relationship issues."

Lucy nodded in understanding. "Join a gym together. I recommend the spin class."

Sofie gave Laine a nudge on the arm.

"I don't have relationship issues," Laine snapped. "I don't have a relationship, period."

BACK IN THE LIVING ROOM, Laine sat on the sofa and reflected that Victorian furniture looked interesting but didn't always feel comfortable. Sofie sat on the couch next to Laine, while Lucy sank to the floor and stretched her legs into something *looking* like a difficult yoga position or a giant pretzel.

Lucy listened intently as Laine and Sofie explained the weird events of the last few weeks.

"How about calling the police?" Lucy asked. "Someone is definitely trying to scare you at the very least."

"I did, but they didn't take me seriously. They don't trust newcomers."

Sofie snorted. "That's an understatement. They would be more likely to listen to a hardened criminal as long as he was a Seaglass Bay native."

"Let's go to the zoo." Lucy's ponytail swung as she bounced out of her chair. "We'll sit on a bench near the elephants, and I'll tell you how to break into Brooke's computer. That's the only way to find out what these bastards are up to."

"I USED TO feel sad for the animals," Sofie said as they walked through the zoo entrance. "But the city has turned the land into a real natural animal habitat." They power walked down the path with Lucy leading the way, and Laine decided to visit the zoo again when she could stroll. Lucy led them to a bench near the elephants.

"Come here often?" Sofie asked as they sat down. "I can see your butt prints on the bench."

Lucy stuck her tongue out in a show of sisterly love. "I do. I'm really drawn to this spot. I sit here for hours, and I'm not a sitter. I think the elephant is my spirit animal."

"Why the elephant?" Laine and Sofie asked in unison.

"I'm supposed to learn from the elephants how to be still. They can stand, almost motionless, for long periods of time because their legs are so straight and sturdy."

"I guess my animal would be a dolphin," Sofie said. "I'm definitely drawn to water creatures."

"How about a crab?" Lucy said. While the sisters went at it with their banter, Laine wondered what her spirit animal could be. She closed her eyes and an eagle appeared; a symbol of courage and freedom. Yes, she could relate well to a bird, hopefully not a scavenger seagull.

Lucy interrupted her musings. "Let me tell you how to break into her email."

Laine concentrated, trying to follow the dots from elephants to spirit animals to computers. It must all connect somehow.

Lucy reached into her jacket pocket and pulled out a small notebook with a pen attached. She handed it to Laine. "You'll want to take notes."

Right in front of the elephants, Lucy told Laine and Sofie how to commit illegal acts on a computer. First she asked if the computers were on a network.

"I have a password, if that's what you mean."

"Okay, then each computer has an individual password. Most people choose a password easy to remember, like a birthday or anniversary. But if we're dealing with a computer expert, we can throw all that out the window."

"Brooke's not an expert. She has to ask the research assistant Tim for tech support."

"Okay, then we can do it," Lucy said. She gave Laine directions to install a small program on her computer.

"You'll have to install the same program on Brooke's computer so you can access information from Brooke's computer to yours. It's an old way, but it's tried and true."

"How do I get access to Brooke's computer in the first place?"

"Send her an email. Then rush into her office and explain your email was infected with a virus and you have to check her computer ASAP."

"But Tim's the one who handles our computer problems."

"So do it when Tim's not there," Sofie said.

"He takes Tuesday afternoons off," Laine mused. "How do I get the program?"

"That's easy," Lucy laughed. "There's a website you can go to." She began to dictate instructions.

"I LIKE YOUR SISTER," Laine said on the drive back to Seaglass Bay. "She's a real fireball. And I don't think I've ever seen such a clean house."

"No kidding. She's got an exercise speed cleaning app. You should see her doing stretches with the feather duster."

"Thanks for the visual."

They laughed and made cleaning jokes until they pulled into Sofie's driveway. Sofie asked Laine to wait while she ran in to get something.

Sofie disappeared into the house, and when she reappeared a moment later she held a blue box with a silver bow.

"Ta dah!" Sofie presented the box to Laine. "It's a very early Hanukkah gift. Don't open it until you get home."

The smell of chocolate assailed her nostrils. Laine had to use all her willpower to keep her mind on driving. As soon as she shut off the car, she pulled the bow and ripped off the wrapping.

Technically I'm home.

Two layers of chocolate truffles. They looked too good to eat, but it didn't stop her. Detecting made her ravenous. Amazing that all detectives weren't as large as the portly Nero Wolfe from the mystery series by Rex Stout. If she didn't watch herself, she'd have at least five chins by the time this was over.

Twenty-Six.

Thursday through Sunday

THE NEXT SEVERAL DAYS passed in a blur of work, beach patrol, and puzzling over the bike path mystery. When she climbed into bed at night she thought about Sam.

How could he treat her that way, especially after making mad, passionate love to her? Why didn't he call and apologize?

Not that she'd listen, but he could at least try to beg for forgiveness. Begging could be sexy. But, Fiona's endless chatter about the benefit at the Swann in nearby Cranville Harbor made it worse. The annual Fishermen's Association dinner and dance would take place there. As Fiona explained on the phone a gazillion times, this year's money would go to plant scallop seeds in the river.

"I'm gonna miss a great party," Fiona told Laine on one of her many daily passes by Laine's desk. "I promised my mother I'd take her to Foxwoods gambling casino for that weekend. You going?"

Laine shook her head.

"No. No date? Aw, poor you. I bet Tim would take you. Tim, hey Tim," she called.

"Don't ask him," she protested. But inside she did a happy dance. This was the break she'd been waiting for. A chance to pump Tim for info, as Sofie called it.

Fiona told Tim that Laine didn't have a date. Of course she made it sound like Laine had "charity case" written on her chest. Tim's head popped around the corner.

"Hey Laine, want to go to the benefit dance with me?"

My, what a surprise. "Sure. I'd love to." For all the wrong reasons.

Monday

O N MONDAY NIGHT Laine dressed up to go to Serena's, even donned her new show-stopping black dress. But in the end, she lost heart and ended up by herself overdressed at an action-adventure movie. The fear that Sam would act as if nothing had happened, or ignore her completely, kept her from going to Serena's. She wasn't ready to face him.

At the movies, she lost herself in special effects, thrills, gratuitous sex, and spilled buttered popcorn on her dress. No thoughts of Sam intruded.

When she got home, she sat on the bed and cried. Aunt Rose always said, "Laugh and the world laughs with you. Cry and you release a lot of toxins."

Laine blew her nose. *I must have lost about five pounds of toxins.*

The newspaper on the bedside table caught her eye. She read the article about the bike path again. The town would have to write a whole new bike path proposal for next year, according to the reporter.

Oh my God, that was it. Next year's bike path plan wouldn't go anywhere near Emson Estates. Brooke probably had another plan already worked out. Could Brooke possibly verify whether or not Tim really discovered any pond trout? Perhaps Tim didn't portage the canoe to the pond. Maybe he didn't take the canoe at all.

Of course! Laine slapped her hands to her head. It seemed so obvious. She couldn't believe she didn't think of it sooner. She dialed Sofie's number.

"Sorry it's so late, but I need you to finagle a walk for us on the bike path with Stanton as soon as possible."

"Have you found something?"

"Yes. Maybe. Listen. W—oh my God, wait a minute. How could I have been so dense?"

"Slow down. Speak English so I can understand you."

"Give me a little time to figure out this last piece, and then I'll tell you everything, I promise."

"No kidding, you better."

LYING IN BED with her eyes closed, Laine imagined the headlines.

"Spunky amateur detective uncovers bike path scandal."

That would teach Sam to mess with her.

"Woman hailed as town hero."

Okay, maybe that went a bit too far. The phone rang, disrupting images of the parade in her honor.

"It's Sofie. The weather channel predicts high winds tonight. A Seaglass Bay Master Blaster. If you want to stay at my place, I've got plenty of room."

"Thanks, I appreciate it. But I'll be okay. Besides I want to be alone to finish nursing my Sam wounds."

"If you change your mind, you're welcome to wallow here."

AN HOUR LATER, Laine wondered if she'd been a fool to decline Sofie's invitation. The wind howled and howled and howled some more. Laine crawled deep under the covers. Laine could only imagine the wind during the hurricane of '38. She hoped the cottage proved wind worthy. The book *The Perfect Storm* was on her bookcase, but she wouldn't be reading it tonight.

Laine closed her eyes when something tapped against the window beside the bed. She shivered as she peered behind the curtain. Nothing but a hydrangea bush blowing against the window.

The cell rang again, and Laine checked the caller. Sam Holliston. To what did she owe the honor? Her sarcastic thoughts didn't stop her heart from thudding in her chest.

I shouldn't even bother answering. But what if it's an emergency, like he wants to tell me he adores me and can't live without me?

"Hello," Laine answered right before it went to voicemail.

"Hi, it's Sam. Sam Holliston."

Duh. "What's up?"

"I wanted to make sure you're okay. It's blowing pretty hard out there."

"I'm fine, thanks. I don't know why everyone's fussing about a bit of wind."

"That bit of wind is wreaking havoc. Several sections of town have lost power, and waves are breaking over the causeway."

"Thanks for the weather report. Is there anything else?" *Something like "sorry I acted like an ass and you were totally right all along."*

The pause lasted so long Laine wondered if the phone had gone dead.

"Nope, I guess that's it. Glad you're okay."

"Thanks for calling. Goodbye."

If Sam thought she would pretend nothing happened, he had another thing coming.

Besides, riding out a storm alone might end up fun. Loads of chuckles. Then again, maybe I responded too harshly to him. He did call to make sure I was okay. No; he can't pretend everything's okay without an apology. Then again even I know apologies are not a strong male trait. I don't care. Sam acted really rude.

Laine finally dozed off, waking every few minutes to the whooshing of the wind. She dreamed she was on a ship tossing and turning in the storm. The rigging screamed. Giant waves crashed against the side of the ship.

Hey, wait a second. I'm not on a ship. I'm lying in bed. What the heck was that crash?

Her eyes flew open as she fumbled for the light switch. *No lights. Power's out. Shit!* She fumbled for the phone. No dial tone.

Alone in an isolated cottage during a blackout. Laine gulped, feeling definitely creeped out. She reached for her flashlight. Thank God she'd remembered to put it beside the bed.

Laine pressed the button and the flashlight opened a swath of eerie light in the darkness. If only she had accepted Sofie's invitation, they could be making shadow finger puppets on the wall. She could make a pretty good fox. Under these circumstances, she would have to climb out of bed and investigate.

Her flannel pajamas with dancing teddy bears weren't standard outdoor storm wear, but she didn't think she had time to change. The crash had to be a tree branch. She didn't know if the tree had taken down wires, but she figured her best bet was to leave using extreme caution.

Laine put her cell phone in her pocket, let the flashlight guide the way, grabbing her jacket and slipping on her clogs as she stepped outside.

Once she'd travelled a few yards from the house, she shined the light back and forth until it found the maple tree. Sure enough, a large branch leaned against the roof of the cottage, tangled in electrical wires.

She held her arms tight into her body, clutching the flashlight with both hands. She didn't know much about electricity, but she suspected she better get away from the house as fast as possible.

It didn't seem safe to go near the car since it sat in the drive next to fallen wires. She'd have to get away on foot, in these stupid clogs. When she reached the edge of the driveway she tried her cell. *Damn, no service.*

The flashlight cast an eerie yellow path as she walked towards the nearest neighbor, at least a fourth of a mile away. Tillie, the owner of Dude's Place, lived next door to Dude's in a weathered ranch with a porch twice the size of the house.

Laine hugged her coat tight as the wind picked up again.

I should sing. Happy people sing songs. I'd be happy if I wasn't scared out of my mind. Plenty of songs about wind. Everyone knows it's windy. Dust in the wind. They call the wind Mariah. Damn, I can't remember the words. Oh well; the important thing is I'm okay. Why can't I stop shivering?

I wish I'd gone to Sofie's house. After ghost stories we'd sit by a cozy fire drinking lots of wine. Maybe not ghost stories though; this is scary enough. If I didn't keep trying to prove my self-sufficiency, I would be at Sofie's right now. I wish I wasn't so stubborn.

"I'm okay alone!" Laine shouted in the wind. *Enough already with that. I don't have to prove anything anymore. I'm wearing dancing bear flannel pajamas.*

A roar sounded above the wind. *Terrible night for a car to be out on the roads. Maybe it's the power company.*

She turned and was immediately blinded by a pair of high beams.

The car's coming right at me!   Without   a   second   to spare, she threw down her flashlight, grabbed the stone wall, and lurched her body up and over the other side. Crouching low, she shivered and practically held her breath until the car drove past.

Laine stood up slow, muscles stiff, and climbed back over the stone wall; groaning in pain.

The flashlight still shone when she picked it up. She half ran, half stumbled towards Tillie's house.

Somebody tried to run me over. No that's wrong. I was an easy target out there in the road. It would have been easy to run me over. That thought sent her shivering uncontrollably. *Someone tried to scare me again. Boy, they never quit.*

No RESPONSE when she pounded the door at Tillie's place. She pounded again. She yelled, but her voice was carried away in the wind. Finally, the door opened a crack and Tillie peered out.

"Hi Tillie. It's me, Laine Camara. My power went out."

Tillie reached out and pulled her inside. Dressed in an old-fashioned nightgown and cap, Tillie looked like the granny in *Little Red Riding Hood*. It seemed oddly appropriate, since Laine had just escaped the wolf.

"Wires fell on my roof," Laine gasped. "It could be dangerous." She omitted the part about the car. She'd wait to tell Sofie.

"Oh my goodness. What a night. I'll get you a thick blanket and a glass of brandy. I'll call the police. My landline works"

Laine sighed in gratitude and collapsed onto the chair. Tillie wrapped a puffy quilt around her shoulders. The brandy sent a delicious warmth through Laine's shivering body.

"The EMT is here," Tillie called from the front room a few minutes later.

"I don't need one," Laine called back as the EMT entered the room.

Oh shit. Sam.

He stared at her pajamas with the dancing teddy bears. "Cute pajamas. Do they make them in my size?"

"Very funny."

"I knew you couldn't go the night without me. So what happened? Are you okay?"

Their eyes locked, and she knew they both remembered another day when he sliced off her wet pants. In another life at another time she would have laughed. This time she tried to glare as she told him about the tree branch falling on the roof.

"I'm just scraped and bruised." *I'm definitely not going to mention the big bruise blossoming on my butt. Chalk that one up to when I tumbled over the stone wall.*

"You poor thing; you've had your fill of bad luck lately," Tillie said.

It's not bad luck. Her jaw tightened. *I could have been road kill tonight. Someone thinks I know too much. I wish I knew what it is I'm supposed to know.*

Tillie felt Laine's forehead. "You feel warm. Probably shock."

Laine wanted to protest, but held her tongue and sipped her brandy.

"Could I bother you for a cup of your famous coffee, Till?" Sam asked.

Tillie nodded and bustled away into the kitchen.

"Okay, what's going on?"

"Someone tried to run me over on my way here. Now do you believe someone is out to get me?"

"I want to believe it, I really do. I'll check into this stuff. But you know Laine, people really do have accidents. The roads are slippery tonight. Not everything is a conspiracy." He stood and backed away from her. "Call me any time you want to talk. I miss you, Laine. A lot."

Tillie's reappearance with a steaming mug saved Laine from replying. While Sam sipped the coffee, he assured Laine he would call the electric company to take care of the fallen wires.

"They probably won't get to it until morning, though."

"Laine, you are welcome to stay here," Tillie offered. "I've got a guest bedroom upstairs."

"Thanks, but what about the tree on my roof?"

"We'll call Brooke first thing in the morning. The BNC can send their carpenters to cut the branch and repair the roof. By tomorrow evening or the next morning, things will be back to normal." Sam put down his cup, pulled on his coat, gave Laine one last dark look, and stalked out the door.

God damn it, what did she have to do? Die before anyone took her seriously? Even if she died, they would treat her like an imbecile. The autopsy would reveal she ran herself over with a car, or shot herself in the back with a rifle. So fucking frustrating.

She rubbed her temples. Seeing Sam had been the worst of all. That look he gave her before he walked out, like she needed a therapist.

Of course I need one. Doesn't everybody? That's not the point.

For one small moment I thought he might be on my side, might actually start to believe me. Well screw him.

Tillie set Laine up in her daughter Dari's old bedroom.

As soon as Laine's head hit the pillow of the twin bed, she fell fast asleep.

Twenty-Seven.

Tuesday

Noon had passed when Laine opened her eyes the next day. As she got dressed, her aching muscles reminded her of last night's ordeal. She wandered downstairs into Tillie's sunny kitchen.

No sign of Tillie, but Laine spied a basket of fresh baked goods next to a note telling her to help herself. She ate two banana cinnamon muffins and then called Sofie.

"This is really freaking me out," Sofie said when she heard the latest news. "I want you to pack up some clothes and get your ass over here."

"Okay." Laine was too sore and weary to argue. "But first I think I need a massage. My butt hurts."

Sofie gave her the number of a massage therapist, and Laine called right away. Turned out the woman had a cancellation at two.

At three thirty, Laine walked out of Seaglass Massage like a new person. Her mood and her butt had improved a thousand times. Instead of feeling old and bedraggled, she felt rejuvenated. She had laughed when the massage therapist asked if she had any stress. With each sigh, she let out more of the tension of the last few weeks.

Maybe she could cut out necessities like food and shelter and make massage part of her health care routine. She realized if she brown bagged it for lunch most days, she'd have more than enough for a monthly massage and a facial or even those divine hot stones. She could think of other uses for those hot stones if she put her mind to it.

IT TURNED INTO a sleepover party at Sofie's house that night. They watched *When Harry Met Sally*, ate popcorn and talked about the BNC mystery.

"After the roof is fixed tomorrow morning, I'm going home," Laine told Sofie. "The police will send a cruiser by my house every hour or so."

"I won't argue with you. But call me if you're even the slightest bit spooked. By the way, Stanton said he'd take us on the walk tomorrow. Now tell me why you're so eager to hike the bike path trail?"

"I promise I'll tell you tomorrow, right after the hike. I want to test my theory first."

"You sound very mysterious."

"Not mysterious. Just careful."

Twenty-Eight.

Wednesday

W HEN LAINE got back to the cottage the next morning, the landscaper was walking to his truck. He introduced himself as Tony the tree guy.

A wiry, wizened peanut of a man of indeterminate age, he told Laine he had split and stacked the wood from the branch.

"But you can't use it until next year. It needs to season."

Laine looked around the yard. The blue-violet sky. Electric wires all in place. Nothing to remind her of the windstorm except for the chopped up tree branch, now leaning against the tree trunk in a pile.

Tony wiped his brow with his hanky. Laine offered him something to drink.

"A glass of $H2O$ is fine."

"THANKS," he said when she returned with the water. "The roof only had minor damage. It looks like Mother Nature had help knocking down that branch."

"Help?" Laine plunked down on the porch step. "What do you mean?"

"There was a fairly new cut mark at the base of the branch." Tony told her the branch had broken off and fallen on the roof because of the initial cut.

"There was a clean cut about a third of the way through that branch. It could only have been made by a saw."

"Are you sure?"

"Sure I'm sure. I've been cutting trees for almost forty years and I know the difference between a natural break and one started artificially. Are you okay? You look like you need the glass of water."

Laine nodded. "I'm fine." She'd been saying that a lot lately; even started getting good at it. Even when her heart lodged in her throat, almost choking her. Someone had cut the branch to make sure it fell on the cottage during the storm. She tried to breathe normally to get her heart out of her throat and back into her chest.

"I wouldn't worry about it," Tony said. "I think somebody from the BNC trimmed branches while I was on vacation. Guy probably started cutting the branch, got called away and then forgot to finish. When Brooke wants something done, she doesn't like to wait."

I'll bet.

AFTER THE LANDSCAPER left, she walked around the cottage, alternately doing chores and worrying about the tree branch. Someone cut the branch to make sure it fell on the cottage. That someone wanted to scare her away from Seaglass Bay; not kill her. If they wanted to kill her, they were the most bumbling murderers on the planet. One thing she knew for sure: she'd started meddling where she shouldn't. She'd received that message loud and clear.

THAT AFTERNOON, Laine, Sofie, and Stanton set off on their hike along Windham Hill Road. Something told her to keep mum about the tree branch until she found out who had recently cut branches on BNC properties.

The three of them walked side by side, until Sofie and Stanton got into an involved discussion about her whale soft sculptures. Although both Stanton and Sofie did their best to include Laine, they kept falling into private conversation.

I'm glad those two are hitting it off.

Laine lagged a few paces behind, and they soon forgot all about her. This didn't bother her, since her own thoughts dominated her attention.

What if her theory proved correct? Would she have enough evidence to go to the police?

"A rolling hill, a pond and an ocean view," Stanton's voice broke through her thoughts. "What a choice piece of property."

"That's exactly where I saw Pearson talking to Emson."

"Well if it was Pearson, he has good taste in house lots; I'll say that much for him." Laine nodded. She couldn't imagine even the finest mansion and landscaping improving the view.

"How far to the marsh?"

"Twenty minutes. Are you ladies up to it?"

They assured him it wouldn't cause a problem. Sofie's cheeks had a glow not totally attributed to the chill in the air.

"It was sunny when we started, right?" Laine asked, looking up at the now slate gray sky. "I'm not imagining things, am I?"

Stanton laughed. "We might even get a dusting of snow later. First a windstorm, then snow. November in Seaglass Bay is full of surprises."

Laine dropped behind again. Nothing like the deep hush of the woods in late autumn to captivate her senses. The few sounds, quick and short, seemed as if they wanted to hurry back to the silence quo.

"End of the road," Stanton told them. "This is where we planned to build a bridge. Tim found the pond trout near this spot."

"Can we check it out?" Laine's body tensed in anticipation.

Stanton shook his head. "You have to drag a canoe through here. Then you canoe across a pond and drag the canoe to the next pond. The second pond is apparently loaded with pond trout."

"Tim had to portage to reach the pond?" Laine asked.

"Yes. He probably used one of the BNC canoes," Stanton said. "They're light and easy to carry."

I don't think so. Laine decided to keep her thoughts to herself for now.

Stanton took the knapsack from his back and pulled out food and drink. The three sat on a rock that resembled a puzzle of small stones glued together.

"It's a puddingstone," Sofie said. "You find lots of them around here."

As they sat, the sky turned an even deeper shade of gray. The air got colder, but the walk warmed Laine. She chewed a stick of celery stuffed with peanut butter and observed the ground with care. The turf close to the pond stayed soft. She got up and walked around, searching for clues.

"What do you see?" Stanton wondered.

"Nothing. Not a thing." *It's what's not here that concerns me.*

Stanton started to say something else, but Sofie interrupted him.

"Look guys, it's snowing." Sofie held out her hands to catch the flakes.

Laine looked up as the first cold snowflake tickled her nose.

"The storm is starting earlier than predicted," Stanton said. "We better hurry home in case the meteorologists are also wrong about the amount of snow."

LAINE HELD UP her hands, greeting the snow. She tipped her face to the sky and caught a snowflake on her tongue.

The clouds looked like dark animals threatening to scoop them up in fury. Stanton had voiced a legitimate concern. Mother Nature readied to pounce.

"I can't believe turkey day is tomorrow," Laine said as they hiked back at a fast pace.

"I know. I usually go to Virginia to stay with my architect daughter," Stanton told them. "But she's designing a house in Texas and has only one day off. Looks like I'll spend a quiet day at home in front of the fire, gnawing on a turkey leg. I'm actually looking forward to it. What about you ladies?"

"My sister and her family are coming to my house," Sofie said. "My sister brings tofu shaped like a turkey and my mother makes Portuguese sausage stuffing. I guess they cancel each other out."

"I'm going to leave early in the morning and drive to New Hampshire to see my Aunt Rose," Laine said. Aunt Rose's lava lamp, red hair, and open arms. She couldn't wait.

As Stanton had feared, the gentle flakes grew steadily more insistent until they stung with fierce urgency. Laine had looked forward to snow in Seaglass Bay, but not *this* kind of snow. She began to run.

"Don't run," Stanton warned. "You could trip over a twig or stump and go sprawling."

Sweatshirt and jeans had seemed like a fine choice this morning, but they turned out to be poor protection now. Laine pulled up her hood, shoved her hands in her pockets, hunched her shoulders and hurried down the path.

BY THE TIME they reached Stanton's house, more than an inch of snow covered the ground.

Stanton let them into his house. Sofie and Laine peeled off their icy sweatshirts, brushed off their jeans, and sank onto the floor of his living room.

Stanton started a fire in the woodstove and bustled about getting dry shirts for everyone. They sat close to the fire, drinking hot coffee. Outside, the snow flew in white sheets.

"Stay for dinner," Stanton urged. "I make a mean soup. Afterwards I'll take you both home in my four-wheel drive."

Laine and Sofie readily agreed. Stanton ransacked the kitchen cupboards and the refrigerator for ingredients for a soup. He chopped chicken, onion, garlic and celery. Soon a fragrant soup simmered on the stove. While the soup cooked, Stanton made butterscotch pudding with real butterscotch chips.

Laine noted the way Stanton kept smiling at Sofie. It became the best part of the day.

"The soup smells good," Sofie said. "What is it?"

"Curried chicken." Stanton poured the soup into crockery bowls.

The smells of turmeric and cumin filled the air, warming Laine through and through even before she tasted the savory concoction.

BY BUTTERSCOTCH PUDDING TIME, it looked like six inches of snow covered the ground. Stanton turned on the weather channel. They listened with rapt attention as the forecaster predicted the freak snowstorm would last until early morning.

"We almost never have heavy snow accumulation in Seaglass Bay," Sofie told her. "Even in January. We're too close to the ocean."

Maybe Mother Nature is also conspiring to scare me. She's certainly pulling out all the stops lately. She can join the club.

"I agree. This is crazy," Stanton added. "Next we'll have an earthquake or a tornado."

"Shhhh," Laine warned. "Don't even say it. I'm wishing for some boring weather."

Laine tasted the warmth of the pudding on her tongue. Hot butterscotch pudding, snow, and thou. Only the "thou" part remained missing.

"I better get you all home," Stanton said, after they'd devoured all the pudding. "Pretty soon I won't want to chance it, even in the four-wheel drive."

Stanton drove Laine home first, and she didn't have to wonder why.

Even though wind and snow whipped around it, she was snug as a bug in a rug. What a night to spend with a special someone..

In her bed, burrowing deep under her quilt, she thought about Sam. If Sam were there, they'd play Scrabble or strip poker or maybe they'd just strip. Well, forget it. She deserved a man who respected her ideas and listened to her intuition.

The wind blew harder and the trees rattled like old bones about to fracture. Laine burrowed deeper under the quilt. No, no, no. She would not feel lonely.

The phone rang and she answered with a muffled hello.

"What happened on the walk? What did you see?" Sofie sounded impatient.

Laine couldn't believe it. In the midst of storm and stew and pity party, she had almost forgotten her big news.

"I couldn't find drag marks from Tim's canoe. Canoes are heavy. Tim never went to check the pond trout because there were no pond trout. It was a fabrication to justify withdrawing the bike path."

"No kidding? Why? What the hell."

"When Pearson decided to buy a house lot, Emson probably panicked. He didn't want to imagine how Pearson would react to a bike path fifteen feet away from his property line. F.F. Pearson is a huge coup for Emson. As we already know, Pearson will be a magnet for other rich and famous people looking for summer getaways."

"And Emson will be well on his way to real estate mogulness, or whatever they call it."

"Exactly. The thing is, I couldn't figure out how to prove it. Then it came to me. Stanton said Tim had to drag the canoe to the different ponds. It hasn't rained, so there would have to be drag marks. The BMC canoe is far too heavy for one person to carry."

"How do you know he used the BMC canoe?"

"I asked him. He told me. He had no reason to lie because he didn't know what I was after. He even complained about how sore his back felt from dragging it. He's a big whiner."

"No kidding. Wow. This is like our first break."

"Yeah, it is. And Sofie, let's keep this to ourselves for a while. You know, until we get more evidence. By the way, did you have fun with Stanton?"

"He's a pretty good kisser. But can you imagine me having a boyfriend named Stanton?"

"Actually, I can."

"Me too, that's what scares me. I guess I could call him Stan for short. Or Ton."

Twenty-Nine.

Thursday

WHEN LAINE WOKE early the next morning, the temperature hovered around thirty-four degrees and a bright sun shone in the sky. Ten inches of gleaming snow covered everything except the sea. Even the black rocks in the bay wore fuzzy snow hats.

Laine said a prayer of thanks to the previous tenant for leaving the snow shovel. She dug a path from her front door to her car.

As she shoveled, Aunt Rose seemed farther and farther away. No way could she make it to New Hampshire today, unless she rented a snowplow.

With a clear path to the car, she returned to the house and called Aunt Rose. "Remember those igloos I used to build? I could make an igloo condo with all this snow."

"We've got several inches here, too. I think you better stay put for the day."

Laine sighed. "I really wanted to spend today with you."

"I did too," said Aunt Rose. "Let's have our Thanksgiving tomorrow. 'Good things come to those who wait.'"

Laine agreed to leave the next morning at eight if the roads were clear. She could be at Aunt Rose's by one o'clock, and spend the rest of the day with Auntie. But that left today—Thanksgiving Day—without company or festivities, or even real, home-cooked food.

Laine hung up the phone. Her worst fears of spending Thanksgiving alone began to clarify. She always kept a frozen turkey dinner in the freezer for emergencies. Now it looked as if she might need it. She had to laugh at herself. Most people had extra batteries or candles. She kept a flashlight and an emergency turkey dinner.

She turned on the TV and caught a human interest news story. Apparently some resourceful guy had thrown a frozen turkey against a car window to rescue a woman trapped inside.

Maybe Laine needed an emergency frozen turkey. She couldn't perform many rescues with her pitifully small frozen turkey dinner. She turned off the tube.

Wrapped in her quilt, she sat in the rocker by the picture window and watched the icicles dripping from the eaves and the sparkling snow-covered landscape beyond. The snow began to hypnotize her with its white glare. The ringing cellphone startled her out of her snow reverie. For one yearning second, she hoped Sam called to wish her a happy holiday. But Stanton's voice greeted her.

"I wondered if you could join me for Thanksgiving. Sofie's already changed her plans due to the weather. She'll be here in a couple of hours."

Laine hesitated. After all, today provided a perfect opportunity to be alone and practice loving the solitude.

"I make the best chestnut stuffing in Seaglass Bay."

His statement pushed her over the hump. "I'd love to. What can I bring?"

"How about a salad?"

She mentally scanned the contents of her fridge. "Done."

RUMMAGING THROUGH the actual contents of her fridge took only a few seconds. She collected a slightly tired head of lettuce, a cucumber, carrots, even one lonely tomato.

As she cut and peeled, her thoughts wandered to Sam. She played back the events of that first night at his houseboat. The tangy air, the sweet sunset, Sam's woodsy scent; all had fueled her desire. And the culmination of that desire formed a picture too perfect for words. A pure passionate feeling. Sadly, that precious, fragile moment had been *damaged* beyond repair. She took a deep, calming breath, and searched the cupboards until she found a jar of artichoke hearts. Hearts. Why did everything remind her of Sam?

THE SLOW DRIVE to Stanton's looked like Christmas rather than Thanksgiving. Good thing she knew the house because snow had transformed the world. The scrub pines wore white snow capes and leaned forward like protective wizards. Snow laced the house and bushes with frivolous icing. Icicles dripped from the eaves in sun-sparkled ice crystals.

ONCE INSIDE Stanton's house, she inhaled the scent of sage and cinnamon. Yum, but not as good as it would smell at Aunt Rose's.

Stanton and Sofie busied themselves at the stove. Laine tried to help but soon figured out she had nothing to do or add. She decided to go outside and build a snowman.

A HALF HOUR LATER, when she stepped back to admire her handiwork, she had to admit she hadn't lost any of her childhood snowman building skills. Shells and stones, from the shoreline where the snow tapered off, decorated the snowman.

When Stanton and Sofie came to admire the snowman, Laine pelted them with snowballs. Then they all fell into the snow, laughing. It was already turning out to be a good Thanksgiving, and they hadn't even eaten yet.

In addition to Stanton's succulent turkey with chestnut stuffing, dinner included mashed potatoes, Laine's salad, and Sofie's homemade pumpkin pie.

AFTER STUFFING THEMSELVES to the gills, they retired to the chairs around the fireplace to toast marshmallows.

Laine, full of good food and good friends, almost forgot about the BNC. And Sam.

"It's the turkey that makes you sleepy." Sofie yawned. "It's got something in it—tryptophan, I think."

"No," argued Stanton. "It's all the carbohydrates making you tired."

A rousing argument ensued. Laine watched them from her chair.

A match made in heaven. I'd like one of those.

LATER THURSDAY NIGHT, back at her house, Laine threw her sleeping bag and overnight bag full of clothes in the trunk of her car, and placed a stash of cookies on the passenger seat. Ready for her trip, she climbed into bed and closed her eyes. She envisioned the headlines of tomorrow's paper:

Local resident Sam Holliston choked on turkey bone today. Last words were "Laine, I'm sorry; I should have listened to you."

If only.

Thirty.

FRIDAY MORNING DAWNED crisp and cold. The sun transformed branches into twisted, icy wands along Route 24. The clean roads, down to bare pavement, made driving easy.

Laine found herself thinking about Aunt Rose. After her parents died, Aunt Rose opened her arms wide to take Laine in. Aunt Rose had no experience with children but a lot of experience with love. Speaking of love, Aunt Rose's then-fiancé unceremoniously dumped her once she and Laine became a package deal.

"Spoilsport. Good riddance to bad rubbish," Aunt Rose had scoffed. She sold her three-carat diamond engagement ring, bought a mobile home in New Hampshire, and set about raising her brother's daughter.

Once, after Laine was teased at school, she asked Aunt Rose what trailer trash meant. Aunt Rose replied their garbage pickup happened on Thursdays. Then, realizing the reason for the question, she made sure Laine knew Loon Acres was not a trailer park, but a resident-owned manufactured-housing community.

Laine marveled at the way Aunt Rose always helped her with homework and took her to every volleyball game. Aunt Rose only took one night out for Wednesday poker at the recreation hall.

Laine's eyes welled up. She and Aunt Rose formed a family, and Laine would be hugging her in a few short hours.

Laine listened to talk radio the entire trip. By the time she pulled into Aunt Rose's driveway, Laine knew how to feed a finicky cat, and all about the Colorado prison system.

"I'm home, I'm home," she called as she entered the trailer and engulfed her tiny aunt in a hug.

"I'm glad to see you too, dear," Aunt Rose said when they broke apart.

Aunt Rose gave a hearty laugh, a laugh too big for her five-foot frame. Her perfume mingled with the smell of turkey in the oven.

Laine breathed in deeply. "I'm so happy to be here." She sipped her tea and sampled an appetizer. Home. Her home.

Aunt Rose's bird-like eyes focused on Laine's face. "You've got dark circles under your eyes, honey. What's wrong?"

"I'm working a lot. You know, making hay while the sun shines." Her voice choked on a sob.

"Oh Aunt Rose, I've made assumptions and I've made a great big ass out of myself."

Laine let the tears flow freely in front of Aunt Rose. Aunt Rose hugged her and patted her hair. It had worked when she was thirteen and it worked now. Laine cried for several minutes and then blew her nose in the proffered tissues. She told Aunt Rose all about Sam—everything but the X-rated parts.

"It's over." Laine took another tissue. "I don't know why I'm even talking about him."

"Maybe because you can't stop thinking about him. Love makes the world go round, you know."

"Oh Aunt Rose, if that's the case, my world is flat as a pancake." She sniffed and quickly changed the subject. "The turkey smells out of this world. Did you make your cornbread stuffing?"

Aunt Rose smiled. "That's my girl. Still got your priorities straight, I see. I did make my cornbread stuffing. I added chopped portobello mushrooms this time."

Aunt Rose wisely refrained from further comments about Laine's love life. They had a lot of catching up to do. Aunt Rose told her about the antics of her bridge club, her gardening club, and her yoga class.

"Do you remember Mildred Munson?"

Laine nodded.

"She got stuck in the lotus position and the yoga teacher had to call 911."

Laine laughed until tears rolled down her cheeks. She felt better than she had in ages.

Aunt Rose pulled the turkey from the oven. Turning to Laine she asked, "Could you go over to the recreation hall to pick up my turkey platter?"

"Sure." Laine walked down the path towards the recreation hall. The path forked; to the right the hall, to the left the lake. She looked with longing to the left. Maybe later. She spent many formative years hanging around the lake, sitting on the dock watching the water turn to rose-tinted aluminum foil. Only the crying loons and Aunt Rose had understood the depths of her loss.

Laine opened the door of the hall expecting to find a turkey platter on the long table. Instead, a food-laden table faced her. People yelled "Surprise!" Behind her, Aunt Rose bustled in with the turkey.

"You guys waited to have Thanksgiving with me?" A teary mist clouded Laine's vision. *What's all this crying about? I'll add it to the list and have Doc Cremble check it out when I get back.*

"Hey Laine," said Mitchell, giving her a kiss on the cheek. "Still saving the world?" Mitchell had the best hair comb-over in the whole USA. When he unwound it, a two-foot strand of hair hung from the top of his head.

The Grayson twins wore their matching leopard vests. They still dressed alike even at seventy years old.

The Souza family, from the hot pink mobile home, waved to her. George and Martha rounded out the party. His demeanor, cranky; hers, sweet. They actually reminded everybody of George and Martha from *Dennis the Menace.*

This motley crew made up her extended family, and they had waited for her to have their Thanksgiving dinner together. Everybody had a famous favorite dish, from Aunt Rose's noodle pudding to Martha's butternut squash with pineapple and marshmallows.

Laine had quite a full belly by the time she had Aunt Rose to herself back at the trailer's cozy living room.

"You could make an outhouse into house beautiful," Laine told her, looking around at the loveseat and two easy chairs. "You must be very cozy here all by yourself."

"That's what I want to talk to you about. Laine, honey, I've met someone."

"Met someone? Like a man?"

"Exactly like a man. He's asked me to move in with him . . . in his house . . . in town."

Laine's body tightened with surprise. She held on to the chair so she wouldn't fall off.

"You met someone," she repeated, unable to grasp the fact. "You sure he's legit? He's not a criminal or something?

I mean not that you're not attractive and couldn't meet someone great."

"Why don't you stop while you're ahead?" Aunt Rose suggested.

To her surprise, Laine burst into tears again.

Aunt Rose handed her the rest of the box of tissues. "Things can't always stay the same, dear. Besides, 'variety is the spice of life.' Plus, I'm enjoying sex again after all these years. It's nice to know I've still got what it takes."

"Okay, too much information," Laine smiled through her tears. "Spare me the details, please."

"Maybe you would feel better if you got Sam off your chest, so to speak," Aunt Rose said. "I take it there's more to the story."

Laine nodded. She told Aunt Rose about their fight.

"I certainly understand your frustration. But you've got to understand he hasn't known you very long and he's known the townsfolk all his life. I knew you would get yourself embroiled in a real-life mystery. That's my Lainie. My advice to you: Follow your gut and stay the course. If he's a good man, he'll come around. By the way, you know the saying about good things coming to those who wait? Well, it's not true. I found that out when I met my Lester. So go get 'em, girl."

"His name is Lester? For real?"

"Yes, Lester," Aunt Rose said, and began to describe the new love in her life.

Laine had to admit he sounded funny and warm. Once she got over the shock, she began actually looking forward to meeting the man.

But not yet.

Thirty-One.

Saturday

~~~~~~

L AINE SLEPT WELL in her old bed and woke up late the next morning to her favorite childhood breakfast. The bowl of oatmeal with raspberry jam swirls actually made her nostalgic for junior high. After breakfast Aunt Rose sat on the settee and patted the space beside her.

Laine sat and wondered what Aunt Rose wanted to tell her. She remembered the long, intimate talks on the settee, where she learned many of the facts of life.

"You're not going to give me another sex talk?" Laine joked to hide her nervousness.

"No," said Aunt Rose. "This is the love talk." Then she told Laine about her own brush with love over ten years back. "I couldn't let myself fall in love with Lester, because I had lost my brother and sister-in-law and my fiancé. I almost let him go. But you know what I finally learned? It takes more courage to open your heart and love than it does to be alone. You and your young man both need to learn this lesson."

Laine squeezed her hand. "I remember that guy who left when my name got added to the dance card."

Aunt Rose nodded. "Guess what happened to that fellow? His wife left him for another man and left him with the kids. Very sad."

Aunt Rose didn't look the least bit sad. "There's a lot you don't know about me. The point I'm trying to make is, someday you've got to get back on a horse and ride again."

"Too snowy for horses Aunt Rose, but we can go for a walk."

"The lake?"

"Of course. Our favorite." Aunt Rose donned her fur coat and Laine added a few layers. The little road around the lake had been cleared by snowplows. Laine breathed in the cold clean air and stared at the sun sparkles dancing on the lake.

"Remember when you thought the lake turned into a sheet of tinfoil at night?"

Laine smiled at the memory. She and Aunt Rose had walked the lake path almost every day for years. But sometimes Laine snuck out at night and sat by the lake alone.

"Next month you'll have to come back and go skating on the lake. Bring your friend."

Laine gave her a sharp glance. "Aunt Rose, you know we aren't together."

"Uh-huh. You know that saying, 'If you love something, set it free'?"

Laine nodded. She knew almost every saying ever conceived, thanks to Aunt Rose.

"Well, it's all bunk. If you love something, fight for it. Not all the sayings are true, you know. If you want him, you better get on the stick."

"On the stick? Oh Aunt Rose, you are as wise and irreverent as ever." They both started to laugh and didn't stop until they got back to the trailer.

Laine packed her overnight bag. She and Aunt Rose hugged and said long, tearful goodbyes. Laine couldn't believe her arms didn't fall off on the way to her car; they were so laden with containers of leftovers.

BESIDES THE TURKEY, Laine had much food for thought on her way home. Aunt Rose seemed now in serious doubt about some of her own maxims. What did you call that? De-maximizing? Aunt Rose had loved and lost because of fear.

That's not what I'm doing. Sam let me down. He didn't listen. He didn't trust me. Maybe he felt a touch of fear, too. Solving the BNC mystery seems infinitely easier than figuring out my relationship with Sam. Aunt Rose didn't even seem upset that I'm embroiled in trying to solve a mystery. I guess she knows me better than I think. And accepts me.

Laine's heart flooded with feelings of love and gratitude.

THAT NIGHT, back home in the cottage, Laine tossed and turned, thinking about breaking into Brooke's computer. Even chamomile didn't soothe her. Nor did reading. She finally slipped into sleep, images of tapping into the computer invading her dreams. Then, at the most crucial moment, getting caught. Brooke, yanking her away from the computer. Brooke, dialing 911.

Thirty-Two.

Monday

WHEN LAINE WOKE UP Monday morning, her bedclothes were strewn all over the place. *Looks like I had tons of fun in bed last night.* She lumbered out of bed and trudged to the shower, letting the water pummel her back to life and some semblance of sanity.

At the breakfast nook, she raised her mug of coffee to the toaster. "A toast to my first time breaking into a computer. May it be a success." She'd had several firsts since moving to Seaglass Bay, come to think of it.

THE MORNING AT WORK dragged by so slowly Laine considered screaming to end the tedium. When Tim poked his head around to say hi, she jumped.

"Edgy today," he observed. "Guilty conscience about something?"

"I'm fine. I have a headache. You know, that time of month."

"Hey, I'm sorry." Tim walked away mumbling.

Laine breathed a sigh of relief. She hated to use the PMS defense, but whatever worked.

Laine glared at the clock, willing the hands to move faster. Fidgeting at her desk, she then realized she stared at Tim.

"Are you sure nothing is wrong? You are acting kind of weird."

"W-what?"

"You were staring at me. Really hard. I wondered if I had my pants on inside out."

"Oh, no, no I'm thinking about something." *Lame, very lame.* "You caught me daydreaming."

"I see." Tim opened his briefcase and stuffed a tumble of papers inside. "Not about me, I hope."

Crap, how embarrassing. "I was uh . . ." Laine stammered.

Tim winked at her. "I'm kidding around." He locked his desk, strolled to the door. "I'm done for the day. See you later, dream weaver."

"Bye," Laine managed. The door shut behind him. A sound sweet to Laine's ears. Now she could jump into action.

Laine took a deep breath and stood up. Straightening her shoulders helped; she needed all the extra self-confidence she could get.

"Laine?" Brooke's voice made her jump out of her skin. She turned to find Brooke standing beside her.

"I'm going out to get some papers from my car," Laine stammered. "Did you need anything?"

"I want to ask Tim a question. Is he still here?"

"He left for the day."

"It will wait." Brooke returned to her office.

Laine patted her chest, sure her heart would stop. That brief encounter was close, too close for comfort. Even though she hadn't done anything wrong—yet.

Once Laine got outside, she took a deep breath. No sign of Tim's jeep. Okay, good. The first step going as planned. She took a pack of teaberry gum from her glove compartment. Chewing something might calm her nerves. Time to get to work.

Good thing she watched mystery shows on television. Couch potato spy training.

Her mouth full of gum, she opened the door to return to her desk.

Fiona stood, straightening her sparkly gray velour warm-up pants.

Time for her lunch break with the collagen donuts. This couldn't be more perfect.

"Where are your papers?" Fiona asked.

"Papers?"

"I heard you tell Brooke you were going to your car to get papers."

Oh crap. "I went to get gum. I didn't want to tell Brooke. She-she hates gum."

"You didn't want Brooke to know you chew gum? Whatever. Wanna join me for lunch down in the dungeon? I have an extra donut you can eat."

Yeah, it's probably a day-old cream-filled you peed on and ran over with your car. Stop; maybe she's trying to be nice. Maybe pigs fly.

"No thanks. I'm working through lunch today."

"What a suck up," Fiona muttered as she clomped down the stairs.

If you only knew.

Back at her desk, her hands trembled on the keyboard as she composed her email to Brooke. Her heart pounded in her ears, and took up residence in her throat. She hesitated at the last possible moment, and then hit send. She watched her message exit the outbox. Could she get it back?

Too late for that now. How long to wait? A beat. Then another. She straightened her spine, and it had an instant calming effect.

"Deep breath, girl," she whispered as she hoisted herself to her feet. She pivoted towards Brooke's office but stopped as she reached the threshold—the flashdrive! She snatched it from her purse and slowly knocked on Brooke's door.

"Come in."

Laine slowly turned the knob and pushed open the door to the office.

"I'm sorry, Brooke. I'm afraid I mistakenly sent you a virus by email!"

Brooke looked up, annoyed. "Tim says we have anti-virus software."

"This is a brand new virus, sorry to say. But I know exactly how to fix it."

"You do?" Brooke did not hide her skepticism.

"I keep up on computer technology. I took a course at the Apple store on computer protection."

"Tim can handle it when he comes back tomorrow morning."

Laine swallowed hard. "By then it will be too late. It might crash your system."

"That would be a total disaster. I can't afford to lose anything on my computer. Can you really fix it?"

Laine nodded as she held up the flashdrive. "I have the solution right here."

"Very well prepared." Brooke stepped aside.

Laine went to work. The program installed with ease, exactly as Lucy had promised.

"That should do it!" Exultation filled Laine, even with the sound of her heart pounding away.

"I must admit, I'm impressed."

Me too.

Minutes later, Laine sat at her desk, ready to test the results of her daring scheme. She opened up the file, wondering how her fingers could move so fast.

Within minutes—they seemed like hours—the program sprang to life, up and running. Right there on her screen, everything from Brooke's computer lay sectioned out, including the password!

"Hard at work?" Laine jumped as Brooke's voice chopped through the air like a machete.

"Oh . . . uh, yes."

"Come on back into my office."

"Okay." Laine gave a meek smile as her fingers pressed keys to exit the program. She rose, feeling lightheaded, to follow Brooke into her office.

Brooke sat at her desk and stared at her computer screen.

Laine knew imminent death when she saw it. She'd been caught.

Brooke turned the monitor screen towards Laine. Laine glimpsed the email she'd sent with the code attached. She swallowed hard and tried to smile.

"The *Seaglass Gazette* copy deadline is tomorrow. I need your data for the upcoming children's events. Email them to me as soon as you can, please."

The blood rushed to Laine's head and butterflies settled in her stomach.

This is not the time to pass out or throw up. Hang in there.

Brooke continued to speak. "I received an email from the state park people asking us to coordinate several programs. Do you have time?"

Laine managed to mutter, through a too dry throat, "I do."

Brooke nodded and pulled a notepad from her drawer. "That's all then." She dismissed Laine with a nod.

Laine practically oozed back to her desk and sank into it like an amoeba. Relief flooded every pore as she took several minutes to regain her composure. The chewing gum helped. As soon as her breathing steadied, she left the office and drove to Sofie's house with the flashdrive.

"Have you read it yet?" Sofie asked.

"Of course not, I waited for you."

Laine slid the flashdrive into the computer, and up popped Brooke's emails. She and Sofie read in engrossed silence for several minutes.

"Wow. Here it is in black and white. Emson paid Brooke to stop the bike path."

"These emails are so incriminating. Pearson had a purchase and sales agreement for a lot two days after the bike path approval. Brooke and Emson scrambled to find a loophole to ensure the path stayed away from Emson Estates. Emson knew months ago about the bike path. Why did he wait so long?"

"Emson never thought the bike path would interfere with the homes he planned to build. Then Pearson came along. See here?" Laine pointed at the computer screen. "In this email, Emson tells Brooke the bike path plans must be stopped. He says if Pearson buys a house lot, Emson Estates will skyrocket in value. The next email says that no way can a bike path go anywhere near Emson Estates. Not with the likes of Pearson buying houses. A whole different class of people entirely."

Sofie read the email, shaking her head in disbelief. "Pearson and his cronies won't want all us common folk bike riding behind their mansions." She scrolled down the screen. "Here's where they had the argument about Tim. They say he's discovered their secret and they have to pay him off, but maybe he'll be useful."

"They never mention him by name though. They call him the assistant. Pure conjecture at this point."

"You sound like a lawyer. Brooke is worried about Tim's—I mean the assistant's—involvement. Emson is reckless, like he thinks money will protect him from getting caught."

"It's shielded him so far. Look at this: 'She's a nosy little bitch but she's harmless. She thinks she knows more than she does.' That must be about me."

"At least we didn't have to read about Brooke tying Emson to her bedpost and making him wear environmental slogan thongs."

"Drat, I would have enjoyed that."

"Kinky."

"They were calling each other honey and dear when they weren't arguing. They've got to be lovers."

"Oy," said Laine, "I don't want to think about it—I need some mental form of birth control. Yuck. I can't believe they were intimate. Maybe Brooke needed the money and she sucked up to Emson."

"Uh-huh. Sure."

Now their evidence pointed to the truth. Unfortunately, their evidence would be considered illegal. Illegal, and therefore useless.

"We could show Sam," Sofie suggested. "Although I see by your expression you don't like the idea."

"Hell no. Maybe I can get Tim to confess, like you suggested. Wear a sexy dress, go to the benefit dance, get him drunk and pump him for information—figuratively, of course."

Sofie shook her head. "Be sure to bring your cell phone in case you need me to rescue you, and be sure to bring your self-defense skills."

"I can do that."

WHEN LAINE got home, the message light on the landline answering machine flashed. Weird how a red pulse could make her feel so wanted. She pressed the button.

Tim's voice, "Don't forget the benefit dance tomorrow night. Call when you get in."

She called Tim. "I'm looking forward to the dance," she told him. *More than you can imagine.*

Thirty-Four.

Tuesday

~~~~~~

THE NEXT MORNING, Laine dressed warmly for an early beach walk. Both sky and sea melded into an unfriendly shade of gray-green. This New England sky resembled a vast bowl of cold pea soup. As she pulled her jacket closer, a sudden desire to go on vacation in sunny Florida overcame her.

AFTER HER WALK, Laine drove to Sofie's house for coffee. As she walked in, Laine inhaled the fragrant scent of fresh-baked cinnamon rolls. Once again she marveled at how Sofie combined domestic goddess and wild woman.

"I'm in heaven," she said, as Sofie placed a bun on a paper doily in front of her.

Sofie smiled. "Thanks again for introducing me to Stanton. Look what he brought me." She pointed to a bouquet of yellow roses, artfully arranged amongst delicate green ferns.

"They're lovely. I hear you're dining someplace special tonight."

Sofie smiled. "An intimate French restaurant. Laine, please be careful with Tim tonight. I'm worried about you."

"Don't worry. I've learned enough in self-defense class so I can gouge out his eyes and kick him in the nuts if he gets crazy."

"No kidding, that's reassuring." Sofie crossed her arms. "I'm sorry Sam's not your date for tonight. I know you're disappointed."

"Nah, I'll have more fun trying to get information from Tim."

"When pigs fly I'll have more fun tonight," she muttered, driving home. "Or is it 'in a pig's eye'?" A tight knot formed in the pit of her stomach.

At home, she scrubbed her kitchen floor and washed the windows with organic cleaning products in a whirlwind of nervous energy.

The cleaning done, Laine stood in the shower and let the hot water beat on her shoulders. Her short hair took only a minute to wash. After she dried her hair off, she slipped on her new little black dress, just low-cut enough to show a slight swell of her full breasts. Laine had wanted to wear it for Sam, but that ship had sailed.

Laine pictured Tim leaning over and becoming completely entranced by the sight of her cleavage, then confessing everything. That would be too easy. Oh well, a girl could dream, couldn't she?

Vanilla and ylang ylang essential oils supposedly had aphrodisiac powers, so she rubbed a generous drop of each on her neck. Maybe when a guy smelled vanilla, he thought a piece of cake was not far behind. Laine wanted all the help she could get.

Laine considered how much time she took with her looks. Tim probably ran his fingers through his hair while waiting at a stoplight. Guys had it so easy. But when she looked in the mirror at the tendrils of hair curling at the nape of her neck, she knew her efforts were well worth it. LATER, she stood by the picture window waiting for Tim, anticipating the evening.

The Swann, a two-story restaurant and dance hall in nearby Cranville Harbor, had survived two hurricanes and looked it. The well-known restaurant had pockmarked, weather-beaten shingles. The spacious interior, on the other hand, oozed elegance, with teardrop crystal chandeliers.

Or so she'd been told. She'd see the inside of the Swann soon enough at the clam boil.

Laine watched Tim's jeep pull into her shell driveway. Taking a deep breath, she grabbed her purse and walked slowly towards him. Tim whistled when he saw her, so presumably her outfit and seductive sway had the desired effect. *Ready, set, action.*

"You're a total fox," he told her. "I feel like a frog next to you."

He didn't look like any frog she knew, not in a leather dress-jacket. *I better start piling on the bull.* She kissed him lightly on the cheek.

"Now you're a prince."

They chatted amiably on the twenty-minute ride.

When they arrived at the Swann, few spaces existed in the enormous lot. Tim finally found a parking spot against the seawall.

"Place is hopping tonight," Tim remarked, taking her arm.

Hopping? Hmmm, maybe he is a frog.

Laine shivered as they strode towards the lighted door. The cold hadn't caused her to shiver, though the wind whipped off the water. No, the sensation seemed more of a pricking at the back of her neck; anticipation of secrets the night—or at least Tim—might reveal.

THE SWANN'S MAIN ROOM held a sea of thirty round tables dressed in frothy white cloths. An attendant checked Tim's tickets and showed them to the two remaining seats at a table for twelve.

Laine and Tim took a few minutes to introduce themselves to their fellow diners. Relief spread through her at the unfamiliar names and faces. She would be able to focus most of her energy on Tim.

She complimented Tim on his cologne even though she didn't care for a man covering up his natural scent with smelly stuff. She complimented his hair too, even though his usually floppy hair, now gelled and combed, looked like a well-manicured golf course.

I'm lying for a good cause. I hope I'm not overdoing it. Maybe I shouldn't tell him what nice cuticles he has.

But it turned out Tim lapped each compliment up like a starving kitty. He would probably accept praise for his earwax and nose hairs without batting an eye.

By the time the food came, she had him eating out of her hand. At least he was watching her with interest while he devoured clams and drank beer. Laine ate her food, sipped soda water, and eyeballed the room. It took several minutes to take in the ambiance of the polished dance floor and crystal chandeliers. She told herself she just browsed, but of course she searched for signs of Sam.

A full house of people enjoyed their steaming bowls of clams, potatoes, and Portuguese linguiça sausage at the Swann tonight.

Each time Tim's drink came close to being empty, he signaled a waiter to refill his glass. Laine finished her last bite of carrot cake with cream cheese frosting right when the band started up.

Wasting no time, Tim asked her to dance the first song. Tim whirled her around the dance floor, still remarkably steady on his feet. After five songs, dizzy from spinning with such verve, she leaned against a nearby pole to catch her breath.

Laine gazed around the room. Her eyes swiveled to a handsome couple a few tables away. Her heart sank into the pit of her stomach as she recognized Sam.

Sam talked and gestured to a woman with dark curls tumbling down her back. It didn't take him long to get back into action, the jerk. The couple kept talking and they didn't notice she existed.

Her knees turned to water as she slowly made her way back to her seat. She turned towards Tim, who began talking about sailboats. She tried to nod at appropriate times, while her mind made a whirlwind look still.

What is that twist in the pit of my stomach? I'm jealous, so jealous I can hardly see straight. But why do I care if he's out with another woman? We never had a real chance to get our relationship off the ground.

Tim explained something about mahogany deck stain. Laine smiled and tried to look interested.

Then he talked about a new navigator system he wanted to buy.

Tim coaxed her back onto the floor for a slow dance. As she danced, Sam glided around the dance floor nearby with his curly-haired beauty.

Laine's gut filled with raw emotion at a speed that surprised and troubled her. Her head throbbed. Her voice sounded like it came from someone two feet away as she asked Tim to take her home.

"Now? The night is young, babe."

Laine explained that she had a headache. At the moment, she didn't care what happened at the BNC.

"I'm going to the ladies' room before we go," she told him.

WHEN LAINE EMERGED from the bathroom, a familiar voice made her stop short.

"Laine."

"What do you want?"

Sam wore a tweed sports jacket, white button-down shirt, and black jeans.

She'd hoped she'd be okay if she saw him. Ha. Who was she trying to kid?

"You look beautiful."

"Thanks."

"I need to talk to you."

"I'm kind of busy and you look like you have your hands full." Laine clasped her hands behind her back, so he wouldn't notice them trembling.

"It's not what you think. I need to see you tomorrow. It's important."

"I told you I'm busy."

"Laine c'mon, please give me a few minutes of your time."

She nodded in spite of herself. "Alright. A few minutes, that's it."

"Thanks. I'll stop by your house. Is tomorrow morning on my way to work okay?"

"I guess so."

Sam let out a breath. "Great. I'll see you then. We'll talk."

Laine's body trembled and her heart had climbed into her throat as she watched him walk away.

What does he want? I won't have long to wait. Tomorrow morning comes pretty early.

When she got back to the table, Tim coaxed her into one more dance. The way he weaved and wobbled on the dance floor convinced Laine he was in no shape to drive home. He gave up his car keys without a fuss.

IN THE CAR, she opened the window, letting the fresh air clear her head of Sam. By the time she pulled into the driveway, she was back on track and ready to ask Tim some questions.

Tim stumbled into the house and plopped onto the couch. "That was a feast." He did a poor job of covering up a belch.

"I really enjoyed myself. Thanks. I'm glad you can keep your sailboat." Laine sidled up next to him on the couch. "Could you take me sailing this summer? I always wanted to learn and I have a great little black bikini."

"Bet it's sexy on you."

"It is. Your dad's business is in Lyme, didn't you say? I have good friends in Mystic."

"No," he mumbled. "Our summer house is in Lyme. Dad's business is in Hartford."

"I love Mystic Seaport. My dad was a musician, and I went with him for one of his concerts. It's tough to have a father with his own business. Sometimes he's got money and you've got a new car and stereo equipment. A few months later, he tells you he'll be lucky to afford the turkey for Thanksgiving dinner."

"I hear you," he grumbled. "I didn't even get a birthday present last year."

What a pisser-and-moaner. "What business is your dad in, again?"

"Eyewear. S'called Everlast Eyewear. Protective stuff like goggles." He ringed his eyes with his hands.

"Do you like working at the BNC?" she asked. Maybe he would let something slip.

"Oh, yeah. I love it."

"That's amazing that you decided to double-check those pond trout. Clever of you. When did you go?"

"The same day we cancelled the bike path," he said with a burp.

Ah, and you have an invisible canoe, because it sure didn't leave any marks.

"Too bad Seaglass Bay won't have a bike path. Still, I guess there are more important things in life."

"Yeah, like money."

"Speaking of money, I'm broke. Do you think Brooke can help me?"

"Yeah. Ask Brooke for a raise. She gave me a bonus for special services." He leered as he lunged for her. "I can give you a raise right now for special services."

Yuck. She pulled away as quick as she could, but not fast enough. His lips crushed hers in a slobbery, wet kiss. It was almost enough to swear her off kissing and drinking for life.

Laine pushed him away and stood, while he sank back into the couch.

"Ummm, so good," he murmured, his eyes half closed.

That was absolutely gross. I'll have to brush my teeth for an hour. This detective stuff is hazardous to my health and hygiene.

Laine pressed the red button for the coffeemaker, and then looked up Ubers on her cell. None in the area. She looked for cabs. She needed one to pick up Tim, and fast. She didn't care how much it cost.

A noise came from the couch. Tim's thick, wet snores made her cringe. She shook him a few times, but to no avail. Sighing, she took a blanket from the closet and wrapped it around him.

Whoever called alcohol an aphrodisiac? Tim's breath smelled like an abandoned brewery. She climbed into bed and lay awake, listening to Tim's heavy snores. She missed having a man spend the night, but not this one.

LAINE FINALLY FELL into a dreamless sleep in the wee hours. When a truck pulled into her driveway at seven thirty, idled for a few minutes and then peeled out, the sounds barely registered in her consciousness.

Thirty-Five.

Wednesday

L AINE WOKE UP again at nine o'clock to a clear, cold day. When she walked through the living room on her way to the bathroom, she noted with relief that Tim had gone.

The note he'd left on the table read, "*Thanks. My head feels like I got hit with a sledgehammer. Hope I wasn't too much of a jerk.*"

Define jerk. If it means stupid, boorish, and drunk, then bingo, you won the prize for bad behavior.

Laine pulled on a pair of jeans and a sea-green wool sweater. Thank God she didn't have to dress up for work. She scrambled two eggs for breakfast. After eating she checked the mirror. Her hair stuck out at odd angles so she spent several minutes trying to gel it into submission. She met with limited success.

All through her morning ministrations, she kept checking the clock, wondering when Sam would honor her with his presence. Maybe he showed while she slept, but the sound of his rumbling truck motor would have awakened her for sure.

Guess Sam didn't have the decency to show. A wave of disappointment washed over her, then a surge of anger at herself. When will I stop getting involved with these jerks?

As SHE DROVE to the BNC, sunlight poured through the sunroof of her Honda. Her radio blasted an oldies tune about love as a fairy tale. Laine sang along, hoping that words of love, so soft and tender, would dissipate her foul mood.

Laine still hummed as she walked into the BNC. She stopped abruptly as she took in the strange sight of Brooke, sitting at her—Laine's—desk.

"Is everything okay?" Laine asked.

"Please pull up a chair and I'll explain," Brooke replied. The raccoon circles under her eyes had faded to faint smudges of bluish gray.

Laine pushed over a visitor's chair and sat. She looked around, wondering where Fiona and Tim were.

Brooke cleared her throat. "We're downsizing our workforce." Her fingers tapped a nervous rhythm on the table. "We had a budget meeting last night and unfortunately we didn't get our anticipated funds. We're forced to cut back on children's programs. Tim will take on your job. Since he's an intern, he receives credits from the college. We don't have to pay him a salary."

Laine fought down the lump in her throat. "Are you firing me?"

Brooke had enough grace to look uncomfortable. "We're letting you go," she said. "We appreciate all the fine work you did for the BNC. We wish we could continue to fund your position. You'll get two weeks' severance pay and excellent references, of course."

"Of course," Laine echoed.

Sell a few Stevins photos from your office. That would pay a hefty chunk of my salary.

Laine pulled her bottom lip with her teeth. Then she straightened her shoulders and stalked out of the building before she said anything she'd regret later.

Once in the car, she let go of her stored expletives. Then, she took great gulps of fresh air until she regained a measure of composure.

I wonder how Sam would rationalize this new development. Son of a bitch; I moved my whole life up here. Tim had told her he got a raise, but Brooke told her Tim didn't get paid. Too many discrepancies.

Laine called Sofie, but no one answered.

LAINE DROVE down the beach road, her mind in a whirl. Maybe exercise would calm her down. She parked along the side of the road and walked along it. As she walked she looked at the beach houses. She waved to Stanton Coles, sitting on his porch, talking on his cell. He ended the call and walked down the slope to see her.

"How are you?"

"Fine, and you?"

To Laine's embarrassment she burst into angry tears.

"What's wrong?" Stanton asked, worry registering in his widening eyes.

Laine took a ragged breath and sank onto the porch swing. "Brooke fired me."

"That's crazy. How could she fire you? The board thought you were doing an excellent job." Stanton sat beside her.

"Budget cuts, or so she told me."

"I can't believe it. I saw the great job you did with the kids. I didn't know anything about a lack of funds. Maybe I could talk to the board, get Brooke to change her mind. In fact I'll call Brooke at home tonight."

"I thought you said you don't know Brooke very well."

"We're not exactly friends. But an irate member of the BNC can call her anytime."

"Thanks," Laine told him. "I'm not giving up."

"That's the spirit. I'll support you in any way I can."

Laine thanked him for his concern and promised she would keep him informed. Then she dragged herself back into her car and drove home.

In her kitchen, she heated up a can of chicken noodle soup. Sitting at the table, she managed listless motions to bring the soup to her mouth. Then she plopped on the couch and tried to figure out what to do next.

Right now, she needed some pampering. She massaged her feet with sesame oil and had started running water for a hot bath when the phone rang.

She picked it up and said hello, louder than she meant to.

"It's Tim. Are you okay?"

"Yes, I'm fine. Why wouldn't I be?"

"Listen, I know I'm not your favorite person right now. But I need to explain about the BNC. I know you got fired, and that sucks. I think I can help get your job back. I admit I've done some things I'm not proud of."

An eager pricking began on the back of her neck. *It's about time someone 'fessed up.*

"Go ahead. I'm listening."

"Not over the phone. Let's meet at four thirty."

"Okay." Laine tried to keep her voice calm. "Where do you want to meet?"

"Let's meet at Windham Landing. I want to show you something on the bike path route."

"I'll be there."

Laine picked up the phone and called Sofie. This time she caught her at home, and Laine brought her up to date.

"No kidding? You got fired? That's such a crock." Sofie went on to describe all the things she was going to do to help Laine get her job back. They included a protest rally and a strike.

Laine shook her head. "I appreciate that, I really do. I don't think we need a strike and a rally yet. I need you to listen." She told Sofie her plans to meet Tim.

"I'm going too. I don't want you alone with that creep."

"I'll bring pepper spray, the loudest whistle in the world, and my cell phone."

"Where did you get pepper spray?"

"In Boston it's the single woman's friend. I almost forgot I had a can. Listen; don't tell anyone. I don't want to blow it. But if you don't hear from me by six, call the police, okay?"

After reassuring Sofie about twenty times she would be careful, she took a hot bath. She couldn't get comfortable, despite the soothing lavender bath oil. Throughout the bath, she nearly vibrated with restless anticipation of her meeting with Tim.

He's finally realized he's in over his head. Slapping her hands, *she displaced about a gallon of water out of the tub. Or else I'll be in over my head.*

Laine gave up trying to bathe. She dried and dressed. Then she paced from room to room.

It took forever, but the time finally came to leave. She bundled up, since the afternoon temperature only inched up to forty and promised to drop as darkness fell.

Her cell phone had a ninety percent charge and a good flashlight if she needed it.

She drove to Windham Landing and pulled into the parking lot at the same time as Tim.

Tim climbed out of his jeep, wearing a beat-up leather bomber jacket and a couple days of stubble. "I'm sorry I was so blotto the other night." He gave her a sheepish grin. "I usually don't drink that much. I hope I didn't say anything too stupid."

Yeah right. "You offered to marry me and buy me a house on the beach."

Tim looked aghast.

"I'm kidding. You wanted to show me something?"

"Whew. It's along this trail."

They started down the tree-lined path. Not even a breath of wind rustled the leaves. No small animals stirred. All remained quiet, except for the occasional chirping of a bird waiting for a ride south.

Even though she had gloves on, she stuck her hands in her pockets and waited for Tim to speak.

Tim broke the silence. "I know you're suspicious of the BNC. You're right, there's some twisted stuff going on."

"Why tell me about it?"

"I don't think it's fair you lost your job. I went along with the plan at first, but things went too far. I'll tell you what I know and maybe we can set it right."

"I'm all ears."

"I wish I never got involved in the first place. Money is my downfall. I'm not like you; I take the lucrative road instead of the high road."

The looming trees accentuated the oncoming darkness. She shivered and her teeth chattered. She didn't feel afraid, just chilly.

"There's a hidden shed right off the path. It's where Brooke and Emson meet."

"Are they having an affair?"

He nodded. "Isn't it a joke? She fell for him many years ago. They've kept it a secret all this time. I guess she's too embarrassed to have people know the tree hugger was going down on the tree hater."

Way too much information.

"When everything began to unravel, that secret came in handy," Tim smirked.

Laine touched the whistle at her throat. She groped for the cell phone and pepper spray in her pocket. Unease and wariness made her careful to notice Tim's every action and gesture. She followed him as he veered off the path and walked next to a large rhododendron bush.

Almost hidden by the scrub brush stood a shack. No other word to describe the old boards hanging together by sheer stubbornness. As Laine stood in the gathering gloom she wondered if the shack slipped out of a cheap horror flick. The air of neglect and secrecy gave her the creeps.

Damn, damn, and double damn, I've got the heebie-jeebies. I should leave my imagination in my pocket with my cell phone. Maybe this isn't such a good idea.

"You know what? I have to go," she said, trying to make her shaky voice sound determined. "It's later than I thought, and my friend Sofie is expecting me for dinner. I told her I was going for a walk with you first."

"Look . . ." Tim's face softened. "Don't be afraid. I want to show you Brooke's love shack."

"I'm not afraid. I just need to reschedule."

Reschedule? My God, I sound like an idiot. Why don't I just tell him I have a root canal appointment?

"It won't take long. A few minutes, I promise."

Laine stopped but Tim grabbed her wrist. She yanked free and adopted a defensive pose. As she fumbled for the cell phone, she lost her footing and stumbled backwards. Before she knew it she'd fallen splat on her butt. Oh, no, she didn't know what to do next. The self-defense class hadn't covered what to do when she fell on her ass. That must be in the advanced class.

Laine needed a weapon, a rock, a branch, anything to help fend off Tim as he bent towards her. She tensed herself for the oncoming attack. Instead of the expected fist or kick, Tim grabbed her wrist and hoisted her to her feet.

"Are you okay?"

"I'm fine. I thought—never mind, I'm fine." Flustered, she followed him inside the shack. The interior turned out to be as dark as the outside.

"What did you want to show me? She tried to fumble in her pocket for her cell phone flashlight.

"Patience, patience." Tim rubbed his hands together. The shack door creaked as it closed behind her. They were plunged into total darkness.

"Hey, that's not funny," Laine exclaimed. "Open the door."

"It's not me. Must be the wind."

"It's not windy." Laine tried to adjust her eyes to the dark. She reached in her pocket and pressed the cell. Damn, no service in this remote location. She grabbed her whistle and blew an ear-splitting shriek.

"Ow!" Tim yelled. "You blew out my eardrum, you bitch."

Without warning, the shed door banged open and a flashlight shone on her face.

"Everybody halt." At that moment Laine managed to turn on her cell phone flashlight and she shined it at the intruder.

The dark shape turned into a recognizable figure.

"Stanton?" Laine stared in surprise at his craggy features. The hand holding his flashlight trembled.

"What are you doing here?" Laine backed up a step.

"You still don't get it, do you?" Stanton asked. "Poor dear Laine."

Oh, I get it all right. I didn't want to believe it, but I started to get it a while back. A shudder of panic coursed through her body.

"Tim, tie her up nice and neat and we'll take care of her," Stanton ordered, pointing his flashlight as if it were a gun.

Laine's head spun. This man who made killer brownies and bird watched and dated Sofie turned out to be a bad guy.

She looked at his twisted smile, illuminated by his flashlight. His inner evil self shone in the flashlight's glare. He was the wild card. It all came together as it unraveled.

Great. Might be nice if there were someone to share this story with rather than take it to my grave. It's one thing to be right. It's another to be able to enjoy it. Alive.

"You're not going to kill her, right?" Tim asked as he came up behind her. "You promised you weren't going to kill her."

Tim grabbed her wrists. Laine had to get out of this mess. She struggled and broke his grasp.

"Don't do it, Tim. He's going to kill me."

"That's not right, is it? You're not going to hurt her. You promised you were just going to threaten her."

"And you believed me? More's the pity."

Laine heard a shot and a loud thud and turned to see Tim lying flat on the floor. As she shined her light she saw blood beginning to pool in a halo pattern around his head.

"Nooo!" Laine screamed. "You killed Tim." *Oh shit, Stanton has a gun and he's a good shot.*

"I didn't realize you were so fond of him. Don't worry; you'll see him again soon. You'll both end up at the same place, or maybe not, depending on your afterlife beliefs."

A theological discussion was the last thing on her mind. She frantically searched her numbed brain for questions to ask. What should she do next? The pepper spray in her pocket wouldn't help with Stanton's gun aimed at her head.

"You think you'll walk away free?" Laine asked, buying time.

"Something like that."

"Why are you doing this? You have everything. What about Sofie?"

"No one has everything. Things are not always what they seem. I guess I can tell you, since you won't live to talk. I didn't retire from banking. They asked me to leave. Turns out they had enough evidence to implicate me in an embezzlement scheme."

"Why didn't they have you arrested?"

"You'd be amazed at how many people go free in exchange for silence. In my case, the bank figured they'd lose customers if one of their top executives was exposed for planning and executing such an elaborate scam. They even gave me a nice severance package, but now I'm running out of dough."

"How were you going to get money from Emson?"

"He planned to buy my property and turn it into a beach clubhouse for Emson Estates. Two million bucks and I could live out my life like a king in Puerto Rico. But all deals were off if the bike path went through. Residents of Emson Estates won't want to cross a public bike path to get to the beach. You were a nice kid, but a meddling pain in the ass."

"What about Sofie?"

"What about Sofie? We'll be closer than ever, mourning the loss of our dear friend Laine."

"How do you expect to get away with this?"

"So many questions and so little time. I'll make it look like you killed Tim and then yourself."

"That's very clever." *Keep him talking, girl, even though you want to shit your pants.*

"Thank you. I thought so too. I really hate to kill you. I was beginning to like you. Tim was not in my league. But you might be. In fact, I might have even chosen you over Sofie under different circumstances. You are quite voluptuous."

Lucky me.

A random thought popped into her head. Fiona had guessed right about one of her targets. Stanton turned out to be quite a scum ball.

Stanton pushed her onto the wooden bench. "Have a seat."

If she could grab his ankle, she might be able to knock him off balance. She stared at his legs, trying to think.

Laine moaned and feigned keeling over. Stanton stepped close to her, his ankle barely in reach. Laine's arm shot out, snagged the ankle and wrenched it for all she was worth.

"Oof." Stanton tumbled to the floor, making a heavy crash.

Laine scrambled to her feet and lunged towards the door. Before she reached the knob, Stanton seized her leg and jerked her back. She tumbled to the ground on top of Stanton, elbowed him in the face, and found herself free again. She clambered to her feet and yanked open the door.

Stanton rolled over and sprang to his feet. "This isn't done yet," he growled. His mild-mannered persona had disappeared, and he looked truly menacing. His eyes blazed with rage. The tendons in his neck bulged. He leapt at Laine like a crazed tiger.

Sidestepping to the right, she guided him forward with a foot sweep.

Stanton's face crashed into the doorframe.

Maybe that wasn't such a good move. It put Stanton between Laine and the door, the only way out. The element of surprise no longer existed. He had strength on his side.

"That wasn't too smart." With a horrendous yelp, he sprang. Laine's eyes had adjusted to the dark, plus Stanton's flashlight was on the ground, still sending out rays of light. A mixture of blood and spittle dotted his face. His eyes wide with rage and deadly determination, he grabbed her throat.

Oh shit, he's going to strangle me.

"Not so damned smart now, are you?" Stanton raved.

His fingers tightened around her throat and she searched her oxygen deprived brain for what to do next. Her self-defense class hadn't trained her to get out of this spot.

Wait, the squirrel and eyeballs technique, but that seemed gross and gushy.

Hey, can't be picky when I'm about to be choked to death.

In a burst of strength, Laine kneed Stanton in the balls and then jabbed him in the eye. Eew, it really *was* gross and gushy.

Stanton howled in pain. Laine grabbed the pepper spray from her pocket and shot him in the eyes. He tumbled backwards clawing at his eyes and howling.

Laine wasted no time, didn't wait for a victory cheer or gloating. Instead, she flew out the door as fast as she could. Her entire body ached as she hurtled through the underbrush. And her heart pounded so hard, it might explode.

Oh God, get me out of here.

She veered around a rock and realized she didn't know her location. Which way to get out? The road veered to her left, no, right. A trickle of blood dripped down over her eye. She could still hear Stanton's moans.

"I'll get you . . . you won't get away from me. I'll find you."

Laine stumbled through prickly underbrush, briars ripping across her face and arms without mercy.

Ahead, in the dark, lay a clearing.

She charged towards it, head spinning, vision blurred from her collision with the rock. There—a vague indentation in the underbrush—the path! She stumbled several times before she reached it, plummeting ahead without looking back. Though she could no longer hear Stanton behind her, her heartbeat filled her ears. Her breathing became as painful as swallowing needles.

Out of breath, face scraped and cut from the briars, Laine stopped to call the police. Damn, no cell phone.

I must have dropped it in the cabin when Stanton attacked me. She finally saw her car, still parked next to Tim's jeep. Relief flooded through her.

BRUISED AND IN SHOCK, she sat in the car with the doors locked. A few moments later, she heard the welcome sound of sirens. *That's right, I told Sofie to call the police. The two hours must be up. Feels like at least three days.* When two police cars and an ambulance pulled up, her whole body shuddered with relief.

Sam and Hank sprang out of the ambulance and ran towards her.

"Look at your face," Sam cried. "You're hurt."

"That's nothing," she said, with an attempt at bravado. "You should see Stanton. He's in there." She pointed to the woods.

"He tried to kill me, and he shot Tim. I don't know if Tim is alive—or dead." She leaned against Sam as the police spread out to search for Stanton. Laine's body shuddered with waves of relief. Sam wrapped her in a blanket and pulled her close. His body trembled against hers.

Hank readied the stretcher. "I've only got a few scratches and minor shock," Laine told him. "Please don't make me go to the hospital."

Hank looked at Sam and Sam nodded slowly. They took her vital signs and decided she could stay.

"Now do you believe me about the crazy stuff going on at the BNC?" Laine asked.

"Yes, yes, yes," Sam said over and over. "I got a real kick in the ass from Sofie. I deserved every bit of it. Then I started doing a little investigating on my own. I even talked to Tony the tree man. What a total ass I've been. But never mind that now. It's you I'm worried about."

"I'm okay," she insisted.

"I'm not okay. I thought I was going to lose you. I'm so, so sorry I didn't believe you. You must be so pissed at me."

"I'm happy to be alive. Lucky for you, I'm too shaky and exhausted to feel angry right now. I'll have plenty of time to be pissed off later. Stanton cut the branches on the property a couple of weeks ago, didn't he?"

"Yeah, he did."

Something thudded, followed by a grunt and several foul expletives. The policemen appeared, dragging Stanton between them. Doubled over, he whimpered in pain.

"Looks like they got him," Sam said. "What the hell did they do to him?"

"I did that," Laine said in her sweetest voice. "I've been taking self-defense classes."

Sam stared at her in amazement. "Looks like somebody needs the ambulance after all," he told Hank.

"Two somebodies," Laine interrupted. "There's Tim."

"No honey. That's a body bag. Tim's gone."

"Stanton shot him in the head." She shivered, remembering her torment. Then her teeth began to chatter in earnest as exhaustion and relief took over.

Laine huddled in Sam's arms under a thick wool blanket, drinking hot tea from a thermos.

When her breathing eased back to normal Sam insisted on driving her car to the police station. Once there, Laine began the long ordeal of telling her story.

WHEN SHE AND SAM finally left the station, it was almost ten o'clock. Hunger screamed from her every cell. They stopped at a fast food joint for takeout.

Back at Laine's cottage, they devoured the bacon burgers and French fries.

Laine managed to tell Sam about getting fired before her eyes drooped, then shut as she sank back into the couch.

Sam carried her to bed, tucked her in, and then tucked himself in beside her.

"Try anything sexy and I'll deck you," she muttered.

"That's what I like about you," he said. "You're always so accommodating."

"Mmmm," she replied, drifting into sleep.

Thirty-Six.

THE NEXT MORNING Sam entered Laine's bedroom with two coffees and bloob muffins on a tray.

"Oh, that's heaven. Thank you." Laine took a muffin. "Did you notice that whenever you enter my bedroom, you always bring food?"

Sam laughed. "I thought you might need nourishment. Plus I happen to know you find food very erotic."

Laine eyed him as she sipped the hot coffee.

His disheveled hairdo matched the stubble sprouting on his chin.

"Thanks for coming to the rescue last night."

"When I heard you were in trouble, I went crazy. But you can take care of yourself. I guess you don't need me."

"No, I definitely don't need you."

His face looked grim as he turned away.

"But I want you."

"What did you say?" Sam turned towards her.

"I want you."

His arms engulfed her, gathering her up like a precious, long-awaited gift.

"I dreamed about you every night. I was afraid to love again after Louisa drowned. I know Sofie told you the story. But I knew I had to get over may fears . . . or I would lose you. And I couldn't bear that."

"I'm sorry," Laine whispered.

He nodded. "Sofie told me what a fool I've been. Actually, I had already come to that conclusion. The past weeks without you showed me I can't live my life in fear. Love isn't something I can turn on and off. I've been such a jerk. How can I make it up to you?"

With a start, Laine remembered something. "You can start by telling me who your date was at the Swann."

"The pretty woman with the long, dark curls?"

"Yes," Laine glared at him.

"That was my cousin, Jenna. You know; the one who wears a size seven and a half."

Laine narrowed her eyes at him.

"Hey, you can ask Sofie. She knows Jenna. By the way, why was Tim's jeep parked in your yard the morning after I saw you at the Swann?"

She laughed. "I was protecting the roads from drunk drivers. You think I was having sex with Tim? C'mon, I have much better taste than that. Well, at least slightly better." She eyed Sam up and down.

"Enough talking." Sam took her in his arms for a long and hungry kiss.

Her nipples grazed his chest, and this time when they got hard, she knew for certain the cold air had nothing to do with it.

When he finally left, Laine slept until late afternoon.

Thirty-Seven.

~~~~~~

I N AN ITALIAN RESTAURANT in Providence, the three friends sat in armchairs in front of a roaring fire. Sam raised his glass for a toast.

"What exactly are we celebrating?" Laine asked, her eyes on Sam. "Besides the fact I'm minus a job and Sofie is minus a boyfriend."

"Here's to good friends and a case solved," Sam said. "It turns out that Laine was right on target with most of her suspicions. Here's to the good guys winning,"

"With no help from you," Sofie reminded him.

"I know." He bowed his head with such mock humility the others burst out laughing.

They clinked glasses and drank.

"I'm sorry about Stanton," Laine told Sofie.

"That's okay. I think I may be over the older guy attraction thing. Turns out they aren't any more mature than the young guys."

Sam and Laine updated Sofie on the BNC saga. David Emson, Brooke Treadwell, and Stanton Coles were in police custody.

"That's practically half the town." Sofie shook her head. "Poor Tim."

Laine agreed. Hopefully he had died instantly of his head wounds. Greed had cost him his young life.

"Tim didn't want Stanton to kill me. He tried to do the right thing in the end. I thought David Emson did all those things to scare me. Turned out to be Stanton. He's the one who put the dead bunny at my door, tampered with my brakes, and cut the tree branch."

"He also slashed your tire," Sofie reminded her. "I can't believe I went out with that scumbag. I've made some bad man choices in my time, but I never dated a murderer before."

The three sat silent, contemplating Sofie's man choices.

"What about Fiona?" Sofie asked.

"Seems she didn't know anything," Sam said.

"You mean she's just a bitch?"

"Yup. She was loyal to whatever decisions Brooke made. She knew Brooke from forever. They were friends, or so she thought. She feels like a big sucker right now."

"Tell us the whole story." Sofie settled back in her chair. "I still haven't put all the pieces together."

"As you know," Laine began, "F. F. Pearson bought a house in Emson Estates. Emson figured Pearson would go ballistic if a public bike path bordered his property. Emson gave Brooke two hundred grand to fudge papers to identify a pond with rare endangered pond trout. She wanted the money to indulge in her expensive tastes in clothes and art, and, well—everything. Her investments did well. That's why she decorated her office with expensive artwork and flower arrangements. I looked up her Stevins photograph; an original costs twenty grand. She owned an original. They gave Tim sixty grand to keep his mouth shut. He died for sixty thousand dollars."

Sam leaned closer to Laine and draped his arm around her shoulders. "You're a marvel."

"Anyone with a computer and smart friends could do the same." Laine winked at Sofie. They had promised never to speak of the email break-in.

"Were Emson and Brooke really boinking each other?" Sofie scrunched her face in disgust. "Tim said they had a long-term affair."

Laine snorted at the term boinking to describe the regal Brooke. "They led everyone to believe they were enemies, when actually they were shagging in the shed. What a great cover-up. They were probably taking illegal bites out of BNC land as well. No one would suspect enemies of being in cahoots. They are one of a kind, those two."

"'Different sides of the same coin' as your Aunt Rose might say," Sam chimed in.

"Good one. David Emson paid to have the bike path stopped. That's what they fought about the night I saw them at the BNC. Brooke started getting edgy, feeling she was in over her head. She wanted out of the deal with her lover boy. Unfortunately she had already spent her ill-gotten gains."

"Here's the real kicker," Sam added. "When Pearson found out about the bike path, he was thrilled. He thought it would be like the Cliff Walk in Newport. The admiring public could gaze at his estate from afar."

They sat silent for a moment, contemplating the irony of Sam's words.

"Emson based his evil ways on a stupid assumption," Laine said. "Which, as you know, makes an ass outta you."

"I want to know, Laine, what made you suspect Stanton?" Sofie asked.

"I didn't want to believe it. Things were going so well between you two. But there were discrepancies in things he said. Little things—but still."

"Like what?"

"He said he liked to stargaze. But when I questioned him, he knew nothing about astronomy. Sirius is the brightest star in the northern sky. You don't need a telescope to see it. He also told me he hardly knew Brooke. Then he said he would try to convince her to give my job back. That shows they had more of a relationship than he let on. Sometimes when people start lying, they lie about the most inconsequential things. They can't keep their stories straight."

"I have to admit, you are a pretty damn good detective." Sam smiled at Laine.

"I'm glad you finally realize that. What will happen with the bike path now?" Laine held her hand palm up.

"The BNC board chair called and asked me to pass on this information. The state found out what happened and gave the BNC an extension," Sam said. "They've got a month to send in a revised plan, and if all goes well, they'll start construction early this summer."

"Too bad I don't work there anymore." Laine sighed. "I have some great bike path program ideas."

"Do you, now?"

"Yup. Instead I guess I'll pack my bags and go home to Aunt Rose until I find another job."

"Is that right?" Sam gave her his impish smile.

Why is he smiling, knowing I'm leaving? Ouch, that hurts. I'll never understand men.

After dessert and coffee, Laine and Sam dropped Sofie off at her house. Laine wondered what would happen next, now she and Sam were alone.

Sam cleared his throat. "Do you want to see my house? It's a left here and then towards the river."

Laine nodded. *Do I ever.*

AT THE END OF A SHORT ROAD, Sam pulled into a stone driveway.

Outside lights illuminated a porch and a pergola with a hanging swing. The country red wooden door beckoned.

Laine couldn't wait to get inside and explore.

Sam turned towards her. "Don't get out yet. I seem to talk better in the car." He took her hand and held it between his two large ones. "I feel stronger when I hold your hand."

Oh yay, so do I.

"Look. The thing of it is, well, I've always felt responsible for Louisa's death. When you told me you considered your workplace dangerous, I snapped. I felt any help or information I gave you might make me a part of you getting hurt. I couldn't take that." He shook his head like a young boy who didn't understand. "It takes a while for things to sink into this thick head of mine. I finally realized I projected my feelings about Louisa onto you."

"It isn't your fault Louisa died, you know."

"I know that intellectually. But my feelings often take on a life of their own. Next time it happens, you can clunk me over the head. I've seen what you can do with a guitar."

"Good. I will. Can we go inside? I'm dying to see your house."

ONCE INSIDE she ran back and forth, exploring each nook and cranny like a delighted child.

After watching her for a while, Sam led her upstairs to his bedroom.

The pale gold walls highlighted a blue denim patchwork quilt on the king-size four-poster bed. The squares ranged through several shades of denim, from pale blue to navy.

A bouquet of yellow mums stood on the bedside stand. The bright yellow flowers next to the blue quilt looked like a magazine picture of a cozy cottage.

But this was real, as real as Sam's hand on the small of her back.

"A man who keeps fresh flowers on the bedside table. Be still my heart. And I like the quilt."

"My mother made it for me from my old jeans before I went off to college." He wrapped his arms around her waist. "Laine, please tell me you'll stay in Seaglass Bay and let me get to know you. Let me make you happy."

Laine's heart thudded in her chest. *Could this really be happening?* "I'll let you know in the morning," she teased.

"No," Sam moaned. "Don't do this to me, please."

"We'll see how tonight goes. Payback is such a bitch, although it would be great to stay in Seaglass Bay. I could start taking voice lessons from Field, the music teacher. And I wouldn't have to leave Sofie."

"You know how to hurt a guy."

Laine pushed him playfully onto the bed and he pulled her on top of him. Feeling the length of his body underneath her and breathing in his rich, pine forest scent became almost too much for her. Thank god she lay down on the bed. She would have swooned if she'd been standing. To keep from attacking him, she began to wrestle, and they rolled around on the bed for several minutes. To end it, he cupped her face tenderly and kissed her eyes, her nose, and then her mouth.

His kisses sent waves of yearning between her thighs, which turned to a slow burning ache as he undid her blouse and cupped her breast with his hand.

"I fell in love with you the first time I took off your pants," he said.

"You told me that was professional."

"That's true. But I'm only human."

His lips grazed her nipple and she moaned with pleasure. He reached down and fumbled with the button on her slacks.

"Maybe I should slice them off. That might be easier."

"Let me help." Laine unbuttoned her slacks and Sam pulled them off, huffing and puffing. "These jeans are so tight. Maybe you should wear a sack next time."

"It's been a long month." Laine sighed as she stroked his face. "I'm glad it's over."

"Every cloud has a silver lining."

Laine laughed. "Aunt Rose is going to love you."

Much, much later Sam whispered in Laine's ear how sorry he was he didn't get her to bed earlier. He knew how much she needed her sleep. "You must be exhausted."

"Oh please, you didn't give me that much of a workout."

"Ouch."

"We got into bed early," she reminded him. "Early to bed and late to sleep, good enough to make a woman weep."

"I like it. Early to bed and early to rise, your girl doesn't have time for other guys."

"As long as I'm in bed with you."

Thirty-Eight.

Friday

~~~~~~

THE NEXT MORNING Laine woke to the phone ringing. She sat up in a strange room, the air infused with the smell of fresh roasted coffee. It took her a few seconds to remember she was in Sam's bed, in Sam's house. Wow. A day before she would have called crazy anyone who predicted this turn of events.

"Who would call at this hour?" she growled.

"It's noon." Sam handed her the phone. "It's Doug Bergman, from the BNC board of directors."

That perked her right up. Maybe he wanted information about Brooke and Tim. Laine said good morning to Doug.

"The BNC board of directors held an emergency meeting early this morning," Doug told her. "They'd like you to be the new Bay Nature Center director at a hefty salary increase."

Laine gasped. Doug had said the last thing she ever expected to hear. "Could you repeat that?"

Doug did.

Laine hung up the phone and turned to Sam. "They asked me to be the new BNC director. But I know nothing about directing a nature preserve."

"Brooke supposedly knew everything about directing. Look at the mess she made of things."

"That's true." Laine considered. "Actually I'd love to be the director. First we'll make sure the bike path goes through without interference."

"Excellent news. I don't think we'll have much trouble. Thanks to you, the bad guys are in jail."

Sam's white terry robe gaped open in all the right places as Laine dialed Sofie's number.

"Hi Sofie. I'm calling to tell you about Sam." She looked at Sam, who eyed her with expectation. "He and I had an okay time last night."

"Only okay? Shucks." Sofie's voice sounded full of disappointment.

Sam leaned over and began biting her ear.

"I'm kidding. I had an amazing time and guess what? I'm staying in Seaglass Bay."

"OMG are you kidding that's fabulous news I . . . "

Sam took her into his arms and she dropped the phone.

"Laine, are you okay?" Sofie's voice rose from the phone on the floor.

Laine picked up the phone. "I'll call you back later. I'm getting some serious EMT attention right now."

"Now where were we?" Laine said as she hung up the phone.

Stanton's Killer Brownies

Ingredients

12 ounces unsweetened chocolate, coarsely chopped

3 cups sugar (2 cups if you like it less sweet)

1 tablespoon raspberry liquor

1 ½ cups butter

1 ½ cups all-purpose flour. I use a gluten free substitute.

6 large eggs

Scant 2/3 cup raspberry fruit spread.

Preheat oven to 350 degrees

Grease 13x9 baking pan.

In small saucepan over low heat melt chocolate and butter, stirring constantly until chocolate melts.

Remove immediately from heat.

With wire whisk, beat until smooth.

Cool to room temperature.

In a separate bowl, beat eggs, sugar, and liquor until blended.

Fold in chocolate mixture, and then add flour.

Stir until just blended and pour into prepared pan.

Drop jam by teaspoonfuls over the top.

Swirl jam through batter with a knife tip.

Bake 30-35 minutes.

Cut into bars when cool.

If you want to go really crazy, try rhubarb sauce instead of the raspberry jam and vanilla instead of the liquor.

Rich, dark, and dangerous.

Enjoy. But remember, they are deadly!

Note: Stanton actually gave Laine the recipe when she visited him in jail. Luckily he knew it by heart. Laine made them only once a month since they contained so much fat. Sam said if Stanton hadn't gone to prison, he probably would have died from clogged arteries within five years.

Stanton became the prison baker and was best known for his Criminally Insane Chocolate Torte.

"We'll have a great story to tell the kid someday about the killer brownies," Laine said.

"What kid?" Sam asked.

"You never know."

Linda Richter is an award winning author with an MA in writing. Her hometown in South Coast Massachusetts has many similarities to Seaglass Bay. She is hard at work on a sequel called *A Bird In The Hand*.

Made in the USA
Middletown, DE
17 September 2022